ST. MARTIN'S

MINOTAUR

MYSTERIES

"Ingenious . . . Hamilton unreels the mystery with a mounting tension many an old pro might envy."
—*Kirkus Reviews*

"Hamilton combines crisp, clear writing, wily, colorful characters and an offbeat locale in an impressive debut."
—*Publishers Weekly*

"[A] well-plotted and tightly written thriller."
—*Detroit Free Press*

"A good combination of crafty and colorful characters, an offbeat locale in Michigan's Upper Peninsula, and really crisp, clear writing . . . There are several plots, all woven together very well. Alex is a very likable character, as are other townspeople, and the writing moves very swiftly, making this an easy and enjoyable book to read."
—*Sullivan County Democrat*

"P.I. Alex McKnight's 'mean streets' are the deep pine woods and the small lakeside towns of Michigan's Upper Peninsula, and here the past comes to find him, chilling as the November wind. A must for PI and suspense fans."
—Charles Todd, author of *Wings of Fire*

"His story is so fundamentally sound and stylistically rounded that Hamilton ought to be teaching whatever writing course he may have taken toward producing this novel."
—Jeremiah Healy, author of
The Stalking of Sheilah Quinn
and *The Only Good Lawyer*

WINTER OF THE WOLF MOON

STEVE HAMILTON

St. Martin's Paperbacks

WINTER OF THE WOLF MOON

Copyright © 2000 by Steve Hamilton.
Excerpt from *The Hunting Wind* copyright © 2001 by Steve Hamilton.

Front cover photograph © Yoshinori Watabe/Photonica.

Library of Congress Catalog Card Number: 99-056343

ISBN: 0-312-97475-2

Printed in the United States of America

St. Martin's Press hardcover edition / February 2000
St. Martin's Paperbacks edition / February 2001

St. Martin's Paperbacks are published by St. Martin's Press, 175 Fifth Avenue, New York, NY 10010.

10 9 8 7 6 5 4 3 2 1

TO NENA

Acknowledgments

For so graciously sharing her time and her knowledge of the Ojibwa life, I owe a great debt of gratitude to Donna Pine from the Garden River First Nation.

Thanks also to Frank Hayes and Bill Keller, Liz Staples and Taylor Brugman, the real-life agents "Champagne" and "Urbanic," Bob Kozak and everyone at IBM, Bob Randisi and the Private Eye Writers of America, Ruth Cavin, Marika Rohn and everyone at St. Martin's Press, Jane Chelius, Larry Queipo, former chief of police, town of Kingston, New York, and Dr. Glenn Hamilton from the department of emergency medicine, Wright State University.

And finally, to my wife Julia, who makes everything possible, and to Nickie, who gets to be a big brother soon. . . .

CHAPTER ONE

Two minutes. That's how long it took me to realize I had made a big mistake.

The blue team was good. They were big. They were fast. They knew how to play hockey. From the moment the puck was dropped to the ice, they controlled the game. They moved the puck back and forth between them like a pinball, across the blue line, into the corner, back to the point. Once they were in the zone they settled down, took their time with it, waited for the best opportunity. They were like five wolves circling their prey. When the shot came it was nothing more than a dark blur. The center slid across the front of the goal mouth, untouched, taking the puck and with one smooth motion turning it home with a sudden flick of the wrist. It hit the back of the net before the goalie even knew it was coming. Right between his legs. Or as they say on television, right through the five hole.

It was going to be a long night for the goalie on the red team. Which I wouldn't have minded so much if that goalie hadn't been a certain forty-eight-year-old idiot who let himself get talked into it.

"It's a thirty-and-over league," Vinnie had said. "Every Thursday night. No checking, no slapshots.

They call it 'slow puck.' You know, like 'slow pitch' softball? 'Slow puck' hockey, you get it?"

"I get it," I said.

"It's a lot of fun, Alex. You'll love it." Vinnie was my Indian friend. Vinnie LeBlanc, an Ojibwa, a member of the Bay Mills tribe, with a little bit of French Canadian in him, a little bit of Italian, and a little bit of God knows what else, like most of the Indians around here. You couldn't see much Indian blood in him, just a hint of it in the face, around the eyes and cheekbones. He didn't have that Indian air about him, that slow and careful way of speaking. And unlike some of the Indians I've met, especially the tribes in Canada, he looked you right in the eye when he spoke to you.

Vinnie was an Ojibwa and proud of it. But he didn't live on the reservation anymore. He never drank. Not one drop, ever. He could put on a suit and pass for a downstate businessman. Or he could track a deer through the woods like he knew the inside of that animal's mind.

He had found me at the Glasgow Inn, sitting by the fireplace. I should have known something was up when he bought me a beer.

"I don't think so, Vinnie. I haven't been on skates in thirty years."

"How much you gotta skate?" he said. "You'll be in goal. C'mon, Alex, we really need ya."

"What happened to your regular goalie?"

"Ah, he has to give it a rest for a couple weeks," Vinnie said. "He sort of took one in the neck."

"I thought you said it was slow puck!"

"It was a fluke thing, Alex. It caught him right under the mask."

"Forget it, Vinnie. I'm not playing goalie."

"You were a catcher, right?" he said. "In double-A?"

"I played two years in triple-A," I said. "But so what?"

"It's the same thing. You wear pads. You wear a mask. You just catch a puck instead of a baseball."

"It's not the same thing."

"Alex, the Red Sky Raiders need you. You can't let us down."

I almost spit out my beer. "Red Sky Raiders? Are you kidding me?"

"It's a great name," he said.

"Sounds like a kamikaze squadron."

Red Sky was Vinnie's Ojibwa name. During hunting season, he did a lot of guide work, taking downstaters into the woods. He liked to use his nickname then, playing up the Indian thing. After all, he once told me, who are you going to hire to be your guide, a guy named Red Sky or a guy named Vinnie?

"Alex, Alex." He shook his head and looked into the fire.

Here it comes, I thought.

"It's just a fun little hockey league. Something to look forward to on a Thursday night. You know, instead of sitting around looking at the snow and going fucking insane."

"I thought you Indians were at peace with the seasons."

He gave me a look. "I got eight guys on my team. They're going to be very disappointed. We'll have to forfeit the game. All because a former professional athlete is afraid to put on some pads and play goal for us. You gonna just sit here on your butt all winter? Don't you ever get the urge to do anything, Alex? To actually use your body again?"

"You're breaking my heart, Vinnie. You really are."

"You can use Bradley's stuff. It's all new. Mask, blocker, glove, skates. What size do you wear?"

"Eleven," I said.

"Perfect."

I didn't have much chance after that. Vinnie had been there when I needed him, taking care of the cabins while I was out making a fool of myself pretending to be a private investigator. So I certainly owed him one. And he was right, I was tired of sitting around all winter. How bad could it be, right? Put on the pads and the mask, play some goal. It might even be fun.

It was fun all right. I flicked the puck out of the goal to the referee and he skated it back to center ice for another face-off. I barely had time to take a drink of water from my bottle when they were back in my zone again, moving the puck back and forth, looking for another shot. The blue center was skating around in front of my goal like he owned it. I had to keep peeking around him to follow the puck.

"Get this guy out of here," I said to anyone who could hear me. "Don't let him just stand here."

A long shot came from the blue line. I knocked the puck down, but before I could dive on it, the blue center knocked it into the net. Three minutes into the game, and I had given up two goals. The center did a little dance, waved his stick in the air, his teammates jumping all over him like they just won the Stanley Cup.

Vinnie skated by. "Hang in there, Alex," he said. "We'll try to give you a little more help."

I grabbed the front of his red jersey. "Vinnie, for God's sake, will you hit that guy or something? He's camped out right in front of me."

"There's no checking, remember? Alex, we're just playing for fun here."

"I'm not having any fun," I said. "You don't have to take his head off, just . . . give him a little bump."

The blue center was skating around in wide circles now, bobbing his head. He was chanting to himself, something like, "Oh yeah, baby, oh yeah, oh yeah, oh baby, oh yeah."

I knew the type. It doesn't matter what sport you play, you always run into guys like this. In baseball, it was usually a first baseman or an outfielder. They came up to the plate with that swagger in their step. I'd ask them how they're doing as they're digging in, just because that's what you do in baseball, but they'd ignore me. First pitch is a strike, they look back at the umpire with that look. How dare you call a strike on me? I'd throw the ball back to the pitcher and then give him the sign for a high hard one. Guys like that need the fear of God put in them every once in a while, something to remind them that they're human just like the rest of us. If not a bolt of lightning then at least a good ninety-mile-per-hour fastball under their chin.

It was reassuring to see that hockey players had to deal with these guys, too. Vinnie smiled at me, took off a glove and adjusted his helmet strap. "Maybe just one little bump," he said.

I knew they played three ten-minute periods in this league, a concession to age and to the fact that most teams only had nine or ten players. So I only had twenty-seven more minutes to go. I slapped my stick on the ice. Go Red Sky Raiders.

Vinnie's men finally woke up and started playing some hockey. While the puck was in the opposite zone, I stood all alone in front of my goal, looking around at the Big Bear Arena. It was brand-new, built by the Sault tribe with money from the casino. There was a second rink on the other side, locker rooms in the middle, and a restaurant on the upper deck. The stands were mostly empty, just some women watching us. None of them looked like they were on our side. I pulled the mask away from my face, wiped away the sweat. The catcher's gear I wore a million years ago—the chest protector and the shin pads—was nothing compared to these goalie pads. It felt like I had a mattress tied to each leg.

The game started to get a little "chippy," as the hockey announcers like to say. The elbows were coming up in the corners, the sticks were hitting other sticks, maybe even a leg or two. There was only one referee, a little old guy skating around with a whistle in his hand, never daring to blow it. He was probably retired from a civil service job, never got in anybody's way his whole life and wasn't going to start now.

I finally stopped a couple shots. It wasn't like catching a baseball at all, I realized. A pitch in the dirt, you become a human wall. The glove goes down between your legs. You don't even try to catch it. You let it bounce off you, you throw the mask off, and then you pick it up. A hockey goalie can be more aggressive, move out of the net, cut off the angle.

"Att'sa way, Alex," Vinnie said. He was breathing hard. He bounced his stick off my pads. "Now you're getting it."

Toward the end of the first period, there was a loose puck in front of the net. I dove on it. The blue center came at me hard, stopping right in front of me. He cut his skates into the ice, sending a full spray right into my face. The old shower trick. I had seen it on television a thousand times, now I got to experience it in person.

As I got up I stuck my stick into the hollow behind his knee. He turned around and cross-checked me. Two hands on his stick and wham, right across my shoulders.

I looked into his eyes. A cold blue. Pupils dilated, as wide as pennies. My God, I thought, this guy is either stone crazy or high. Or both.

The referee skated between us. "Easy does it, boys," he said. "None of that."

"Hey, ref," I said. "That metal thing in your hand, when you blow in it, it makes the little pea vibrate and a loud sound comes out. You should try it. And then you can send this clown to the penalty box for two minutes."

"Let's just play some hockey, boys," he said, skating off with the puck.

The center kept looking at me. Those crazy eyes. I took my mask off. "You got a problem?"

He smiled when he saw my face. "Sorry, didn't

realize you were an old man. I'll try to take it easy on you."

When the first period was over, we all got to sit on the bench and wipe our faces off for a few minutes. Nobody said anything. We could hear the other team on their bench, laughing, yelling at each other. Just a little too loud, I thought. A little too happy. Then they started making these noises. It sounded like that stupid chant you hear them do down in Atlanta at the Braves games. The Indian war chant.

Vinnie stood up and looked at them over the partition. Then he looked at us. Eight faces, all Bay Mills Ojibwa. And one old white man. Nobody said a word. They didn't have to.

Here it comes, I thought. I've seen this look before. I've never met an Ojibwa who wasn't a gentle person at heart, who didn't have a fuse about three miles long. But when you finally gave that fuse enough time to burn, watch out. You see it in the casinos every couple months. Some drunken white man makes a scene, starts yelling at the pit boss about how the no-good Indian dealer is cheating him. Doesn't even realize that the pit boss himself is a member of the tribe. If he pushes it far enough he goes right through a window.

I felt a little looser in the second period, watching my Red Sky Raiders take it to the blue team. Vinnie was right about one thing—it felt good to use my body again. For something other than cutting wood or shoveling snow, anyway. If this was a mistake, it certainly wasn't a big one. It wouldn't rank up there with the other major mistakes of my life. Like getting married when I was twenty-three years old, just out of baseball, not sure what I was going to do with my life. Not a good reason to get married.

Or letting myself get talked into becoming a private eye. And everything that happened after that.

Or Sylvia. Letting myself fall in love with her. Yes, I'll say it. The puck is in the other end. I'm skating back and forth in front of my net, wondering why I'm thinking of these things. But yes, I'll say it. I loved her. "I've been hiding up here," she told me. "I've been hiding from the world. I think you are, too, whether you admit it or not." And then she left. Just like that. "I hope I've touched your life." The last thing she said to me. What a melodramatic college-girl thing to say. I hope I've touched your life.

Yeah, Sylvia. You touched my life. You touched my life the same way a tornado touches a trailer park.

The puck coming this way. The blue center behind it. The sound of his skates in the empty arena. *Snick snick snick snick.*

Funny how things come into your mind at a time like this. It used to happen in baseball. I'd be settling under a pop fly and I'd think of something else in my life with a sudden clarity like it was the first time I'd ever thought of it.

Like my biggest mistake of all. A madman's apartment in Detroit. Aluminum foil on the walls. My partner and I frozen with fear, watching the gun in his hand.

Snick snick snick snick.

Sylvia. I am in her bed and she is looking down at me. We have just finished making love in the bed she shares every night with her husband. He is my friend, but I don't care. She owns me.

The skater is fast. He's the best player on the ice, probably the best player this little Thursday night hockey league will ever see. He looks up at me. A peek over his shoulder. The other players are far behind. Time slows down. It's something every athlete knows, an unspoken understanding between us. It's just him and me.

I didn't pull my gun in time. I waited too long. I am shot and my partner is shot and we are both on the ground. There is so much blood. It all comes back to me. Not as urgently as it once did. I don't dream about it much anymore. I don't need the pills to make it through the nights. But it still comes back. I am lying on the floor and my partner is next to me.

I come out of the net to cut off the angle. He shoots. No! It's a fake. He pulls the puck back. I can feel myself falling backward. He's going to skate right around me and slip the puck into the open net. Unless I can knock the puck away. My only chance. I jab at it with my stick as I fall.

I hit the puck and my stick goes between his legs. He trips and slides face first into the boards. Then he is up, his gloves thrown to the ice. I take off my gloves, my mask. He throws a punch at me and misses. I grab him by the jersey and we dance the hockey fight dance. You can't find any leverage to throw a good punch when you're on skates. You just hold on and try to pull the other guy's shirt over his head. It's a funny thing to watch when you're not one of the guys dancing.

The man's eyes were wide with bloodlust and whatever the hell chemicals he was flying on. "Take it easy," I said. "I'm sorry."

"The fuck you're sorry," he said. Spit and sweat hitting me in the face. All around us the other players in the same dance, every man picking his own partner according to how much they really felt like fighting. The old referee was skating around us, blowing his whistle. I guess he finally remembered how it works.

"I didn't mean to trip you," I said. "Just calm down."

"Fucking Indians," he said.

"I'm not an Indian," I said.

"Yeah, fuck that," he said. "I know, you're a Native fucking American."

I started laughing. I couldn't help it.

"What's so funny?" he said. "Did I say something funny?"

"You always get high when you play hockey?" I said.

"The fuck you talking about?"

"You're higher than the space shuttle," I said. "If I were still a cop I'd have to arrest you. Skating while impaired."

He gave me a good push and skated away. The dance was over. "Fucking Indians," he said.

We finished the game. Vinnie scored once in that period. Another of his teammates scored in the third period to tie the game at 2–2. I made a couple nice saves to keep us tied.

In the last minute of the game, my new friend the blue center had an open shot at me. He wound up and launched a rocket. No slapshots, my ass. I got a glove on it, knocked it just high enough to hit the crossbar with a loud ringing sound that reverberated through the entire arena.

The game ended. There would be no overtime. The next game was ready to start, as soon as they got us out of there and gave the Zamboni a chance to take a quick run over the ice.

He glared at me, breathing hard.

I look back on that moment now, the two of us facing each other on the ice. I wonder what I would have done if I had known what would happen in the next few days. I probably would have hit him in the face with my hockey stick. Or broken off the end and jabbed him in the neck. But of course, I had no way of knowing. At that moment, he was just another hot-shot asshole hockey player, and I was the old man who just took away his third goal.

"No hat trick today," I said to him. "Looks like the Cowboys and Indians have to settle for a tie."

CHAPTER TWO

The night was cold. It had to be below zero. My wet hair froze to my head the moment I stepped outside. Across the street the Kewadin Casino was shining proudly. It was a big building and it was decorated with giant triangles meant to remind you of Indian teepees. It was almost midnight on a frozen Thursday night but I could see that the parking lot was full.

The Horns Inn was not far away, just over on the east side of Sault Ste. Marie, overlooking the St. Marys River. As soon as you walk in the place, you see deer heads and bear heads and stuffed coyotes, birds, just about any animal you can think of. I usually don't spend much time there, but Vinnie was buying that night, so what the hell. It was the least I could do, even if it *was* American beer.

"Here's to our new goalie," he said, raising a glass of Pepsi. We had pushed a couple of tables together in the back of the place. His eight teammates were all there, all quietly working on their second beers.

"Stop right there," I said. "You said this was a one-night gig, remember?"

"Yeah, but you were great, Alex. You gotta keep playing. Do you realize that those guys had a perfect record before tonight? We just tied them!"

If his teammates shared his enthusiasm, they didn't show it. I looked at each of them, one by one. A couple you'd know were Indians the moment you saw them. The rest were like Vinnie—a lot of mixed blood. Maybe you'd see it in the cheekbones. Or the dark, careful eyes.

They were all drinking. Most if not all would get drunk that night. More than one would get to a state well past drunk. I knew it bothered Vinnie. "I feel guilty sometimes," he once told me, "living off the reservation. A lot of my tribe, they think I abandoned them. When I was growing up, I could go down the street and walk in any house I wanted to. Just walk right in. Open the refrigerator, make a sandwich. Go turn the TV on. Everybody was my family."

He never really told me why he left the reservation. Maybe he wanted to buy his own house instead of living on land owned by the tribe. Or all that family togetherness he was talking about, maybe it was just too much.

He lives in Paradise, right down the road from me. He's my closest neighbor, maybe my closest friend next to Jackie. He deals blackjack at the Bay Mills Casino when he isn't doing his Red Sky hunting guide thing. "You know the difference between an Indian blackjack dealer and a white blackjack dealer?" he once asked me. "This is going to sound like a stereotype, but it's true. The white blackjack dealer never gambles. Those guys in Vegas? They see a thousand people playing blackjack all night long, maybe fifty of them walk away big winners, right? You think those dealers are gonna cash their paychecks and play blackjack with it? I've got a couple of cousins who lose every dime, every week, guaranteed. They cash their check, maybe they buy some food and beer, then they go right to the casino and lose the rest of it. Every fucking week, Alex. And nothing I do or say is gonna change it."

Vinnie sat at the table, staring at a moose head on the wall. Nobody said anything. Just a quiet frozen winter night at the Horns Inn.

Until the blue team showed up.

They busted into the place with a lot of noise and a gust of arctic air that rattled the glasses on our table. "Goddamn," one of them said, "will ya look at this place?"

They pushed a few tables together at the other end of the room. There were nine men and nine women. Most of them had leather bomber jackets on. Even with the fur collars, they couldn't be warm enough.

My new buddy the center went up to the bar, told the man to start the pitchers coming. He had one of those hockey haircuts, cut close on the sides and long in the back.

"So who the hell is that guy?" I finally said.

"Who, the center?"

"Yeah, Mr. Personality."

"That's Lonnie Bruckman. Some piece of work, eh?"

"He always play high?"

Vinnie laughed. "You noticed, huh?"

"Hard not to."

"Guy can skate, though, can't he? I think he played for one of the farm teams somewhere. Most of those guys on his team are ringers. Old teammates from Canada. He brings in a new guy every week."

Bruckman took a couple pitchers back to the tables. When he came back for more, he spotted us. Our lucky night.

"Hey, it's the Indians!" he said. As he came and stood over us, I got a good look at him without the hockey gear on. Whatever he was on, he had just taken another dip, probably in the car on the way over here. Coke or speed, maybe both. "Nice game, boys," he said. "Can I bring a couple of pitchers over?"

Nobody said anything.

He looked at Vinnie's glass. "What ya got there, LeBlanc? Rum and Coke? Lemme buy you one."

"It's Pepsi," Vinnie said.

"You're kidding me," Bruckman said. "An Indian that doesn't drink?" He laughed like it was the funniest thing he'd heard in weeks.

"We're all set here," Vinnie said. "Thanks just the same."

"Hey, old man," he said to me, "that was a nice save you made on me. You took away my hat trick, you know that?"

"Yeah, I know," I said. "Sorry about that."

"I'll get you next time."

"Won't be a next time," I said. "I was just filling in tonight."

"You gotta play again," he said. "You're good. Believe me, I know. I played in the Juniors in Oshawa. I played on the same line as Eric Lindros before he went up. I would'a gone up myself if I wasn't an American."

There it is, I thought. There's always an excuse. All the guys I played ball with, and most of them never went to the major leagues, of course. Maybe one in a hundred guys who starts out in the rookie leagues ever makes it. The other ninety-nine, they all have a story. Coach never gave me a chance. Hurt my knee. Didn't get enough at-bats. It's never just "I wasn't quite good enough."

This American thing, though, that was a new one, because of course you're only going to hear that one from a hockey player. I should have let it go. Just nodded at the guy, smiled, let him stand there making a jackass of himself, laughed at him later. But I couldn't help it.

"That's a shame," I said. "They should really let Americans play in the NHL. It's just not fair. Ain't that right, Vinnie?"

"It's gotta be a conspiracy," Vinnie said.

"How many Americans are there?" I said. "I bet we could count them on one hand. Let's see . . . John LeClair, Brian Leetch, Chris Chelios . . ."

"Doug Weight," Vinnie said. "Mike Modano, Tony Amonte."

"Keith Tkachuk," I said. "Pat LaFontaine, Adam Deadmarsh."

"Jeremy Roenick, Gary Suter."

"Shawn McEachern, Joel Otto."

"Bryan Berard, is he American?"

"I believe so."

"Derian Hatcher, Kevin Hatcher. Are they brothers?"

"I don't know," I said. "But they're both American."

"Mike Richter in goal," Vinnie said.

"And John Vanbiesbrouck."

"All right already," Bruckman said. "You guys are

real comedians. I didn't know Indians could be so funny."

"We forgot Brett Hull!" Vinnie said.

Bruckman grabbed Vinnie's shoulder. "I said all right already." His smile was gone.

"Get your hand off me," Vinnie said.

"You're making fun of me and I don't fucking appreciate it," he said. "Last guy who made fun of me lost most of his teeth."

The whole place got quiet. His teammates were all looking at us, as well as the men at the bar. There were maybe a dozen of them. They had all been watching the Red Wings game on the television. The bartender had a shot glass in one hand, a towel in the other. He didn't look happy.

"Bruckman," I said. I looked him in the eyes. "Walk away."

He held my eyes for a long moment. He was sizing me up, calculating his chances. I could only hope the chemicals racing around in his brain didn't make him decide something stupid, because I sure as hell didn't want to have to fight him without skates and pads on.

"You were lucky," he finally said. "I should have had the hat trick. You never even saw that puck."

"Whatever you say, Bruckman. Just walk away."

"Look at you guys," he said. "You Indians are so pathetic. I don't know why they ever let you have those casinos."

The bartender showed up with a baseball bat. "You guys gonna knock this shit off or am I going to call the police?"

"Don't bother," Bruckman said. "We're leaving. Too many drunken Indians in this place."

He gave me one last look before he went back to his table. I didn't feel like telling him I was really a white man just like him.

When they had all put their leather jackets back on, knocked over a few chairs, muttered a few more obscenities, and then left without paying for their beer, the place got quiet again. Vinnie just sat there looking at the door. His friends all sat there looking at the table or at the floor. I tried to think of something to say to break the spell, but nothing came to me.

"You know what bothers me the most?" Vinnie finally said.

"What's that?" I said.

"Those women that were with them? One of them, I know her."

"Oh yeah?"

"I grew up with her," he said. "On the reservation."

It was a little after one in the morning when I left. Vinnie thanked me for playing with his team. Most of the team thanked me. A couple of them were already too far into their beer glasses.

I went up to the bar, apologized to the man for whatever part I almost had in fighting on the premises.

"Don't worry about it," he said. "If I don't have to read about it in the paper tomorrow, then it never happened."

I threw a couple bills on the bar. There were two men sleeping on their bar stools, their heads buried in their arms. The only difference was the man on the left was snoring and the man on the right wasn't. I didn't think either of them was an Indian. Just two white men who come into the place every single night, I would bet, and drink themselves unconscious. Somebody once told me that 3 percent of the people who live in Michigan live in the Upper Peninsula, and that they drink 28 percent of the alcohol. That's not just the Indians drinking all that. And yet I didn't hear anybody telling me what a disgrace it was, those white men, they're all just drunken degenerates.

"Hey," the bartender said, "aren't you that private investigator? The one that was working for Uttley?"

"I was," I said.

"Where'd he go, anyway? I never see him anymore."

"I honestly don't know," I said. It was the truth.

"He had a tab going here," the man said. "He never paid it."

"How much is it?" I said. I pulled my wallet back out.

He held his hands up. "It's between him and me," he said. "I'm not gonna let you pay it. If you ever see him, though, you tell him he owes me."

"If I see him, I'll tell him." The thought of it made me smile a little. Just a little.

When I stepped outside, the cold wind off the lake slapped me across the face. I closed my eyes and held my gloves against my face. When the wind died down, I took a deep breath. The air had a smell and a weight to it that held the threat of more snow.

I looked out across the St. Marys River. It had been frozen solid for almost a month. The locks were shut down for the winter. The next freighter wouldn't pass through them until March at the earliest. From the other shore the lights of Canada beckoned to me. I could walk right across the river if I wanted to. No customs, no toll. I wouldn't be the first to do it. There were stories of men who left their wives and families behind them and walked across the ice to a new life in another country.

I started the truck, got the heater going full blast. It took a good ten minutes to take the edge off the cold. The clear plastic that was covering my passenger side window didn't help matters any. I made a mental note to call the auto glass place again the next day to see if the new window was in yet. They told me two to three weeks when they ordered it for me. That was almost three months ago.

I drove across town in the dim light of street lights and barroom windows. I had the plow hanging on the front of the truck, a good eight hundred pounds of cinderblock in the back for traction. The roads were clear of snow that night, but I knew that wouldn't last long. It never did. Not until spring.

When I got onto the highway, it took a long while to get the truck up to fifty-five miles per hour. I could feel the engine struggling against the weight. I-75 to M-28, west through the Hiawatha National Forest to 123. I had driven it so many times I didn't even have to think about it. I had the road to myself, pine trees loaded with snow on either side. The wind whistling through the plastic. When I finally get this window fixed, I thought, the sudden quiet is going to drive me out of my mind.

There's one main road in Paradise, with one side road that takes you west to the Tahquamenon Falls State Park. The intersection has a blinking red light. When they change that to a regular stop light, that's when we'll know we've hit the big time. For now it's just a gas station, three bars including the Glasgow Inn, four gift shops and a dozen little motels for the tourists in the summer, hunters in the fall and snowmobilers in the winter. Plus a lot of cabins scattered throughout the woods.

The lights were on at the Glasgow Inn, but I passed it by. I don't have to stop in there every single night, after all. After eighty or ninety nights in a row, a man is entitled to a night off.

A mile north of the intersection, there's an old logging road that heads west into the forest. The first cabin on the left is Vinnie's. I knew he wouldn't be home yet—he was doing his designated driver routine for his teammates, dropping them off at the Bay Mills Reservation, and probably having to talk to a hundred tribal relatives who still didn't understand why he moved away. He'd be lucky to make it home by daybreak.

The next six cabins were mine. My father built them in the sixties and seventies, one per summer until he got too sick to build them anymore. When I left the police force, I came up here figuring I'd stay a little while and then sell them. That was fourteen and a half years ago.

Maybe Sylvia was right. Maybe I was hiding from the world.

I didn't want to think about it. I was tired. My muscles were already starting to stiffen up in the cold. For that night I wanted only a warm bed. Beyond that simple desire, there were only two other things I could ask for. My first wish was not to wake up the next morning feeling terrible. A little soreness I could take. Just let me get up and walk without screaming. My second wish was not to have to deal with that Bruck-man clown ever again. Guys like that bring out the worst in me. Just don't let me run into him again.

Just those two tiny requests. Surely that's not too much to ask for in a man's life.

Is it?

CHAPTER THREE

I woke up the next morning. I tried to lift my head. Bad idea. I winced, held my breath, regrouped, tried to push myself up to a sitting position. Another bad idea.

Good Almighty God in Heaven, I thought. I've really done it this time.

I tried to stand. I failed. There are certain muscles that get a real workout when you crouch down into the ready position, when you move your body from side to side. I know this because I used those muscles every day when I was playing ball. The hip flexors. The quadriceps. Now those same muscles were letting me know how unhappy they were. Twenty-four years of not using them and then last night.

I grabbed on to a chair and pulled myself up. Oh, and the back muscles, tight as piano wire. The hamstrings. The groin muscles. I am such an idiot. If I ever get my strength back I'm going to strangle Vinnie.

A shower. Hot water on my body. I pointed myself at the bathroom. Nice and easy, no sudden movements. Take a step. God that hurts. Another step. God that hurts. I made my way across the cabin, the wood floor cold and unforgiving under my feet. Through the window I could see that it was snowing softly.

I got to the shower somehow, turned it on and waited for it to get hot. I looked at myself in the mirror. Forty-eight years old is not supposed to feel like this. This is ridiculous.

I let out a scream as I stepped into the shower. There was a little rim on the bottom of the shower I had to step over, which meant actually lifting my leg into the air. I let the water pound on me for a good thirty minutes. When I was done I felt a little better. I cleared that rim like it was nothing.

I put some clothes on. Once I got the pants on, life got easier. I shaved, made some breakfast, sat at the table and looked out the window while I finished my coffee. It looked like about four inches of new snow. Around here, that qualifies as scattered flurries.

I went out and got the truck going, ran the snowplow down my road. I headed west first, deeper into the forest. I lived in the first cabin, the one I helped my father build in the summer of 1968. The second cabin was a little bigger. He built that one himself the next year. It was empty now. The man from downstate had called to cancel at the last minute.

The third cabin was a little bigger, and so on until the sixth and last cabin at the end of the road, each one marking another summer of my father's life. At this time of year, the renters were all snowmobilers. You could hear them during the day, roaring up and down the trails on the state land. I have this thing about snowmobiles. The noise, that oily blue smoke. And the people who drive them, wrapped up in those snowmobile suits, looking like the Michelin man, most of them full of beer and schnapps. If the wind is right you can even hear them out there in the middle of the night, riding those stupid machines. That's when the accidents happen. Every week, you'll read about somebody driving into a tree or falling through the ice. The one I remember most was the man who went off the trail onto a farm, ran right under an old wire horse fence. Imagine the poor guy riding behind him who had to pick up that helmet with the head still in it.

"You really hate snowmobiles, don't you?" Jackie once asked me.

"Yes, Jackie. I admit it. I hate snowmobiles."

"Did you know that every motel in town is booked up two years in advance during the wintertime? It's not the summer people who keep this place going, Alex. And it's not the hunters anymore. It's the snow-mobilers. Who do you rent out your cabins to this time of year?"

"Birdwatchers," I said. "Cross-country skiers. Guys with snowshoes."

"The hell you do," he said. "Where would you be without snowmobilers? What would you do between December and March?"

"I'd go to Florida," I said.

"Yeah, I can see that. Alex McKnight sitting on a beach. Drinking a margarita."

"Why not?"

"You've been up here too long," he said. "It's in your blood." I remember Jackie leaning over the bar, grabbing me by the collar. "You're a 'yooper,' Alex. You're one of us now."

The snow was as dry and light as talcum powder. I plowed it off the road without even feeling it or hearing it. Then I turned around and went east back toward the main road. I passed my cabin and plowed right past Vinnie's place. His car wasn't there. Probably spent the night at the reservation. Normally I plow his driveway on my way through, but today I felt like leaving him snowed in. Let him shovel for once.

I rumbled by, then I stopped. I backed up and did his driveway.

I went into town, picked up my mail. I stood next to my truck and filled it with gas, feeling the cold morning wind off Whitefish Bay. It was frozen as far as you could see, but somewhere out there, maybe two miles, the water was still open. That's the water that fed the snow gods. I could remember one night a couple years before, we got over four feet of snow in twelve hours. That's the kind of night where you play a kind of musical chairs—wherever you are when the snow hits—bar, restaurant, house—that's where you're going to stay for the next couple of days.

A big truck rolled into the gas station, pulling a trailer. On the back there were two snowmobiles, looked like they cost at least seven thousand dollars each. The driver got out of the truck. He had a new snowmobile suit on, another thousand dollars right there. He looked at me standing there in my jeans and hunting boots, my down coat that had seen twelve hard winters, standing next to a beat-up truck that was even older than my coat, with a sheet of plastic where the passenger side window should have been.

"Howdy," he said.

"Howdy," I said.

"Nice little town you got here."

"Glad you like it."

"We've been driving for seven hours," the man said. "This place is hard to get to."

"Not hard enough," I said.

He smiled and nodded. I guess he wasn't really listening. "Well, have a good one," he said.

With those good wishes and a tank full of gasoline, I was all set for the day. I stopped in at the Glasgow Inn to have some lunch and to bother the owner. Jackie had the whole place done up like a Scottish pub, with the fireplace and the tables and the big over-stuffed chairs. Jackie was born in Glasgow. He didn't have the accent anymore, but he certainly *looked* like one of those old weather-beaten golf caddies. The place was almost empty at this time of day, just a few locals sitting with their newspapers. Jackie was sitting with his feet up by the fireplace.

"Where were ya last night?" he said.

"What, I've got to call in when I'm not going to be here now?"

"Forgive me for asking," he said. "I was just wondering where you were."

"If you must know, I was playing hockey."

"Sure you were," he said. "Right after the aliens abducted you and took you for a ride on their space-ship."

"Vinnie's got a team," I said. "A thirty-and-over league." I bent down very slowly and carefully. Finally, I made it into a chair. "I'm a little sore today."

"Alex, when they say thirty and over, that usually means over thirty and under fifty."

"I'm forty-eight, smartass. Now get up there and

bring me a beer. And make me a sandwich while you're at it."

"Such manners," he said. He went behind the bar and opened up the cooler. I put my feet up on his little hassock and closed my eyes. The heat felt good. I could have gone to sleep right there.

"Here," he said. He put a plate down on the table next to me, along with a bottle.

"Jackie," I said. "What is this?"

"It's a sandwich, genius. Ham and provolone." He went back to the bar, which was a good thing because I wasn't going to give him his footstool back.

"No, the bottle," I said, across the room. A man in the corner looked up from his newspaper, smiled and shook his head, looked down again.

"That's beer, Alex."

"What kind of beer?"

"Molson beer. You can read."

"What kind of Molson beer?"

He let out a long sigh. "American Molson beer."

"Where's my Canadian beer, Jackie?" We have this little arrangement. Whenever he goes across the border, he picks me up a case of Canadian Molson. He's not supposed to be selling Canadian beer in the United States, but he keeps a few in the cooler, just for me.

"I ran out of the Canadian," he said. "I'll get you some more tomorrow."

"You're supposed to keep an eye on it," I said. "You're supposed to let me know if you're getting low."

"Like I got nothing better to do than to monitor your personal beer supply."

"No, Jackie, as a matter of fact you don't. That

should be your number one priority in life."

"Just drink the goddamned American beer, will you? I swear, I'm gonna make you put on a blindfold some day, see if you can even tell the difference. I'll bet you five hundred dollars you can't."

The door opened before I could take him up on his bet. A blast of cold air swept through the room, and a man walked in who was just about as welcome as the cold air. Leon Prudell.

"Oh yeah," Jackie said from the bar, "I was supposed to tell you. Leon Prudell was here last night looking for you. I told him to come back today at lunchtime."

"Thanks a lot," I said.

Prudell came over to the fireplace and sat down in the chair next to me. "How's it going, Alex?"

"Prudell," I said.

"Call me Leon, ay," he said. He hadn't changed much. He was still all flannel and messy orange hair and that yooper twang.

"Leon. What can I do for you?" The last time he showed up here, he drank a great deal of whiskey and then he tried to take me apart in the parking lot. Come to think of it, that was the same night my whole life started turning inside out. I hoped his coming into the bar again wasn't an omen of more of the same.

"I just wanted to talk to you," he said. "I got a business proposition."

I didn't know what to say, so I didn't even try.

"Here's the deal," he said. "I've been thinking about getting back into private investigation, ay. I really miss it, Alex. I mean I still have my license and everything. Here, I had these made up." He handed me a business card. It read "Leon Prudell, Investigation, Security, Bail Bonds."

"You're serious," I said.

"I thought it would be a good idea to add the bail bonds in there. Did you know that there are no bail bondsmen in the whole county? Until me, I mean. If you had to get bailed out of jail, you'd have to wait for somebody to come up from Mackinac."

"I'll remember that," I said. "But what does this have to do with me?"

"Alex . . . ," he said. He gave the room a quick scan and then he bent his head closer to mine. "Alex, here's the way it is. I've been trying real hard to be an investigator again, because it's what I love to do. And I think I'm real good at it. I helped you out that one time, remember? Getting into that guy's house? You could tell I was pretty good at that kind of stuff, right? Am I right?"

I looked at him. "Yes," I finally said. "You knew what you were doing."

"Okay," he said. "But the problem is, most people, they look at me and they don't see that. You know what I mean? They look at me and they think of that goofy fat kid who used to sit in the back of the class."

"Prudell—"

"Alex, I'm not saying I *remind* them of that goofy fat kid. I'm saying I *was* that goofy fat kid, okay? Everybody I went to school with, they're still in Sault Ste. Marie. They still see me like that. You know how hard that is to deal with?"

"So what do you want me to do?"

"I want you to be my partner."

"Oh God," I said. "Are you kidding me?"

"McKnight-Prudell Investigations," he said. "Although, I don't know, maybe Prudell-McKnight sounds better."

"Prudell, come on . . ."

"Okay, McKnight-Prudell. We'll put your name first."

"Just stop," I said. "Please."

"We'd be perfect," he said. "You're an ex-cop. You *look* like an ex-cop. You're not from around here. You don't talk like you're from around here. And you've got that." He looked at my chest. "You know, you've got that bullet thing going for you."

I just looked at him.

"You really have a bullet in there, right?" he said. "Next to your heart? Do you have any idea how great that sounds? People hear that, they think, 'Now. this guy is like somebody out of a movie.' "

"Yeah, that's kinda what I was hoping for," I said. "That's exactly why I let myself get shot in the first place."

"No really, Alex—"

"Just stop right there," I said. "Listen to me. I don't want to be a private investigator. It's the last thing in the world that I want to be."

"I get it," he said. "You just don't want to be my partner."

"It's got nothing to do with you. I just don't want to be one. Becoming a P.I. was the worst thing I've ever done in my life, you understand me? Nothing but bad has come of it." I wasn't about to tell him the whole story. I didn't even like thinking about it.

"Will you think about it?" he said. "Will you do that much at least?"

"There's nothing to think about," I said. "I'm not a private investigator anymore. And I'll never be one again."

"Fine," he said. He got up from the chair and put his coat on.

I tried to stand up. My legs had other ideas. If Prudell ever wanted another chance to kick my ass, today would be a great day for it. "Look," I said. "If anybody ever asks me about it, I'll send him your way, okay?"

"Sure," he said. "You do that. Thanks a lot."

I gave up and sat back down. Prudell left the place, slamming the door behind him.

"What was *that* all about?" Jackie said.

"Nothing," I said. "I just ruined his life again." I took a drink of my American beer and nearly choked on it. "Goddamn it, Jackie. I am not going to sit here and drink this."

"Canada's thirty miles that way," he said, pointing north. "You know the way."

"I might just do that," I said. "As soon as I can walk again."

I sat there for another couple of hours. The place started to fill up with snowmobilers. I overheard a lot of talk about which trails were smooth and how fast the Yamaha was compared to the Polaris compared to the Arctic Cat. It was fascinating. Finally, when I had heard enough about fucking snowmobiles and I was tired of sitting next to a perfectly good fire with a fucking pathetic American beer in my hand, I told my body that it was moving whether it liked it or not. "I need some air," I said to Jackie as I left. "I'm going to Canada."

"Don't bother coming back," he said.

"In your dreams," I said, and then I was out in the cold air, snowflakes coming down like a million white butterflies. I stood there for a long time, just listening to the silence. It was hard to even imagine the storms of November, the constant sound of the waves pounding on the rocks. And now, nothing. No sound. Just snow.

Then suddenly, from the woods, the silence was ripped apart by the whine of a hundred-horsepower engine. God, I hate snowmobiles.

I climbed into the truck. It was too hard. It hurt too much. Just climbing into my stupid truck. I yelled at myself, banged the steering wheel with both hands. You used to be an athlete, goddamn it. What happened to you?

This is some mood you're in, Alex. What's the problem? A little muscle soreness? A little lactic acid overload in the bloodstream? Is it the thought of three more months of ice and snow? Maybe it's Prudell, that look on his face when you told him you didn't want to be his partner. Like you took his dream away. Again.

Or maybe it's Sylvia. You're going to drive yourself crazy if you keep thinking about her. She's gone. Accept it.

The daylight was already fading when I got to the International Bridge. Below the bridge I saw the frozen locks and then the burning smokestacks of the Algoma Steel Foundry. I paid the $1.50 toll and then sat in line at the Canadian customs booth. Traffic was light, so there was only one lane open. The man moved the cars through quickly, though. When it was my turn, he asked me where I was headed and why. He looked familiar. You cross enough times and they get to know you. I told him just a quick trip into Soo Canada for beer. He just smiled at me and waved me through.

You come off the bridge and you're right in the middle of downtown Soo Canada. It's a big city by Canadian standards, at least four times bigger than Soo Michigan. I drove down Bay Street, past the fish hatchery and the Civic Centre, and pulled into a brightly lit parking lot. It used to be called Brewer's Retail. Now it's just the Beer Store. There's one or two in every town in Canada, from Vancouver to Prince Edward Island. It's a wonderful place. You walk in and you look at a row of bottles on the wall. You say that one, please, make it two, please. And two cases comes rolling out on the conveyor belt. They don't roll them slowly. You have to be ready for them. I've heard a lot of things said about Canadians, good and bad. But when it comes to beer, they know what they're doing.

With two cases in the back of the truck, I headed back to the bridge. I could feel my bad mood lifting as I drove under the streetlights of Queen Street. I paid the buck fifty toll again, and then this time I had to wait at the U.S. customs booth. When it was my turn, I drove to the window, said hello to the man. Another familiar face. He asked me the usual questions. I told him I had two cases in the back.

"You know you're only supposed to bring back one case at a time," he said.

"Can you blame me?" I said. "This is Canadian beer we're talking about."

He thought about it for a moment. "Go on, get out of here," he finally said. "Be careful with that beer. You got it secured back there? You're not going to break any, are you?"

"This beer is safe with me," I said. "You can count on it."

I drove back through Soo Michigan. The same roads, everything at least a half hour trip up here. No wonder my truck was pushing 200,000 miles. The snow was beginning to come down harder.

As soon as I passed the sign ("You're entering Paradise! We're glad you made it!"), a snowmobile came out onto the road. I jammed on the brakes, heard the bottles rattle behind me. The rider just sat there transfixed like a deer in the glare of my headlights. I couldn't see his face through the visor.

If even one of those bottles was broken, I said to myself, there would be hell to pay. I gripped the steering wheel, made myself count to five, and then I opened the door. The snowmobile disappeared in a cloud of white.

I checked the beer and got back in the truck. I could feel my bad mood making a comeback. Just go to the Glasgow, Alex. Put one case behind the bar. Keep one in the truck. Better put it in the cab so it doesn't freeze. Sit by the fire, take your boots off. Jackie will make you something to eat. You'll sit there, you'll have a cold Canadian. You'll be a new man.

I took the case and backed myself through the door. The place was full of snowmobilers. A man walked by me to the bathroom with his suit open down to his waist, his boots clunking with every step and the shiny material on his legs going *zip zip*. Jackie was

behind the bar, leaning over it and talking to a
woman. The string of lights that ran along the wall
behind the bar were blinking on and off, even though
Christmas was long gone. I put the case down. I stood
up and stretched my back, looking around the room.
There were a lot of strange faces, but that was normal
for this time of year. All these men from downstate,
filling the place with stories and bad jokes and cigarette smoke.

The usual scene. And yet . . .

And yet what? Something wasn't right. A certain
noise, or a lack of a certain noise. A feeling I was
being watched, even though nobody was looking at
me. Just a feeling that something was . . .

What? What was the problem? I couldn't say. I
didn't pursue it. I chalked it up to a strange mood on
a strange day. I didn't listen to the voice in the back
of my head, that little voice I relied on every day
when I was a cop. I could have gone into the room
and looked at every man, one by one, slowly and casually, not making any fuss about it. Just make eye
contact, smile and nod, move on to the next. Maybe
I would have narrowed it down to the man in the
corner, sitting by himself. Or the man by the window
who kept glancing outside. Maybe I would have
sensed that something bad was going to happen that
night, and maybe I would have found some way to
prevent it.

But I didn't. I shook off the feeling the same way
the pitchers used to shake off my signs. A single quick
tilt of the head and it was dismissed.

Jackie appeared next to me. "Alex, come on over
here," he said. "I want you to meet somebody."

I looked at the woman he had been talking with. The face was vaguely familiar, but I couldn't remember where I had seen her before. She was in her thirties, maybe mid to late. Brown hair, a streak of blond on one side. Blue eyes, a dark blue, almost violet. I probably would have found her attractive if Sylvia hadn't just burned out most of my circuits. She was sitting at the end of the bar, the stool next to her empty, like there was an invisible bubble around her, keeping all the men away. She had her hands folded in front of her on the bar and she was looking up at the Christmas lights.

"Who is she?" I said.

"Her name is Dorothy," he said. "She's been waiting for you."

She looked down in her lap, unfolded her jacket and pulled out a package of cigarettes. It was a leather jacket. Not nearly warm enough.

It came to me. I remembered where I had seen her before.

CHAPTER FOUR

"It wasn't hard to find you," she said. We had taken the small table next to the fireplace. She sat across from me, looking around the room at all the men in their snowmobile suits. Jackie had come by, dropped a beer in front of me, asked her if he could get her anything. She asked for a glass of water. "I started at that bar, you know, from last night. The one with all the animals."

"The Horns Inn," I said. "You were there with the other hockey team."

"Doesn't that place give you the creeps? All those eyes looking at you?"

"I never thought about it that way," I said. "Next time I'm there, I probably will."

She smiled. Her eyes were red. She looked tired. "The bartender at that place knew you," she said. "He told me you were a private investigator. The lawyer you worked for, he hung out there a lot, used to talk about you. Is it true you have a bullet in your heart?"

"Next to my heart," I said.

"Okay, that makes sense then," she said. "If it was *in* your heart, you'd be dead, right? How did that happen, anyway?"

"It's a long story," I said.

She nodded, biting her lip. I could see a small chip on one of her front teeth. "He told me you lived here," she said. "In Paradise. I knew it's a small town, so I didn't figure I'd have any problem finding you. I hitchhiked, can you believe it? I haven't done that in twenty years. When I got into town, the guy at the gas station told me to try this place. I got talking to Jackie over there." She looked over her shoulder at him. "He's a very nice man."

"You're the Indian, aren't you?" I said. If I hadn't been looking for it, I probably wouldn't have noticed it. There was just the slightest hint of it in her face, a certain calmness in her eyes. "Vinnie recognized you. He said you grew up on the reservation."

"Vinnie who?"

"Vinnie LeBlanc."

"I don't know him," she said. "I don't remember many people from that time. I've been gone for, God, it must be ten years. Until a couple months ago, I haven't even been in the Upper Peninsula."

"He remembers you," I said. "From when you were kids, I guess."

"Maybe," she said. "Anyway, you're probably wondering why I was looking for you."

"I figured you'd get to that part."

"It's like this, Alex. . . . Can I call you Alex?"

"Of course."

"What I'm wondering is, do you happen to be free at the moment? I mean, can I hire you?"

"Hire me?" I said. "Wait a minute. I'm not really a private investigator anymore. I'm not sure I ever *was* one."

"I don't understand," she said.

"It's a long story," I said. "Another long story."

"Oh," she said. As tired as she already looked, this seemed to take a little more steam out of her. She leaned back in her chair and closed her eyes.

"Actually," I said, "I was just talking to a real private investigator this afternoon. I promised him I'd send any business I got his way. Do you want me to call him?"

"No," she said. "I don't want to talk to anybody else. Look, I'm sorry, this was a mistake. Just forget it." She started to get up.

"Dorothy, sit down," I said. "Just tell me what's going on. Why did you come all the way out here? Just because you heard I was a private investigator?"

She picked up her glass of water, rattling the ice. She took a long drink and then put the glass back on the table. "All right, this is going to sound crazy, okay?"

"Go ahead."

"I was at the game last night," she said: "I saw what you did to Lonnie."

"Bruckman? You were with him?" It was hard to imagine, after all he had said about Indians.

"Yes," she said. "He makes me go to all his games."

"It was just a league game," I said. "A bunch of old guys playing hockey because they miss the good old days. All I did was block a couple of his shots."

"You don't know what that does to him," she said: "You stopped him cold. Then in the bar afterwards, the way you stood up to him. I was listening, Alex. We all were. You made him look bad."

"Dorothy, this is really—"

"You don't know him, Alex. Do you have any idea how mad you made him? He couldn't stop talking about it. All night long. He didn't sleep."

"Of course he didn't sleep," I said. "He was too high."

"You noticed."

"Hard not to," I said. "Does he do that a lot?"

"Yes," she said. She looked at the fireplace. The door opened and more snowmobilers came into the bar, stomping their boots.

"What's going on?" I said. "Are you in trouble? Did he—"

"Did he what? Did he beat me? Is that why you think I'm here? Because I need you to protect me?" She looked back up at me. I could see the reflection from the flames in the fireplace in her eyes.

"I'm just asking," I said. "Because if he did—"

"Then I should go to a shelter for battered women and leave you alone."

"Do you want me to help you or not?"

"I'm sorry," she said. "I'm just . . . I don't know. I'm sorry."

"What do you want me to do? Do you have someplace to go?"

"Not really," she said. "Maybe downstate. I have some friends."

"What about the reservation?"

"No," she said. "I'm not welcome there. My parents and I . . ." She didn't say anything for a long moment, just shook her head. "No, not there."

"Let's say I really was a private investigator," I said. "I mean, let's say I really wanted to be one. What would you want me to do?"

"I would hire you . . . ," she said, and then she stopped. "I can trust you, can't I? I really can?"

"Yes," I said.

"I believe that," she said. "I don't know why I believe that, but I do."

"What would you hire me to do, Dorothy?"

"I would hire you to help me get away," she said. "That's all. Just help me get away. Before he finds me."

"You think he'll come after you?"

"Yes," she said. "I know he will. He'll come after me. And if he finds me he'll kill me."

"God, it's cold," she said. The snow was coming down hard, the flakes already joined together in the air like falling paper dolls.

She kept her white bag slung over her shoulder, after refusing to let me carry it. "You need a warmer coat," I said. "Here, take mine."

"Don't even try it," she said. "I'll be fine."

"My truck's over here." The parking lot was full of snowmobiles and trailers. "I'll get the heater going."

She stopped and looked up into the darkness. "There's a full moon tonight."

"What moon?" I said. "I haven't seen the sky in two months."

"I can feel it," she said. "Can't you feel it?"

I opened the passenger side door for her. "Sorry about the missing window," I said. I got in my side, turned the key, cranked on the heat.

"You don't feel the moon, do you?" she said.

"No," I said. "Sorry."

"It's the wolf moon, you know. The first full moon of the year."

"This will heat up in a minute," I said. "I should keep a blanket in here."

"You think I'm crazy, don't you?"

"No," I said. I stopped fooling with the heater and looked right at her so she would know I was telling her the truth. "I've seen crazy. Believe me."

"Don't tell me," she said. "Another long story."

"Yes."

"And this window," she said, tapping the plastic.

"Another long story," I said.

She shifted the bag in her lap. "Are you sure you don't mind?"

"I had a cancellation," I said. "The cabin is empty anyway."

"I really appreciate it," she said. "I just have to sleep for a few hours. Then I'll be able to think straight."

I pulled the truck out of the parking lot, headed north up the main road. There's a place not far up the road where the trees break and you can see all the way across the bay. Just a few weeks ago we would have seen the freighters docked outside the locks, getting their last runs in before the freeze, waiting for the right weather to make their run to Duluth. But tonight it was so dark we could barely see the ice.

"Are you sure you can't feel that wolf moon?" she said. She was lying back against the seat. Her voice was a low murmur that undercut the sound of the wind. The effect was hypnotic.

"I wouldn't know how to feel it," I said.

"You've forgotten. Your ancestors knew how."

"Oh yeah?"

"You think it's an Indian thing, don't you?" she said. "Having a name for the moon."

"Isn't it?"

"No," she said. "It's Celtic mythology. I was into all that stuff when I was growing up. Pagan rituals, witchcraft, tarot cards. Anything but Indian stuff. I didn't want to be an Indian."

The snow was rushing into the headlights. It made it seem like we were moving very fast.

"It's your moon, Alex. Mr. McKnight from the Scottish highlands. The wolf moon belongs to you, not to me."

"I've never even been to Scotland," I said. "Jackie was born there. It must be *his* moon."

"You share the same blood," she said. "Why do you think you go there every night?"

"Because I don't have a television."

She laughed. Or came as close to laughing as she was going to that night. "Every moon has a message, you know. You know what the wolf moon means?"

"No," I said. "What does it mean?"

"The wolf moon means it's time to protect the people around you because there are wolves outside your door."

"I see."

"I'm not saying you need to protect me," she said. "That's not what I'm saying. I can take care of myself."

"Okay," I said.

"That's the moon talking," she said. "Not me."

"Okay."

The snow was beginning to accumulate. She stared

out at the road for a while and then she said, "Although if you wanted to just keep driving all night long, I wouldn't object. See how far away we can get."

"Dorothy . . ."

"Keep driving," she said. There was a sudden, ragged edge in her voice. "Just keep going. Get me the hell out of here."

"This road goes straight up the point about twelve miles," I said. "And then it's a dead end."

"Story of my life," she said. The edge in her voice was gone, just as suddenly as it had appeared. "Hey, you know they got wolves out on Isle Royale now?"

"So I heard."

"Speaking of wolves, I mean. You know how they got there?"

Isle Royale was an island in the middle of Lake Superior. The whole island had been protected as a national park. "They crossed the ice," I said. "How else they gonna get out there? Take the ferry?"

"Yeah, you're funny," she said. "What I mean is, do you know *why* they got there? Why they went all the way across the ice to get to the island?"

"They're hunters," I said. "There's only one reason they'd go there."

"Yeah, the moose," she said. "The moose crossed the ice first. And then the wolves came looking for them."

"Naturally."

"So imagine you're one of those moose. You think you've finally found a safe place, with no wolves around. And then one day . . ."

I kept driving.

"The wolves will always find you, Alex. Remember that."

"I'll remember," I said.

"God, I can't believe I'm back here." She slid into a fake yooper accent. "I'm in da Yoo Pee, ay?"

I didn't say anything.

"I hate this place so much, Alex. I can't even tell you how much."

"This is it," I said. I took the left through the trees. The snow had all but hidden my access road again. I was sure I'd have to plow it again the next morning.

"You live here all year?"

"Sure, why not?" We passed Vinnie's place first. "That's where Vinnie LeBlanc lives," I said. "The guy who recognized you." There was no car in his driveway. It looked like there hadn't been a car there all day. "I haven't even seen him around since last night. Since the hockey game, I mean. I wonder where he is. He should meet you."

"Why's that?" she said. "So we can exchange the secret Indian handshake?"

"He'd want to meet you," I said. "That's all. I can't imagine where he is."

"Probably drunk somewhere," she said.

"Vinnie doesn't drink," I said. It came out sharper than I expected. "I mean, you can't say something like that if you don't know the man. Even if you are an Indian yourself."

"You're right," she said. "I'm sorry."

"Here's my cabin," I said as we passed it. "The empty one is just up the road here."

I parked next to the cabin. When I turned the headlights off, the night reclaimed us. We sat there in the total darkness.

"I'll turn these lights back on until we get inside," I said.

"No," she said. "Leave them off. I forgot how dark it gets up here. It's one of the only things I like about this place."

"Too bad that full moon isn't out tonight," I said.

"That's one of my first memories," she said. "Looking out a window and seeing the snow glowing in the moonlight." She didn't say anything for a long moment. The silence was as complete as the darkness. "I'm sorry," she finally said. "You don't want to hear all this. I start talking about the strangest things when I'm tired."

"I don't mind," I said. "But you're gonna get cold soon."

We made our way through the snow to the front door. She shifted the bag on her shoulder.

"I wish you'd let me carry that," I said. It was all I could do to keep myself from wrestling it away from her.

"No thanks, Sir Galahad."

I unlocked the door and let her into the place, flipping on the lights. It was the second cabin my father had built. He thought the first one looked a little too rough and dark on the inside, so he used unstained white pine for the interior walls. It made the place look a lot bigger than it was.

"Wow," she said. "This is nice." There were two sets of bunk beds on opposite walls. She put her bag down on one of the lower bunks and climbed halfway up the ladder into the loft. "This place sleeps, what, about eight people?"

"Six is comfortable," I said. "Eight if everybody likes each other." I started the woodstove. I had already had paper and logs in there, figuring I'd have paying guests from downstate that night. "I'll get this fire going. There's electricity for the lights and the water, but this is the only heat. There's no phone. You can use mine in the morning if you want."

"No problem." She poked her head into the bathroom. "You've really got hot water in here?"

"Eventually," I said. "It'll take a few minutes to get going. I have to go turn the water on."

I went back outside and around to the back of the cabin. There was a little door that opened up to the crawlspace. All I had to do was shimmy my way under the cabin, wondering what sort of creatures were down there this time. I've seen plenty of mice under the cabins, along with a few bats, a raccoon, a possum. It's not my favorite thing to do, but if I don't keep the water turned off when the cabin's empty, it freezes in the pipes.

When I turned the water on, I backed my way out the door, brushed myself off, and went back inside. I tried not to drip snow all over the place, because the puddles dry on the white pine floor and it looks like hell. It was the only mistake my father ever made when he built these cabins.

She was leaning against the sink, her coat unzipped. She didn't look ready to get completely comfortable yet. I couldn't blame her. No matter how much she said she trusted me, it must have felt a little strange to be here.

"You got all dirty," she said. She was holding something in her hand. It was round and black. It looked like . . .

"Is that a hockey puck?" I said.

"Yeah, here," she said. She tossed it to me.

I caught it and looked at it. There was a white circle on one side, and on it a red wheel with a wing coming off it. It was the Detroit Red Wings logo. Beneath the logo there was an autograph. Gordie Howe.

"Is this real?" I said.

"Yes," she said. "Ever see him play?"

"Sure, at the old Olympia Stadium."

"Lonnie says he was better than Gretzky."

"He's right," I said.

"You can keep it," she said.

"I can't keep this," I said. "It's probably worth a lot of money."

"I know," she said. "It's all I can give you right now for helping me."

"Where'd you get it?"

"It's Lonnie's," she said. "It *was* Lonnie's. The last thing I did before I left, in fact I was out the door already, then I came back in and took that stupid hockey puck. God, he wouldn't even let me take it out of the little plastic case. Think how mad he's gonna be now."

"I don't understand," I said. "Why did you take it?"

"To hurt him," she said. She folded her arms across her chest. "It's the only thing I could think of. Pretty lame, isn't it?"

"Here," I said. I put the puck on the table. "You should keep it."

She stared at it on the table and let out a long, tired breath.

"Is he that bad?" I said. I thought I had had this guy pegged pretty well when I met him, the kind of guy who doesn't want to do anything else but play his sport, and can't deal with the fact that he's not quite good enough. I saw it all the time in baseball, guys who got cut and then spent the rest of their lives taking it out on the rest of the world. There's one on the end of every bar in every town in America. But the way her voice sounded when she said she wanted to hurt him, maybe there was something else. Something a lot worse. "I know it's none of my business," I said.

"You know those wolves I was talking about?"

"Well, yeah, I kinda figured you weren't talking about real wolves and real moose."

"Let's just say Lonnie's the first wolf," she said. "Not the worst wolf, just the first."

"I don't get it."

"You shoot one wolf, there's more behind him. Bigger wolves. With bigger teeth."

I let that one go. I figured she was just talking about the rest of his hockey team. I should have asked her about it. But I didn't.

The woodstove started to heat the place up a little bit. She felt comfortable enough to take off her coat and sit down at the table. She told me about growing up as an Ojibwa, getting out of the U.P. as soon as she could, going downstate for college, dropping out, working a lot of jobs. No matter how bad it got, she never thought of coming back up here. Then she met Lonnie. She didn't tell me much more about him. She didn't tell me what he had done to her, or why he had brought her back up here.

She asked me about myself, about why I had so many long stories. I surprised myself and told her a couple of them. Not all of them. I guess it just felt good to talk to somebody. It was the first time since Sylvia left.

"You're the lonely man with long stories," she said before I left. "If I could make you an Ojibwa, that would be your name."

"What's your Ojibwa name?" I said.

"I don't have one anymore," she said. "I gave it up a long time ago."

"It's going to be cold tonight," I said. "You better leave the water running a little bit. Just a trickle. It'll keep the pipes from freezing."

"I'll do that," she said. She came to the door as I left. "There's a good lock on here, right?"

"Yes," I said. "Although you don't have to worry. You're in the middle of nowhere."

"Thank you, Alex," she said. "Good night."

As she closed the door, I felt a vague, distant sadness for both of us. Standing there in the darkness, waiting for my eyes to adjust to it again, feeling a cold wind coming through the pine trees. We had both been through so much. Different problems but the bottom line was the same. People are bad for each other. And yet we keep trying. We can't stand to be alone.

It was late. I needed to sleep so I could get up the next day and do everything I could to help her. It surprised me how much I wanted to help this woman. Maybe it was a chance to show myself I could still do something right, after all the mistakes I had made

in the last year. Something meaningful besides splitting wood and plowing the snow off the road.

I went back to my cabin and slept. In the middle
of the night I thought I heard her voice, but when I
lifted my head it was nothing but the drone of a snowmobile engine. All night long those idiots keep driving those things through the woods. I cursed the man
who invented them and went back to sleep.

The next morning, there was six inches of new snow
on the ground. The fire had gone out in my woodstove, so I threw a couple of logs in and stood shivering before the window, looking out at the snow. I
put on some clothes, drank some coffee, went out and
started the truck. It didn't even look like there was a
road anymore, just a long gap in the trees. I plowed
all the way down to the main road, past Vinnie's
cabin. There was still no sign of him. If he had come
home during the night, if *anyone* had turned off onto
our road, I would have seen the tracks. There were
none.

I started to worry about him. It was thirty-six hours
since I left him at the bar after the hockey game. I
could go look for him at the reservation, I thought, or
go to the casino and see if he's working. As soon as
I help out Dorothy. It's going to be a busy day.

I plowed the other way, into the woods. I honked
as I passed Dorothy's cabin. Rise and shine. The other
four cabins all had vans and trucks outside them, with
trailers for the snowmobiles. The people who rented
the cabins would probably never drive once they got
here, just park the vehicles and ride their snowmobiles
all week. But I liked to keep the road plowed just in

case they needed to get out. On my way back I honked again. Here's your snooze alarm. Time to wake up while I make breakfast.

I stopped back at my cabin and picked up some eggs and cheese for omelets, some juice and coffee. I drove back around the bend to her cabin. Funny how you think that way. She spends one night there and suddenly it's *her* cabin. I knocked on the door. There was no answer.

"Dorothy?" I shouted. "Are you awake?"

I pushed on the door. It was unlocked. I opened the door and stepped inside.

The table was turned upside down. One table leg broken off. Chairs scattered in every direction.

Nothing else.

She was gone.

CHAPTER FIVE

I went back to my own cabin and called the sheriff's office. After I hung up, I stood there looking down at the phone book. It was still open to the first page. Right there under the Police and Fire and Ambulance, the number for Protective Services. I had seen how these people operate, down in Detroit anyway. They come and get you, take you to a shelter. If I had called that number last night, I told myself, then she'd be safe right now.

I went back outside, the wind blowing snowflakes into my face. The sun had come out, one of those brief interludes when the clouds break and the light shines so brightly off the white snow, your eyes hurt just to look at it.

I stood there for twenty minutes, going over it again and again in my mind. She was so scared. I should have done something, right away, instead of waiting for morning. Was I lazy or just stupid? I wanted to go back to the cabin, start searching for something, anything that might tell me what had happened. I wanted to do *something*. I felt so useless just standing there. But I made myself wait. Don't mess it up, I thought. There might be tracks there, or footprints, or God knows what kind of evidence they

might be able to find. Just stand here like the useless
idiot you are and don't mess things up any more than
you already have.

I couldn't help thinking about a murder I saw first-
hand in Detroit. It was my first year on the force. I
answered a domestic disturbance call with my partner.
He talked to the man in the kitchen while I sat with
the woman in the living room. She didn't say anything. She just rocked back and forth on the couch,
hugging a pillow. I couldn't sleep that night. I kept
seeing her face. Three days later, I watched them
carry her body out in a bag.

She had tried to leave him. How many times did
they tell us? When the woman decides to leave, that's
the most dangerous time. That's the flashpoint. When
a woman is murdered, the detectives always start with
the same question: Where's the husband or the boyfriend?

"Bruckman followed us," I said out loud. My voice
sounded small in the winter stillness. "He had to. How
else would he know she was here?" Was he at the
bar? He could have followed my truck all the way
down the main road, but then how would he know
which cabin she was in? He couldn't have followed
me all the way down my access road, could he? Could
I be that fucking oblivious?

I didn't call the police. I didn't stay with her. I left
her alone in a cabin with no phone.

The county car pulled in then and saved me. A few
more minutes alone with my thoughts and I would
have killed myself.

They came out of either side of the car, their Chippewa County hats worn just right, a young man and

a young woman. The both of them put together weren't as old as me.

"Where's the sheriff?" I said.

"He's busy," the young woman said. Her dark hair was tucked up beneath her hat.

"Call him," I said. "I want him out here."

"I told you, sir," she said. "He's busy."

"Busy, my ass," I said. "He needs to be here."

"Take it easy, sir," the young man said. He had the standard-issue police buzz cut. He approached me with his hands up, the way you'd approach a dog you think might be rabid. "Are you Mr. McKnight?"

"I told the dispatcher I wanted Bill himself," I said. "And nobody else." Bill Brandow was the county sheriff, if not exactly my best buddy then at least a friendly acquaintance. I had bought him a couple Canadians one night, traded a few cop stories. There was something fundamentally competent and trustworthy about the man. It was his face I needed to see right now, not these two kids who looked like they were on their way to a high school costume party dressed as deputies.

"I told you, Mr. McKnight. The sheriff can't be here. You're gonna have to calm down a little bit here."

"A woman has been kidnapped," I said. "Do you have anybody out looking for her? Is Bill going to do anything besides sending two teenagers out here to tell me to calm down a little bit?"

"Has it occurred to you that maybe the sheriff is out looking for her right now?" he said. "And this guy, what's his name?"

"Bruckman," I said. "Lonnie Bruckman."

"Where do you want him to be, Mr. McKnight? Out there looking for them or standing here in the snow making you feel better?"

I clenched my gloved hands into fists, looked up into the winter sky, then I took a deep breath and let it out. "Okay," I said. "You're right. Let's just . . ."

"Tell us what happened," he said. "Where's the cabin she was staying in?"

"This way," I said. "Right around the bend."

We all got into the county car, the two deputies in the front, me in the back. It wasn't more than a quarter mile to the first rental cabin, but we rolled slowly down the road, the tires scrunching over another half inch of snow that had fallen since I plowed. I gave them the quick version of what had happened. Dorothy meeting me at the bar, asking for my help. The way she talked about Lonnie. The genuine fear in her voice when she told me he'd kill her if he ever found her.

We got out of the car and stood there a moment, the deputies looking up and down the road. Nothing to see but trees. "She stayed alone in this cabin last night?" the woman asked.

"Yes," I said. "I really don't have much room in my cabin. And besides . . ." I didn't finish it.

The deputies traded a quick look at each other while they walked through the snow to the cabin.

"No footprints here," he said.

"I didn't see any," I said. "It snowed too much last night."

"No tire tracks either?"

"No," I said. "None at all."

"Even with the snow," he said. "You'd see something, wouldn't you? It didn't snow *that* much."

"When I plowed the road it looked totally untouched," I said. "Like nobody had driven on it for days."

"This unlocked?" he said when he got to the door.

"Yes," I said. "It was unlocked this morning."

"Was it locked last night?"

"Yes, she locked it when I left."

The deputies looked at each other again. I felt a sudden urge to knock their heads together. "Can we get something straight right now?" I said. "She slept in this cabin by herself last night. And I slept in mine."

"Nobody's suggesting otherwise," he said.

"If we were in the same cabin," I said, "then none of this would have happened."

"We hear you," he said. "Please. Let's work together on this." The deputy pushed the door open and looked inside.

"Careful," I said. "Don't contaminate anything."

"I won't."

"I'm serious," I said. "What if there's evidence here?"

"If we see something, we'll bag it."

"No, I'm talking about hair or fibers or . . ."

They both looked at me. He's seen this stuff on television, they're thinking. He expects us to set up a crime laboratory and start picking up little strands of stuff with tweezers.

"I was a cop once," I said. Back when dinosaurs ruled the earth. "Never mind. Go ahead."

"We'll be careful," she said.

I followed them as they entered the cabin. There

was a complete silence in the place that made me feel sick to my stomach.

At least we're not looking at a dead body, I said to myself. If he wanted to kill her that badly, he would have done it right here. It was the only positive thing I could think of.

The troopers walked around the overturned table, looked at the scattered chairs. The young man stopped at the bed where the blanket had been turned back. "Looks like she went to bed," he said. "Then got up later. Doesn't look like she left anything behind. Did she have a backpack or a suitcase or something? You said she was running away from this guy."

"She had a bag," I said. "A white duffel bag."

"She must have taken it with her," he said. "Or he did, I mean. This Bruckman guy. You say you played hockey with him a couple of nights ago?"

"Yeah, I did." It felt like a lot longer.

"He a big guy? How easy would it be for him to take her out of here?"

"I don't know," I said. "He's a lot bigger than her, but I can't imagine her going with him without a fight."

"So why is the door unlocked?" he said. "She must have opened it, right? There's no sign of forced entry."

"It doesn't make sense," I said. "She wouldn't have opened that door if she knew it was him."

"Maybe he comes to the door and says he just wants to talk to her. Then when he's inside he starts busting up the place."

"Impossible."

"You said you were a cop once. You've seen these situations, right?"

"I know where you're going," I said. He was right, I *had* seen it before, more times than I could count. The man begging for forgiveness, the women caving in. "But I just can't see it here."

"Then why did she open the door?"

"I don't know," I said. "The way she talked about him last night, I just don't know."

I looked down at the table leg that had been broken off, almost bent over to pick it up before I stopped myself. Then I noticed something else.

"Look at this floor," I said.

The troopers stopped and looked at me.

"There's too much melted snow here," I said. You could see the faint imprints of snow puddles all over the room.

"She had to walk through snow to get here, didn't she?" the man asked.

"Yes, of course," I said. "And I did, too. I even had to go around back and turn the water on. But I remember thinking about the floor as I came back in. I always try not to track too much snow in here. The white pine, it gets dirty fast. I'm sure there wasn't this much snow on the floor when I left. Not all over the place like this."

"So he *did* come in," the man said. "She definitely had company."

"I can't believe it," I said. "I can't believe she'd let him in here."

"How would Bruckman know to find her here, anyway?" he said. "Does he know where you live?"

"I don't think so," I said. "Even if he did, how

would he know which cabin she was in?"

"Could he have been following you?"

I tried to remember, tried to put myself back in my truck that previous night. Were there lights behind me? "I'm sorry," I said. "I can't say for sure. I didn't notice anybody following me, but I can't swear that it didn't happen."

"Could it have been somebody else?" he said. "Maybe she called somebody."

"There's no phone here," I said. "And she couldn't have called anyone from the bar before I got there. She hadn't even met me yet. Although . . ."

"What is it?"

"At the bar," I said. "I remember having this funny feeling. Like we were being watched."

"Bruckman?"

"No. I would have noticed him. But maybe somebody else was there. One of his hockey goons maybe."

"Well, let's call in what we've got," he said. "Whatever little that may be."

The brief window of sunlight had disappeared. The sky was clouding over again and it suddenly felt twenty degrees colder. From behind the cabin we could hear the whine of a snowmobile. It grew louder and louder as the machine came closer.

"A snowmobile," I said. "That's how he could have gotten here."

"How do you know?"

"There's a trail that runs right behind these cabins," I said. "On the state land. That's why there were no tire tracks this morning."

"Makes sense," he said. "Let's see that trail."

I walked them around the cabin, deep into the pine trees. We had to work hard at it. In spots where the snow had drifted it was almost up to our waists.

"Here," I said, fighting to catch my breath. The trail ran parallel to my road. As long as he had a general idea where I lived, he could have done it this way. Maybe he didn't even know which cabin she was in. Maybe he just skipped mine, started with hers, and got lucky.

The deputies looked up and down the trail. "Lot of tracks out here," the woman said. "We'd never know which one was his."

At that moment a snowmobile came through the trees. I winced at the noise. The driver slowed down when he saw us. Both of the deputies raised their hands for him to stop.

"What's the problem, guys?" he said after flipping his visor open. "I wasn't going too fast, was I?" I recognized the man. He was staying in the farthest cabin with a few other guys from Saginaw.

"Were you on this trail last night?" the male deputy asked him.

"Yes," the man said. I could hear the apprehension in his voice. "But I was taking it easy, I swear. I know there are cabins nearby."

"There's no problem," he said. "We're just wondering if you saw any other snowmobiles. Like around . . ." He looked over at me.

"Any time between, say, one A.M. and this morning," I said.

"We got back a little after one," he said. "I don't remember seeing any other machines on this trail. Besides the guys I'm with, I mean."

"We should probably talk to the rest of your party," the deputy said. "Are they in the cabin right now?"

"Most of them, probably," the man said. "We're supposed to be leaving today. Some of them might still be out on the trails."

We made our way back to the car, wading through the snow again. We spent the next hour going to each of the cabins, asking the renters if they had seen anything suspicious.

Nothing. No leads, no information at all. I started to feel tired and hungry, sitting in the back of the car. And now that we had done everything we could possibly do, I could feel the despair gathering inside me. It was hopeless. Dorothy asked me to help her get away from him. And I let Bruckman or his buddies or whoever it was just come and take her away. They could be anywhere now. I knew the sheriff was looking for her, but what could he do? Find out where Bruckman's living, go check it out. If he's gone, then what? Put it on the wires. Keep working on it for a few days, then file it away.

The deputies rode in silence down the access road from the farthest cabin, back to mine. I could have guessed what was in their minds. They weren't talking about it, but they would be as soon as they got rid of me. Maybe she wasn't abducted. Maybe her boyfriend talked his way into the cabin, made a scene, threw some furniture around, then got down on his knees and begged her to forgive him. He loves her so much it makes him crazy, but it'll be different from now on, and all the usual crap a guy like that says. And then she leaves with him. It happens all the time.

But I knew. I knew he took her against her will.

And I knew it was my fault. I knew I'd lie awake all that night thinking about it.

"We'll let you know if we come up with anything, Mr. McKnight," the young man said. He slowed down in front of my cabin.

"Let's take a ride down to the Glasgow Inn," I said. "See if the bartender noticed anything last night. Or maybe somebody else did."

He nodded. "It's worth a shot."

We went around the bend toward the main road. As we passed Vinnie's place, I noticed that his car still wasn't there. "Damn, that's right," I said. "I forgot about Vinnie."

"Is there a problem?" he said.

"No, it's just that my friend Vinnie hasn't been home for a couple nights. He's a member of the Bay Mills tribe, probably just spent the night there."

The other deputy looked out the passenger's side window. "Vinnie," she said. "Vinnie what?"

"Vinnie LeBlanc," I said.

"Vinnie LeBlanc," she said. "That name rings a bell."

"There's a lot of LeBlancs around here," I said.

"Yeah, I know, but I think I saw that name somewhere this morning." She thought about it for a long moment, then picked up the radio. "I think I know where I saw it," she said. She called in and asked for the front desk. When she had the man on the air she asked him if there happened to be a Vinnie LeBlanc on the premises.

I heard the answer myself. But I couldn't believe it. Vinnie was being held in the county jail on a 415, 148 and a 240.

"Oh, is that the guy who—" the driver said.

"Yeah, he's the one," she said as she put the receiver back. "I thought I recognized that name."

"What's going on?" I said. "Those numbers, what are they again?"

The deputies looked at each other again. That same look that had been driving me crazy. Now I didn't care anymore.

"I know I should remember," I said. "It's been a long time. Just tell me."

"A four-fifteen is drunk and disorderly," she said. "A 148—"

"Hold on," I said. "That's impossible. Vinnie doesn't drink."

"A one-four-eight is resisting arrest," she went on. "And a two-forty is assault, in this case assault against a police officer. Your friend the Indian who doesn't drink put a Soo cop in the hospital."

I sat back in my seat. I didn't know what to say. This whole day had become a nightmare.

"Look at the bright side," she said. "At least you know where he is now."

CHAPTER SIX

I made the deputies turn around and take me back to my cabin, then jumped in the truck and gunned it for the Soo. I swore at myself all the way down M-28. Above me the clouds were growing darker, ready to dump more snow on the world. The wind rattling through the plastic in my passenger side window numbed the side of my face.

And then, of course, I noticed that there was a single car behind me. A green sedan, two men in the front seat, following me all the way down M-28, through Strongs and Raco, all the way across Chippewa County to the Soo.

This is great, I told myself. *Now* I notice when a car is following me. Of course, today it doesn't mean quite so much. For one thing, this is the only highway that runs from east to west in the entire county. And once you start at one end, you're not going to stop unless you really need to pick up some of that beef jerky at the Stop 'n Go. So yes, of course there's going to be a car behind me all the way to the Soo. And besides, now that they've gone ahead and kidnapped Dorothy, there's no more fucking reason for them to be following you.

But apart from that, Alex, congratulations on your sudden powers of observation.

I maintained this wonderful state of mind all the way into Sault Ste. Marie, crossing over the hydro-electric canal into what passes for downtown. The City-County Building is a giant gray shoebox, perhaps the ugliest building I have ever seen. Uglier than any-thing in Detroit, which may be the world capital of ugly buildings. It sits right behind the courthouse, which has just enough charm to make the City-County Building look like an architectural felony.

The county sheriff's office and Soo police depart-ment both share the building. As I pulled into the parking lot I saw the county cars lined up on one side and the Soo cars on the other. Next to the parking lot was an outdoor courtyard, no bigger than twelve feet square. There was a cage around the entire courtyard, making it look like a dog kennel, and then around the cage was another chain link fence with razor wire on top. A man sat on the one picnic table, the snow high enough to cover the seats. He was trying to light a cigarette, fighting a losing battle against the wind.

I went in through the county entrance and right into the sheriff's office. If there was a receptionist there trying to stop me, I didn't even notice her.

Bill Brandow was hanging up the phone when I opened his door. He looked up at me and then down at the pile of snow at my feet. "Look what you're doing to the floor," he said. "Didn't your mother teach you to take your boots off?"

"What's going on, Bill?"

"I guess she didn't teach you to knock, either."

"When did you start hiring high schoolers?" I said.

"And better yet, why did you send two of them to-gether? Don't you even give your rookies experienced partners?"

"Jerry is older than he looks," he said. "And Patricia could dump you on your ass with one hand."

"Jerry and Patricia," I said. "I can't believe what I'm hearing."

"Alex, you got anything else for me?" He stood up and came around his desk. "Or did you just come down here to rip my deputies?"

I stood there. He looked back at me with cool, patient eyes. "Bill, she's gone," I finally said. "And it's my fault."

"Sit down," he said. When I didn't, he pulled the chair around behind me. "Sit."

I finally did. He closed his office door and sat on his desk facing me. With the door closed I could hear the wind rattling his windows.

"Her name is Dorothy Parrish. She's a member of the Bay Mills tribe. The man you saw her with is named Lonnie Bruckman. Correct?"

"Yes."

"She was at your guest cabin last night. This morning she was gone. The door was unlocked. There were no tire tracks, although she may have left on a snow-mobile."

"May have been *abducted* on a snowmobile," I said.

"Abducted," he said. "Fine. We'll assume she was taken involuntarily."

"You don't have to assume," I said. "She was."

"Okay, Alex, I hear what you're saying. Now it's your turn to listen to me." He looked down at me from his desk, one hand on his hip, the other held out to me as if to beg for my attention. "We're looking for them. Both of them. Okay? You gotta trust me here., Just let us do our jobs."

"Where does he live?" I said.

"No," he said. He put his hand on my shoulder. I could feel the strength in his grip. "No way. You're not gonna do that."

"Tell me where he lives," I said. "He's not in the phone book."

"I've got every deputy out there. The state police are watching the roads. I've even asked the Soo police to help us."

I let out a long breath. "The Soo police," I said. "That's the other thing. You've got a friend of mine upstairs."

"Who's that?"

"Vinnie LeBlanc. Your deputies said he assaulted a Soo officer."

"Yes, we have him."

"They also said he was drunk and disorderly," I said. "Which is impossible. Vinnie never drinks."

"No, I think it was a simple four-fifteen. Public disturbance. I saw him when he came in last night. He didn't look drunk to me."

"Then why did your deputies say he was drunk?"

"They made a mistake," he said. "They got the code mixed up."

"It's because he's an Indian," I said. "If he got in trouble, he had to be drunk."

"For God's sake, Alex. You want me to call them in here so you can give them this lecture? Because I really don't need to hear it right now."

"I'm sorry," I said. "It's just . . . goddamn it. Where is he, anyway? Can I see him?"

"He's still in one of the holding cells," he said. "We're a little tight on space upstairs. You know, if he calls the reservation, they'll come get him. Don't you think he'd rather stay in that jail instead?"

"Somehow I don't think so," I said. "You'd have to know him."

"Well, he busted up an off-duty Soo cop pretty badly," he said. "Broke his nose, gave him a concussion."

"How did it happen?"

"I'm not sure. The Soo guys brought him in. All I know is, it had something to do with a hockey stick."

"Oh God," I said. "Will you take me to him, please?"

"It's a Soo bust," he said. "You gotta go through them."

"It's your jail, Bill. The last thing I want to do right now is go see Chief Maven."

For the first time since I got there, he smiled. "I don't blame you," he said. "All right, I'll see if I can sneak you in there. If Maven finds out, though, he's gonna be all over you."

"Let him try," I said. "This day can't get any worse."

There were four holding cells on the ground floor, simple cages with benches running along the sides, single toilets against the back wall. The county jail itself was upstairs. These cells were mainly for suspects awaiting arraignment, although today there were four or five men in each cell.

"What the hell's going on here?" I said.

"I told ya," he said. "We got a full jail upstairs. A lot of them are Soo busts, drugs coming over the bridge. We already called the state prison in Kincheloe. They're gonna see if they can help us out temporarily."

"Where's Vinnie?"

"Last cell on the end," he said. We walked down a narrow corridor that ran the length of the cells. Above us the fluorescent lights were humming and flickering. There was no other light, no awareness of the outside world. "I'd appreciate it if you could talk him into posting bail. I really don't need him here, Alex."

"What bail? He's already been arraigned?"

"Ten thousand dollars," he said.

"Jesus, Bill."

"He put a cop in the hospital, Alex. A thousand-dollar bond is all he needs. You know that."

"Didn't he call anybody?"

"Nope. He's just been sitting there since last night."

"You gotta be kidding me," I said. When we came to the last holding cell I saw him sitting on one of the benches, staring at the floor. He didn't look up.

"Vinnie," I said.

He was silent. There were three other men in the cell, a couple longhairs sitting together on the other bench, trying hard not to look scared. A very large, very ugly man in fatigues standing against the back wall.

"Vinnie," I said.

Nothing.

"I'll leave you two to get reacquainted," Bill said.

"Remember, if Maven finds you here, I had nothing to do with it."

"Thanks, anyway," I said. When he was gone I pulled up one of the folding chairs that were scattered in the corridor and sat on it. I looked at Vinnie for a long time, waiting for him to do or say something. He didn't do either.

"All right, Vinnie," I finally said. "Are you gonna stay in here all winter or am I gonna help you get out of here?"

"I'm gonna stay in here all winter," he said. When he looked up at me I saw he had nice shiner under his right eye.

"That's what Indians do," the man against the back wall said. "They get arrested so they can spend the winter in jail."

"Thanks for the observation," I said. "Now go fuck yourself."

"You wouldn't be talking like that if there wasn't no set of bars in the way."

"You're right, I wouldn't," I said. "I'd be sticking your head down that toilet."

He smiled. It didn't do anything for his looks. For the rest of the time I was there, he kept staring at me, his arms folded against his chest.

"All right, tell me what happened," I said to Vinnie. "And why the hell didn't you call me?"

"What was I supposed to say?"

"That you were arrested and I should come get you?"

"I couldn't do that," he said.

"What about the tribe? They'd bail you out in a second, wouldn't they?"

"No way," he said. "There's no way I'm gonna call the tribe to come bail me out."

"No, perish the thought," I said. "It's so nice in here."

"No fucking way."

"So tell me the story, at least."

"What story?"

"What story. That's cute. The story of how you got arrested. Start with me leaving you at the bar the other night, and then work your way up to hitting a cop with a hockey stick."

Vinnie let out a long, tired sigh, rubbed the swelling around his eye. "I didn't mean to hit that cop, Alex. I didn't even know he *was* a cop. He wasn't in uniform."

"So what happened?"

"He just got in the way, Alex. I was going after Bruckman."

"Hold it," I said. I moved my chair closer to the bars. "Vinnie, this is very important. Tell me everything that happened."

"After you left the other night, I took a couple of the guys back to the reservation. I was going through town, there's a gas station on the loop there, I saw Bruckman and some of his friends gassing up their snowmobiles."

"So they *did* have snowmobiles," I said. "But at the bar, they weren't wearing suits—"

"No, they still didn't have suits on. Just leather jackets. It's pretty stupid, but then I'm not surprised."

"That young woman you saw with them at the bar, was she with them then?"

"Yes," he said. "She was there."

"Her name's Dorothy Parrish."

"I know," he said. He looked down at the floor.

"How do you know her, Vinnie? I asked her about you. She said she doesn't know you at all."

He let out a burst of air. I might have taken it for a laugh if he wasn't sitting in a jail cell. "I'm not surprised," he said.

"I don't get it," I said.

"Alex, I've known Dorothy Parrish since I was a little kid. She was a couple of years older than me. In high school, she was . . ." He shook his head. "She was so pretty, first of all. And a really good student. And popular. Everybody loved her. All the guys were hanging around her all the time. The white guys, I mean. The football players. She was the first girl from the tribe to be homecoming queen, did you know that?"

"I take it the two of you didn't hang around together."

"No," he said. "Not hardly. Back then, the reservation was a bunch of shacks. It must have still been that way when you first came up here. You must have seen it."

"Yes, I remember."

"I suppose things are a lot better now, but back then . . . a lot of other kids from the tribe . . . well, it was hard. But not for Dorothy. She was the exception. When she was at school, at least."

"Did you hate her for that?"

"Hate her?" he said. "I think Dorothy Parrish was the first girl I ever loved. As much as you can love somebody when you're sixteen years old and she doesn't even know your name. Or *want* to know your name. I would have just reminded her of where she came from. Where she had to go home to every night. She couldn't wait to graduate and get out of town."

"Why do you think she came back?" I said.

"I can't even imagine why," he said. "She hated this place so much. I never saw her again until the other night."

"Vinnie," I said. "She came to the Glasgow. She was looking for me. She wanted me to help her get away from Bruckman."

He looked at me without saying anything.

"She stayed with me last night," I said. "In one of the other cabins, I mean. This morning, she was gone. I think Bruckman took her."

He closed his eyes. "Oh, no," he said. "Please no."

"What happened with Bruckman? You said you saw him at the gas station."

"Yes," he said. "Dorothy was sitting on one of the snowmobiles. She was right underneath one of the lights. I could see her face. She looked so cold sitting there. So miserable. Bruckman came over to her and started yelling at her. I couldn't hear what he was saying, but she started . . . God, Alex, she was just cringing. And then he pushed her off the back of the snowmobile. She got up and went into the store next to the gas station. When she came out all the guys were ready to go. She just stood there in front of the door for a long time, and then she got on the back of Lonnie's snowmobile and they took off. So I followed them, Alex. I don't know why. I just had to. I couldn't leave. Jimmy and Buck were in the back seat, but they were totally out of it. I followed Bruckman and his gang down the loop. They were riding right next to the road, so it was easy. They took a right on a little trail that goes west, so I lost them for a while. But I know that trail comes back out along Three Mile Road. So I just kept going west, watching for them. And then I saw their snowmobiles parked in front of Cappy's, you know, that little place on the edge of town. I didn't see them, so I figured they were inside warming up. I parked the car, waited for a while. I thought about going inside, but then I figured they'd recognize me. I mean, I had just played hockey with them, and then they saw me at the Horns Inn. So I just waited."

When he stopped talking it was quiet in the cell, with only the humming of the lights above us. His three cellmates were listening intently, even Mr. Friendly against the wall. This was as much entertainment as he was going to get all day. I pulled my chair up closer to the bars. "Excuse us, gentlemen," I said.

Mr. Friendly spat on the floor.

"So you waited," I said, lowering my voice. "And then they eventually came out." I know where this is going, I thought. They come out, Bruckman roughs her up again, Vinnie takes a hockey stick to him, and an off-duty Soo cop tries to break it up. And now here he sits in jail. But that's not what he told me.

"He came out by himself," Vinnie said. "He stood there and smoked a cigarette in the parking lot. And then Juno showed up."

"Who's Juno?"

"Juno's my cousin. On my father's side. He's had a lot of problems in his life, Alex. He's gotten into a lot of trouble. He did a little bit of jail time a couple of years ago. Hell, I'm sure he sat here in this cell more than once. Anyway, he comes in and Bruckman goes up to his car. Juno rolls the window down, and I saw Bruckman giving him something. Kinda obvious what they were doing. So Juno leaves the place and heads west down Three Mile Road, out towards the rez. Bruckman's still standing out there. It's cold as hell, but he doesn't seem to mind it, even though he's only got that leather coat on. I wasn't sure what to do next, but Jimmy and Buck are still snoring in the back seat, so I figure I'll just keep waiting, see what happens."

He stopped and it was silent again, his cellmates still watching him. I didn't say anything. I just waited for him to find the right words for whatever came next.

"So what happens is, Bruckman goes into the bar for a few minutes, and then he comes back out. He's smoking another cigarette, just standing there in the parking lot. And Juno comes back. He couldn't have been gone more than thirty, thirty-five minutes. Just enough time to go to the rez and back. This time when Bruckman goes to Juno's window, Juno gives *him* something. Had to be money, I'm thinking. Bruckman was giving him drugs and Juno was taking them to the reservation. So, um . . ." Vinnie let out a breath and swallowed. "So I started to get mad. This is my cousin and he's taking drugs back into the reservation. And Bruckman is the guy giving him the drugs, Alex. That's what really got to me. My own cousin, Alex." His voice became ragged. "Goddamn it, my father's brother's son, is . . . I just couldn't stand it, Alex. And then Dorothy comes out of the bar, and she's standing there under the light by the door. One second outside and already she's looking cold again. And Bruckman's yelling at her about something. So she went back inside. But that look on her face. This is the one member of my tribe, the one girl in my whole fucking tribe who found a way out of here, and now here she is back again with this asshole who's selling drugs to our people. Like we don't have a hard enough time, Alex. Like we already don't even have the slightest fucking chance."

"It's all right," I said.

"So I lost it, Alex. I went after him."

"I understand."

"I got my hockey stick out and went after him. All his buddies got out there in about two seconds. I think maybe they were already on their way out. I got a few good shots in, but then somebody jumped on me."

"And then the cops tried to break it up? Did they identify themselves?"

"I don't even know," he said. "I don't remember. I guess there were two off-duty Soo cops there. I was just swinging, Alex. I didn't care who I hit."

"What about Bruckman and his guys? The cops arrested you and let him get away?"

"Why would they arrest him?" he said. "I was the one who attacked them."

"Didn't you tell them he was selling drugs?"

"After I hit the cop in the face with my hockey stick? I'm gonna tell him what to do?"

"So they got away."

"Yes."

"So later that night, Dorothy runs away from him. And then he comes after her."

"If anything happens to her, Alex . . . So help me God, I'll kill him."

"Save it," I said. "Let's just get you out of here."

"I told you, I don't want the tribe bailing me out."

"I know a bondsman," I said. "In fact, I think we'll be his first customer."

"You don't have to do this, Alex."

"Yes, I do," I said. I stood up and pushed the chair away. "I need you to help me find her."

CHAPTER SEVEN

There was a pay phone in the lobby, with a phone book sitting on the shelf under it. There was no chain. With city police on one side and county deputies on the other, I guess they figured you weren't going to steal it. I looked up the number and dialed, shaking my head. This is a mistake, I thought. There's a bondsman down in Mackinac. He could be here in an hour and a half.

"You have reached Leon Prudell," the voice said. "I'm not here to speak with you at the present time. If you are in need of my services, please leave a message. I'll try to get back to you as soon as I possibly can. If this is an emergency, please try paging me at this number . . ." Then came an 800 number with a nine-digit code I had to scramble to write down.

I hung up the phone, told myself this was my last chance to change my mind, and then dialed Leon's pager number. I punched in the number for the pay phone and then hung up the phone again. It took less than a minute to ring.

"This is Leon Prudell," he said. "How can I help you?"

"Prudell, this is Alex McKnight. I need a bail bond."

"Alex!" he said. "Damn, this pager really works! You're my first call! You're calling me to tell me you've reconsidered the partnership idea, right?"

"Just get down to the county jail," I said. "I need a ten-thousand-dollar bond. I can get that for a thousand, right?"

"Yes, ten percent," he said.

"How do you get the money?" I said. "I mean, where does it come from?"

"I told ya before, I'm hooked up with a security firm. Part-time for now. This will be my first bond. And listen, I don't even need to fill out all the paperwork. You're my partner, after all."

"I'm not your partner," I said. "How long will it take you to get here?"

"Well, I'm on my other job right now," he said. "But for you, I'll drop everything. What are partners for?"

"I'm not your partner," I said. "Prudell, goddamn it, just get down here."

"On my way, partner." And then he hung up.

I banged the phone on the hook. The receptionist peeked up at me and then went back to her typing.

I sat down on one of the hard plastic chairs in the lobby, looked at the cover of a magazine. *Michigan Out of Doors,* about two years old. I picked up another one, *Field and Stream,* only a year and a half old. Not that I was in any mood to read. I got up and went outside, pulling my coat around my neck as I stepped out into the parking lot. It was the kind of heavy cold that gets into your bones, makes you feel like sleeping until April. The snow was coming down hard now. A good six inches since this morning.

I stood out there and watched the snow come down, waiting for Prudell to show up with the bond.

"Excuse me, Mr. McKnight?"

I turned around. It was a Soo city officer, holding the door open.

"Can you come back inside for a moment, sir?" he asked. "Chief Maven would like to see you."

"Tell him if he wants to see me," I said, "he can come out here."

The cop didn't say anything. He just stood there with the door open, each breath turning to mist in the frigid air. The look on his face told me he wasn't getting paid nearly enough to put up with this.

"I'm coming," I finally said. "I wouldn't want to disappoint Chief Maven."

"Thank you, sir," he said as he held the door open for me.

"What's it like working for him, anyway?"

"You don't want to know," he said. He led me into the city offices, deep into the middle of the building.

There was another little lobby outside his door, with four plastic chairs. Apparently when the chairs from the front lobby were broken down and wobbly enough, they moved them here. The magazines, too, after they had aged for at least three years. It was the kind of place that made you want to take up smoking.

The officer left me there. I sat in one of the chairs for a few minutes. You've been here before, I said to myself, and you know how this works. Maven is sitting in that office right now, probably with his feet up on his desk, reading the paper. You'll wait here for an hour while he does his little power trip on you.

Then when you're nice and tender he'll call you in and try to make you his lunch.

Not today. Not after what I've been through in the last two days.

I got up, went to his door, and opened it. Maven was on the phone. He looked up at me like I had just run a spear through his chest.

"You wanted to see me, Chief?" I said.

"Goddamn it, McKnight, what's the matter with you?" He hadn't changed since the last time I saw him. He was a tough old cop like a thousand others I had known. Thinning hair, mustache, a weathered face that had seen too many hard winters. He was an ugly bastard, but he made up for it with his winning personality.

I sat down on the chair in front of his desk. "I'm pressed for time," I said. "You've got five minutes."

"I don't believe this," he said. "I'm sorry," he said into the phone. "I've been rudely interrupted here. I'm gonna have to get back to you . . . Yes . . . Yes, I will. Yes. I said yes, already. Okay, good-bye!" He slammed the phone down and looked at me. "Did somebody tell you to come in here without knocking?"

"You know, I think I figured out why you're always in such a bad mood," I said.

He didn't say a word. He didn't blink.

"Look at this place," I said. His office was four concrete walls. No windows. Not a single picture or personal artifact on his desk. "I just spent a few minutes in the jail," I said. "And I gotta tell ya, it's a lot nicer in there than it is in here."

"That's what I wanted to see you about," he said. "What were you doing in the jail?"

"I was visiting a friend."

"This friend wouldn't happen to be Vinnie Le-Blanc, would it?"

"That would be him."

"Who told you could see him? He's in city custody."

"Yes," I said. "But it's the county jail."

"That doesn't mean shit, McKnight. The next time you visit somebody in my custody without asking me first, I'm gonna throw you in the cell next to him. Do you understand?"

"Why did you arrest him?" I said.

"You're joking."

"Why?"

"Well, let's see, because he assaulted a police officer? Because he broke a fucking hockey stick across his fucking nose? You need more than that?"

"He was going after a man named Lonnie Bruckman," I said. "A man who was selling drugs to another Indian. Did you bring Bruckman in, too? Did you even question him? Did your guys even *notice* him? Or did they just pick out the Indian and jump on him?"

"This has got nothing to do with you," he said. "We know about Bruckman. We're handling it."

"Who's 'we'?" I said. "The county's looking for him. He abducted a woman last night."

"I know," he said. "I know all about it."

I leaned back in the chair and looked him over. "It happened in Paradise," I said. "There's no reason for you to be involved in this."

"You want to find her or not? The county needs all the help they can get."

I didn't say anything.

"Besides," Maven went on. "Bruckman lives in the Soo."

There it was, I thought. He had to let that one out, just to flex his muscles. "Of course," I said, "Dorothy was staying there, too."

"Naturally," he said.

"Bill told me about it. That place over on . . ." I let it hang.

Maven just shook his head. "Nice try, McKnight. Like I said, this has nothing to do with you now."

"She was in my cabin," I said. "He took her out of my cabin."

It was his turn to lean back in his chair. "Yeah, about that," he said. "Let me see if I got this straight. The last guy you were protecting ended up on the bottom of Lake Superior. Now this woman comes to you and asks you to protect her, and you put her all by herself in a cabin in the woods so her ex-boyfriend can come kidnap her in the middle of the night. Have I got that right?"

I just looked at him.

"I got one thing to say to you, McKnight. I hope to God that you're at least giving these people a nice discount on your rates."

"Are you done?" I said.

"I'm done," he said. "Now go home and stay out of the way. Let the real cops do their jobs." And then he picked up his phone and waited for me to leave. Just like that.

I got up and left. There was nothing I could say to

him, nothing I could do short of going over the desk and strangling him. I just left him sitting there and went out and closed the door behind me.

I walked up and down the hallway a few times, not even sure if I was more angry or confused. The whole exchange with Maven had a spin to it that just didn't feel right. Besides the insults and the stonewalling and the whole tough guy act, that much I expected. There was something else. But I couldn't figure it out.

When I got back to the front lobby, I saw Leon Prudell coming in the door, shaking the snow out of his red hair. He had on a down coat that looked maybe two sizes too small on him. It probably fit him right when he wore it in high school twenty-five years ago.

"Alex," he said when he saw me. "I'm just on my way to the clerk's office. I have the bail right here."

"How'd you get here so fast?" I said.

"I was in town, anyway," he said. Then after a long moment, "I've got a new job. For the winter, at least."

"Yeah?"

"I sell snowmobiles," he said.

"Oh God," I said.

"In the summer, I'll probably have to sell outboard motors. What can I say, it's a job."

"I know," I said. "Because I took your old private investigator job. We've been through this before."

"No, no," he said. "That's ancient history. We're partners now."

I looked at the ceiling. "Prudell . . ."

"Time's a-wasting," he said. "I gotta bail out our man. Vincent LeBlanc, right? City charges, you said?"

"Yes," I said. "Go bail his ass out while I go use the bathroom."

He went on his way while I found the men's room. I walked in and found Bill Brandow standing at a urinal. I stepped up next to him.

"You're having a tough day," he said without looking at me.

"Bill, what's going on?"

"What do you mean?" He still didn't look at me.

"Something's not right here. Maven's acting funny. You're acting funny."

"I wasn't aware that I was acting funny," he said. "It's not the kind of day to be acting funny."

I didn't know what else to say. I did my business and he did his, and then he washed his hands and left.

I went back out to the lobby and looked out the front window at the snow. It was coming down in flakes as big as cotton balls. When I finally turned around, Prudell was leading Vinnie out through the door to the holding cells. I saw a nice purple bruise on Vinnie's right cheek that I had missed before.

"The trial is in seven days," Prudell said. "I trust you'll be here in court?"

Vinnie looked at him without saying anything.

"Please don't make me come find you," Prudell said.

"He'll be here," I said. "Don't worry about it."

"Good enough, Alex," he said. "I'll leave him in your hands."

"Did you hear that, Vinnie?" I said. "You're in my hands now."

Vinnie just stood there looking miserable.

"Okay, partner," Prudell said. "What's next?"

"What do you mean, what's next?"

"We have work to do," he said. "We've got seven days to prove his innocence."

"He's not innocent," I said. "He broke a hockey stick over a police officer's nose."

Prudell looked around the lobby and winced. "Jesus, Alex. Keep your voice down."

"It's not a secret," I said. "Just ask him."

Prudell looked at Vinnie, waiting for a reaction. He didn't get one.

"Okay," he said. "Okay. But still. There must have been extenuating circumstances. Were there witnesses?"

"Can we stop talking about me like I'm not even here?" Vinnie finally said. "And can we get the hell out of here?"

We all stepped out into the snowflakes. There had to be nine inches on the ground already. I led Vinnie to my truck, kicking up clouds of white powder with every footstep. Leon followed us. "So what should I do, Alex?" he said. "Give me something to do."

I stopped next to the truck and thought of all the things Prudell could do. And then I felt bad, because the man had just done me a favor. "You want something to do?"

"Anything, Alex. Let me help you."

"There's a man named Lonnie Bruckman," I said. I gave him the five-minute version of what had happened. Playing hockey, seeing him later at the bar. Dorothy coming to me for help. And then Bruckman taking her in the night. "I believe he lives here in Sault Ste. Marie," I said. "Or at least, he *was* living here. I'm sure he's gone now. But if you could find out where he was staying, that would help."

"Consider it done, Alex. I'm on the case."

"Okay, good."

"I'll call you with a report," he said.

"Good," I said.

"I'll find the place," he said. "You can count on it."

"Okay," I said. "Go find it."

He finally turned to go.

"Hey, and thanks," I said. "For the bond."

"What are partners for?" he said. Then he was gone, shuffling through the snow to his car.

Vinnie and I got in the truck and waited for the heater to warm things up, our breath fogging up the windshield.

"Why did you tell that guy about what happened?" Vinnie said. "He's an idiot."

"That idiot just bailed you out of jail," I said. "Besides, what have we got to lose? He might find out where Bruckman was living, even if he has to bother everybody in town."

Vinnie shook his head. I pulled out of the parking lot and headed south toward M-28. The midday light was muted by the heavy clouds and snow, giving everything we saw a dreamlike quality. On a different day it would have felt peaceful.

"When you gonna get this window fixed?" Vinnie said. He wrapped himself tight in his coat as the wind whipped at the clear plastic.

"You sure have a lot of complaints for a man who just got bailed out," I said.

"I didn't ask you to bail me out," he said. "You should have left me there."

"Don't start that again," I said. "Just start talking. What else do you know about Dorothy Parrish?"

"I told you everything."

"What about relatives? I looked in the phone book. There's gotta be thirty Parrishes on the reservation."

"That's her family," he said. "They all are."

"I know that," I said. "What about *close* relatives? What about her parents? Do you know her parents?"

Vinnie hesitated. He looked out the plastic window at the snow as we barrelled through it. "Yes," he finally said. "I know her parents."

"Do they still live on the reservation?"

"Yes," he said.

"Good, then that's where we start."

He nodded his head slowly. "Okay," he said. "That's where we start."

We made our way west, back toward the reservation. I couldn't go more than thirty miles an hour in the snow. There weren't many cars on the road, but I did notice one car following us all the way down M-28. Once again, I wondered for a moment if I was being followed. Once again I swore at myself for being stupid enough to wonder.

When we turned north to go up to the reservation, the car kept going west toward Paradise. See, Alex, I said to myself, you're gonna drive yourself crazy if you keep thinking like this. Why on earth would anybody be following you?

CHAPTER EIGHT

The Bay Mills Reservation is just north of the town of Brimley, on the shores of Whitefish Bay where it starts to narrow into the St. Marys River. The tribe is just one of several that make up the Ojibwas, or the Chippewas as the white people call them. There was a time when you'd drive onto the reservation and see nothing but run-down little shacks. Now with the money coming into the Bay Mills Casino, those shacks are gone. The reservation is all ranch homes now, with yards and paved driveways and decorated mailboxes. If you didn't see the sign on the way in, you wouldn't know that you were on a reservation at all. You'd just think you're in another modern subdivision.

"Where's the house?" I said.

Vinnie had been silent for most of the trip, dozing against the side of the car despite the rattling of the plastic. Now he stirred and told me to stay on the main road all the way to the north end of the reservation.

We went past the Bay Mills Casino, the bigger and newer of the two casinos on the reservation, then the health center and then the original Kings Club Casino. Then the gym and the community college, more fruits

of the casino business. A little further down the road
we saw a few children sledding down the road that
led up to the graveyard on Mission Hill.

Vinnie pointed out a house on the left. I pulled into
a freshly cleared driveway. A snowblower sat in the
open garage, still caked with slowly melting snow.
Vinnie went to the front door and knocked. I stood
behind him on the porch as Mr. Parrish answered the
door. "Mr. Parrish, good to see you," Vinnie said. "Do
you remember me? My name is Vinnie LeBlanc."

"Vinnie," the man said. "Of course. I know many
of your cousins. I see them at the college."

"Mr. Parrish, this is Alex McKnight. Do you think
he could ask you a few questions? It's about Dorothy."

Mr. Parrish looked at me for the first time with
slow, careful eyes. He didn't say anything.

"Please, Mr. Parrish," I said. "This won't take long.
It's very important."

"Very well," he said. He opened the door all the
way and let us in. We stepped into the house, after
stomping the snow off our boots. It was a nice place,
pleasant and clean, simply decorated. Above the
couch there was a painting of a crane. According to
Ojibwa mythology, a crane came to this area where
the lake tumbled down the rapids of the St. Marys
River, laid her eggs and then brought the Ojibwa people to the same spot to settle there.

When Mrs. Parrish came into the room, I could see
Dorothy's face in hers. The same eyes, the same
mouth. Vinnie introduced me and I shook her hand.
She offered us coffee. We declined. When they sat
down on the couch together, Mr. Parrish glanced up

into my eyes for a moment. Mrs. Parrish picked a spot on the far edge of the coffee table and sat, staring at it. Neither of them could have been more than five years older than I was. When I had first met Dorothy and told myself I was old enough to be her father, I was right.

"I know this must be a difficult time," I said. I was sitting in one wing-back chair, Vinnie in another, with the television between us. "I mean, I assume you know all that has happened."

"We received a call today from the tribal police," Mr. Parrish said. The tribal police had recently been deputized under the Chippewa County Sheriff, so it made sense that they would handle this end of it. "We understand that Dorothy is missing."

"She was in my cabin last night," I said. Mrs. Parrish looked up at me quickly and then back down at the coffee table. "Please don't misunderstand," I said. "She was not in the same cabin as I was. I own six of them up in Paradise. Dorothy came to me, asking for help. I let her spend the night in one of the guest cabins. This morning, she was gone."

Mr. Parrish nodded.

"I can't help but feel responsible," I said. "I was a police officer myself once. Looking back at it, I should have done more to help her, right away. I should have called the sheriff's office, or Protective Services."

Mr. Parrish lifted his hands from his knees and then put them down again.

"I'd like to help in any way I can," I said. "Is there any place you think she could be right now? Any place this man Bruckman may have taken her?"

"We don't know this man Bruckman," he said.

"You've never met him?"

"No," he said. "We haven't seen Dorothy in several years."

I didn't know what to say next. "You mean," I finally said, "she came back up here with him for these past few months, but you never saw her?"

"No," he said.

"But you must have known she was here."

"No," he said. "Not until the police called this morning."

I let out a long breath and looked away from them. And then I noticed, on a set of shelves in the kitchen, a picture of a little girl, maybe seven or eight years old. Pigtails, front teeth missing. It had to be Dorothy. I looked around the rest of the room, but I couldn't see any other pictures of her.

A fragile silence settled on the house. There was only the faint sound of the snow ticking against the windows. Vinnie sat in his chair, as still as the Parrishes.

I cleared my throat. "Is there anything you can think of," I said, "anything at all, that might help me find your daughter?"

"I'm afraid not," Mr. Parrish said.

"Can I give you my name and number, in case you hear from her?"

"Yes," he said.

I asked them for paper and a pen, and then wrote down the information. I had a sick feeling that it was a completely futile gesture.

"I'm sorry to have taken up your time like this," I said. "I hope this . . ." I searched for the right words.

I couldn't even think straight anymore. "I hope this all works out."

"Thank you," he said. I shook his hand and then Mrs. Parrish's. She hadn't said a word since offering us the coffee.

It was dark already and still snowing when we went back outside. The day was gone.

I started up the truck and got the heater going. We had been in there so briefly, it didn't take long to warm up. I didn't feel like talking, so we rode back most of the way to Paradise in silence.

"What about your car?" I finally said. "Where is it?"

"I'm sure my cousins took it back to my house," he said.

I nodded. There was more silence. A deer hopped through the snow and across the road in front of us.

"Okay," I said. "So what the hell happened back there?"

"What do you mean?"

"The Parrishes. Why were they acting so strange?"

"How were they acting strange?"

"Come on," I said. "Their daughter just got kidnapped. I could barely get them to blink."

"Alex," he said, "you don't understand."

"What don't I understand? Explain it to me. Start with how they could go for years without even hearing from her. I thought family was everything to you guys."

"It is everything," he said. "But you have to understand the way my people are. You know, when I was growing up, my mother used to ask me if I wanted to go to the dentist. She didn't *tell* me I was going. She *asked* me. I would usually say no and I wouldn't go. Does that seem strange to you?"

"Yes," I said. "But what does that have to do with anything?"

"The Ojibwa people do not believe in interfering with other people's lives. Even with their own children's lives. They believe we each have to choose our own path in life. Even if it's the wrong path."

"That doesn't explain anything," I said. "Vinnie, she was *kidnapped*, for God's sake! Shouldn't that matter to them?"

"Of course it matters," he said. "What did you want them to do? Break down and start crying for you? They're not going to show their emotions like that, especially in front of a stranger. And they're not going to ask you to help them, either."

"No, of course not," I said. "Not an outsider."

"No," he said. "Not an outsider. It's not the Ojibwa way."

"It's not, huh?"

"No," he said. "And that's all I can say."

"Vinnie, you know what?"

"What?"

"That's a load of horseshit. Everything you just said."

"I'm sorry you don't like it."

"They're not aliens from fucking outer space," I said. "They're human beings. Their daughter is in trouble. She got mixed up with a very bad guy. Now she's in big trouble. She might be dead, even. Excuse me for expecting them to seem just a little bit concerned by that."

"Excuse them for not showing it in a way that's

acceptable to you," he said. "We are different. It's that simple."

I should have stopped right there. I was worn out. I didn't know what I was saying at that point. But I kept going. "And what's with this 'we' business, anyway? I didn't even think you were an Indian anymore. You moved off the reservation. You don't hang out with them anymore, except to play hockey once a week."

"You're crossing the line, Alex."

"Oh, and when you take the white guys out hunting, then you're Red Sky again, that's right. Then you're an Indian. Or when you're trying to explain the Ojibwa way to me. I guess you can just turn it on and off like a faucet, huh? Be an Indian when it suits you and then turn it right back off. God forbid you'd let your tribe help you when you're sitting in jail. Or even know you're there."

"Is that what this is about, Alex? You're mad at me because you thought you had to come bail me out? You want your thousand dollars back? I'll give it to you. It'll be on your doorstep tomorrow morning."

"Goddamn you," I said. I grabbed the steering wheel like I meant to tear it right off. "I should have left you there. I thought I was just trying to be your friend. But I guess I *can't* be your friend, right? I'll always be an outsider to you."

He didn't say anything else. Neither did I. Not until we got to Paradise and I pulled into the Glasgow Inn parking lot. "I'm gonna get something to eat," I said. "You coming in?" It was as close to a peace offering as he was to going to get from me.

"No, thanks," he said. "I'll walk home."

"It's a long walk," I said.

"Not for me," he said.

"Another Indian thing."

"Go fuck yourself."

"Have a nice night," I said. I got out of the truck and watched him walk up the main road toward his cabin. A good two miles in heavy snow. I shook my head and went into the place.

I sat at the bar by myself and had some dinner and a couple of cold Canadians. Jackie knew by the look on my face that it was a night to leave me alone. So did a couple guys from my regular poker game who were sitting by the fire.

I thought about what had happened in the past twenty-four hours. I didn't like anything I had done. I was stupid enough to leave her alone in the cabin. Then I spent the whole day chasing my own tail, and wondering why everybody was acting strange around me.

The reason they were acting strange, Alex, is because you were making a fool of yourself. They were right and you were wrong, and they even tried to tell you that. Brandow said it in his own way, and Maven laid it out straight. Go home and leave it to the real cops.

There was nothing else I could do. I saw that. Finally, sitting there at the bar, having my third Canadian after I had pushed the plate away. For once in my life, I had to just accept that something bad had happened and there was nothing in the world I could do about it. Bruckman and Dorothy were probably a thousand miles away by now.

And the business with Vinnie, maybe he was right,

too. What right did I have to judge the Parrishes' reactions? How could I know what they were really feeling? Or what they had been through with their daughter in the years leading up to that point?

I needed to talk to him. And then I needed to go to bed. I threw a twenty on the bar and went back out into the unending snowfall. The snow had gotten lighter at least. Maybe we wouldn't be totally buried by the next day.

I fired up the truck again, went up the main road to my access road. Vinnie walked this whole way, I said to myself, in this snow.

I put the plow down and pushed my way down the access road. The snow was powder but deep enough to make me work at it. I struggled to keep the plow straight. When I came to Vinnie's cabin, I saw him outside with a shovel in his hand. He had just started shoveling, and had a long night ahead of him if he was planning on clearing his driveway.

I stopped and rolled down my window. "Get out of the way," I said.

He didn't say anything. He kept shoveling. He had taken his coat off and hung it over the mailbox. He must have had a good sweat going already.

"Vinnie, get out of the way," I said. "So I can plow your fucking driveway."

Nothing. He didn't even look up at me.

"Vinnie, come on," I said. "Talk to me."

He kept shoveling.

I looked at him for a long time. There was only the sound of his shovel scraping against the ground. The shovel wasn't long enough. A couple hours of working with that shovel would give him one hell of a sore back.

"Fine," I said. "The hell with you."

I rumbled past him and all the way down to the end of the road, plowing as I went. I saw lights in most of the cabins, the snowmobilers either in for the night or recharging for one more run. When I got back to my place, I cleared my driveway and got out of the truck. And then I stopped.

My front door was open.

I stood there, waiting, listening for any sound inside the cabin. A snowmobile whined in the distance and then stopped. Then there was silence again.

I crunched through the snow to my door and gently pushed the door all the way open. I owned a gun, but it was hidden in a shoebox at the bottom of my closet. So it wasn't going to do me any good at the moment.

I saw a single light in the back of the cabin. It was the lamp on my bedstand. The shade was angled down over the bulb, giving the whole place an eerie glow. There was smoke coming from where the shade was burning against the heat of the bulb.

I stepped into the cabin and looked around the place. I looked at the wreckage of what had once been my home. I couldn't touch anything yet. I just walked from one end to the other. The only sound was my own breath, and my own heartbeat. In the kitchen every drawer had been pulled out and upended. The refrigerator was open. Food, milk, eggs—everything was all on the floor mixed in with the contents of the drawers. The cushions of the couch had been pulled off and slashed. The mattress was pulled off the bed. It was slashed as well. The burning lampshade woke me out of the trance long enough to take the shade off the bulb and put it upright again. I went into the bathroom. Everything that had once been in the medicine cabinet was now floating in the toilet. The shower curtain was pulled off its rings and torn in two.

The closet was on the other side of the bathroom wall, next to the front door. I went to it and sorted through all of the clothes that had been thrown onto the floor. At the bottom of the closet I found the shoebox open. The gun was still there, the cylinder open and empty. I picked it up and put bullets in it, one by one. Somehow it made me feel better.

I looked at the door. The molding was in splinters. Somebody had just kicked it in. I always knew it wasn't a good door. I always figured that way out here in the middle of the woods where nobody could see the place, if somebody really wanted to break into the place, they'd find a way no matter what I did. I was apparently right.

"Bruckman," I said aloud. He did this. But why didn't he take the gun? I went back through the place and looked everything over as well as I could. There was nothing missing. Unless . . .

Unless whatever it was he was looking for wasn't here for him to find. With that thought, I reached into the pocket of my coat. The compact weight had been there all along, on the edge of awareness. Now I remembered the hockey puck and held it up in the dim light to read the inscription once again. Gordie Howe, Number 9.

Could it mean that much to him? An autographed hockey puck?

Or did he break in just to trash the place? Just to get back at me for trying to help Dorothy get away from him?

I stood there for a long time, looking at the puck. I felt the anger building. And along with the anger, there was a sick sort of fascination with just how crazy this man could be to do this. Or how stupid. Or both. He should be far away from here by now. But instead he decides to stay around just so he can do this to me.

With that anger and that fascination, there was something else. A little burning spark of anticipation, something almost like gladness. Because now I knew that he was close. And if he was close, then I had more than an even chance of finding him.

CHAPTER NINE

When I woke up the next morning, I saw the underside of the bunk bed above. For a moment, I forgot where I was. Then it all came back to me.

My cabin. I couldn't imagine one man doing so much damage. He probably had his whole hockey team with him.

I had called the sheriff's office the night before. It was Saturday, so Bill wasn't in. The deputy had wanted to send someone out to see the damage, but I had told him not to bother. No sense sending some poor sap all the way out here on a cold winter's night just so he could look at the place and say, "Yep, somebody doesn't like you very much." I had left a message for Bill and wished the man a good night.

Then I had started to clean up as well as I could, picking out the silverware from the mess on the kitchen floor along with whatever plates weren't broken. Everything else I had swept into one big pile. There wasn't much I could do with the cushions that had been slashed. I had collected up all of the material and the stuffing and had put it all into trash bags. When I had done enough to feel like I had at least started to undo the violence, I tried to sleep. But I couldn't make the mattress into something comfortable again, no matter how much I tried. So I got in my truck and came around the bend to my second cabin, the same cabin that Dorothy had stayed in.

The snow had finally stopped, but the wind was still blowing. It was a low, relentless wail that sounded like the cry of a wolf. Before I had gone to bed, I had stood in front of the sink and tried to turn the water on. Nothing. I remembered then how I had turned the water on for Dorothy that night, and had told her to keep it dripping so the pipes wouldn't freeze. She obviously hadn't. Too busy getting kidnapped, I guess. Now, the pipes were frozen solid. I didn't feel like dealing with it at that moment, so I crawled into the bed. As I listened to the wind, I thought about how this was the same bed that Dorothy had slept in, assuming she got any sleep at all before her Prince Charming arrived to take her away.

Did she really open the door for him? She must have. Otherwise he would have broken it down, just like he did mine. She opened the door for him, then he grabbed her and took her away. If I ever see her again, that will be the first question I ask her. Why did you open that door?

I dragged myself out of bed. It was cold enough to see my own breath, the fire in the woodstove having gone out. I got into my boots and coat and went out into the morning, where the wind was waiting to make my face go numb. Another glorious winter day in Paradise.

I started the truck and got the heater going. I felt so stiff that I'd shatter if you dropped me.

It hadn't snowed the previous night, but the wind

had made drifts across the road. I plowed my way down to the end and back. When I passed Vinnie's place, I saw that his car was gone. He was probably at the casino, dealing an early shift of blackjack. The wind had erased most of his hard work on the driveway. I plowed him out, just to piss him off.

When I was back at my own cabin and out of my truck, I noticed that my door was open again. I could hear my phone ringing inside. I took the gun out of my coat pocket and peeked around the door. It looked like the same mess I'd seen the day before. With the lock broken, I thought, the wind must have blown the door in. There was snow on the floor, halfway into the room. At this rate, I might as well let the bears have the place to sleep in for the winter.

The phone rang again. I picked it up.

"Alex, is that you?" It was Leon Prudell. "Is everything all right? I've been calling all morning."

"Everything's just wonderful," I said.

"I found his place," he said. "Where Lonnie Bruckman was staying. I'm over here right now, with the landlady."

"You're kidding," I said. "How did you find it?"

"I'll explain when you get here," he said. "You've got to see this place." He gave me the directions to a neighborhood on the east side of Sault Ste. Marie. It wasn't far from the ice rink and the bar where I saw Bruckman the night of the hockey game.

"I'll be there as soon as I can," I said.

"I'll be waiting, partner."

I let that one go. I figured he'd earned the partnership, at least for the day.

Before I left, I called the sheriff's office again and

asked to speak to Bill directly, but the woman on the phone told me he wasn't in. I left my phone numbers, one for the cabin, one for the cellular in my truck, and asked that he call me as soon as possible. Then I went back out into the cold. No hot shower, no breakfast. I'll stop at the Glasgow, I thought. Grab a coffee and something to go.

When I got there, Jackie was sitting in front of the fire, rubbing his hands together. "It's gonna snow," he said when he saw me.

"Your psychic powers are amazing," I said. "Imagine, snow in the U.P. in January. Is this coffee fresh?"

"No, I mean it's gonna *snow*. A lot. Yes, of course it's fresh."

I poured a cup. "How much is a lot? You got any rolls or anything? I'm in a hurry." I poked around on the counter behind the bar.

"A lot means feet instead of inches," he said. "Look in the kitchen."

I went back into the kitchen and grabbed a couple cheese danishes. The place smelled like he had just made one of his famous omelets. It made my stomach hurt, but I couldn't wait. I had to get out to the Soo to see that house. I wasn't sure what good it would do, but at least I'd be doing *something*.

"Thanks, Jackie," I said on my way out. "I'll be back later for an omelet."

"No thank *you*, master," he said just before I closed the door. "I live to serve you."

On a good day I would have taken Lakeshore Drive all along the bay to Six Mile Road, but with the wind blowing all over the place, I figured I'd be better off staying on the main roads. I noticed the car behind me just as I left Paradise. When I hit M-28 and headed east, the car was still behind me. In the rearview mirror I could see that it was a midsize sedan. There were two men in the front seat.

Just for the hell of it, I stopped at a little store in Strongs and went in and got a newspaper. I didn't see the car in the parking lot, but when I got back on the road it was behind me again.

Well, well, I thought. So maybe I wasn't just imagining it. I really am being followed. But who could it be? Bruckman, maybe? With one of his hockey goons? Wouldn't *that* be convenient? Here I am looking all over for him and he could be right in back of me.

I tried gunning it for a few miles, just to see if the car would stick with me. It did, keeping at a constant distance of about a quarter mile behind me. Then I slowed down to thirty miles per hour. If the car wasn't tailing me, it would have gotten closer. It didn't. It stayed back there, just close enough so that they could react to anything I did, but far enough away that I wouldn't notice it in my rearview mirror. Or so they apparently thought.

I stopped again in Raco, went into another little store and then peeked out the side window. The car had pulled off the road. I stood there watching it, wondering what to do.

"Can I help you find something?" the man behind the counter asked. He was an older gentleman with a kind face.

"No, thank you, sir," I said. "I'm just waiting for some friends to show up."

"They say it's gonna snow today," the man said.

"So I hear," I said, as I opened the door and went out. I'm sure the man was shaking his head as I left.

Okay, boys, I said to myself as I got back in the truck. Let's try something different.

When I got back onto M-28, the car was behind me again. I started looking for the right kind of road to turn onto, something with a little bit of cover so I could open up some distance on them without being obvious about it. We were about to leave the Hiawatha National Forest and I knew everything would be wide open soon, so I'd need to find something within the next couple miles.

A side road came up on my left, leading north through the pine trees toward Brimley. This could work, I thought. I took the turn and punched it, spinning my wheels in the snow for what seemed like an eternity. Finally, the truck found some purchase and I was moving again. I went as fast I could safely go, looking for some kind of turnoff. Somewhere that I could hide the truck and then wait for them.

I saw a couple driveways, but they were long and open. I went around a curve and almost missed another driveway. A good one. I pumped the brakes, trying to stay on the road. I squeezed the steering wheel, trying to *will* the truck to stop. When it finally did, I slammed it in reverse and backed up. Perfect, I thought, if I can just back into this driveway before they catch up to me. Hurry up, goddamn it. Careful, careful . . .

I stopped the truck. I was about twenty feet from the road, behind a stand of pine trees that were all but smothered by a thick cloak of snow. I had just enough of a sight line to see them coming, and just enough distance to get my truck back onto the road to stop them. Whoever was in that car, I'd be getting a good, close look at them in just a few seconds.

I took a long breath. I patted the gun in my coat pocket. You never know, I thought. If Bruckman's in that car, it might come down to this.

My heart was beating fast. Relax, Alex. Slow down. Breathe. Make yourself breathe.

I waited. Any second now.

No sign of the car. It might be slow going for them. It's not an easy road with this much snow. Just be patient.

I waited.

Nothing.

Where are they? They should be here by now.

Keep waiting, Alex. Just a little more. Give them time.

I waited.

Damn it. They saw through my little game. They're not taking the bait.

I waited another minute, and then I slammed the gear shift into first. Nice going, Alex. Now they know you spotted them, too.

I went back the way I came, back toward the main road, swearing at myself, at Bruckman, at the snow, and everything else I could think of.

And then I saw them.

The car was stopped, the front wheels off the road. One man was standing waist-high in the snow, trying to push the car backwards.

They're stuck, I thought. Son of a bitch, they're stuck in the snow. I've got 'em. Just drive right on up, nice and slow, see what they do.

The first thing I noticed as I got closer was that neither one of the men was Bruckman. The second thing I noticed was that they both had hunting caps on. I didn't recognize the man pushing the car, or the man driving, as much as I could see of him. But I didn't take much notice of the other hockey players that night, so I couldn't be sure.

I pulled up next to them and stopped. I rolled down the window.

The man kept pushing and swearing softly to himself. The driver kept working the wheel. They weren't going anywhere. Neither of them even looked at me.

I just sat there, watching them. The road was nothing but snow and pine trees. No houses to be seen in either direction. A few lazy snowflakes started to fall. If this was the big snowstorm everybody was talking about, it had a lot of work to do.

Finally, the man outside the car gave me a furtive little look and then a little wave. His face was red from all the pushing. "S'all right," he finally said to me. "We're okay here. Thanks anyway." A totally natural response when you're stuck in the snow and a man in a truck pulls up.

I didn't move. I kept watching them.

"We've got to get it rocking, for God's sake," the man said to the driver. "Forward and back, forward and back. Come on!" But the two men couldn't settle into the same rhythm. The man gave me a wave again. "We're fine," he said. "Go on." He still wouldn't look me in the eye.

"Looks like you boys could use some help," I said.

"No, no, really," he said. "Thank you."

"You'll never get unstuck that way," I said. "You'll be here until spring."

"We've got it," the man said. "I feel it coming now. Look out, please! You're in the way there!"

"Nah, you're stuck all right," I said. "I'm gonna have to pull you out." I opened the door and stepped out of the truck.

"No, really!" the man said. "Please! You don't have to do that!" The driver was shaking his head now and pounding on the steering wheel.

I went around to the bed of the truck and pulled out a long length of heavy chain. I held most of the chain in my left hand, and kept just enough free in my right hand to knock somebody's teeth out if I had to. My gun was in my right coat pocket. "We'll have you out in a second," I said. "You boys are lucky I came along."

"Yes," the man said. "Yes, we certainly are."

"Here, give me a hand with this," I said. "I'm gonna see if I can tie this on to your back end here."

The man hesitated for a moment. I saw him give the driver a quick look. "Sure," he finally said. He climbed out of the snow and came around to the back of the car where I could get a good look at him. I gave the chain a little swing with my right hand. If he tried anything, I was ready.

When he was close enough, I looked him in the eye. He might have looked a little soft from a distance, but those eyes gave him away. Even with that ridiculous bright red hunting cap with the flaps hanging down on either side of his head, I could see he was a rock.

"See if you can hook this up under there," I said.

"I can't bend down real well today. I'm still sore from playing hockey."

I gave him the chain and stepped back a little bit. I put my right hand in my coat pocket. The man looked at the chain like he had never seen one before, and then he got down onto the snow and looked up at the back end of the car. "Down here?" he said.

No, genius, I want you to stick the chain up your ass. "Yeah, right there," I said. "See if you can hook it onto the frame there. You ever play hockey?"

"No, never did," he said from under the car. While he rattled around with the chain, I looked at the Michigan license plate and recited the number in my head a few times. It's a Ford Taurus, I told myself. Dark green. I looked up at the driver. He was as motionless as a wax dummy now, facing forward. I still hadn't gotten a good look at his face. "Come on out of the car," I called to him. "You don't want to be in there when I start pulling." Actually, he *would* want to stay in there and steer while I was pulling the car, but I figured it was worth a shot. The driver opened the door and got out.

"Hi, I'm Alex," I said. I kept my hands in my pockets, my right hand wrapped tightly around my gun. I didn't want to shake hands with the man, so I shivered a little bit for him and said, "God, it sure is cold out here."

"Sure is," he said. Even with the glasses and the little mustache, he looked as tough as his partner. His hunting cap was blue and his flaps were snapped up. Now that I had seen both of them, I still didn't recognize either one of them. I didn't think they were hockey players, or anybody who would hang around a guy like Bruckman, for that matter. But if they weren't with him, what the hell were they doing following me around?

I looked up and down the road. I could pull the gun on them right now, I thought. Tell the man on the ground to stay put, point the gun right at the other man's head, and then politely ask them to start talking.

I decided against it. I had the plate number. I could describe both men. I could pick them out again if I had to. And I had the advantage of knowing that they were following me now. And the further advantage of them *not* knowing that I knew.

"Haven't seen you boys around here before," I said. "You up here visiting?"

The driver just looked at me and then down at the man on the ground. "You got that hooked up yet?"

"I think so," he said.

"Yeah, we're just visiting," the driver said. "See if that'll work now."

I took the other end of the chain and looped it around my trailer hitch. I got back into the truck and gave it a little gas. The chain pulled taut and then the car started to ease its way backward out of the snowbank. For a split second, I was tempted to punch it and drag the car behind me for a few miles. See if they'd chase me on foot. In a race, my money would have been on the guy with the snapped-up blue cap.

"That wasn't so bad," I said as I got back out of the truck.

The car had barely stopped moving before red cap was back on the ground unhooking the chain. He handed it to me and said, "We gotta get going."

"Appreciate it," blue cap said. They swung the doors open on either side, hopped in, and then sprayed me with snow as they left.

I stood there watching the car. It went into another death slide and almost ran off the road again. That man does not know how to drive in the snow, I thought. And the way they just took off like that with barely a word of thanks. If I didn't know any better, I'd swear those boys didn't appreciate my help at all.

CHAPTER TEN

I kept driving to the Soo, wondering when I'd see my new friends in my rearview mirror again. The snow was coming down harder now, in big wet flakes that stuck to my windshield and made it hard to see where the hell I was going.

I called the sheriff's department again. Bill still wasn't in, and they still wouldn't give me his home number. I left another message for him to call me as soon as he could. I didn't want to try to explain to a deputy over the phone that two men were following me all over Chippewa County. I wanted Bill on the other side of a desk, or better yet a table in a bar, listening to me and writing it all down.

I made my way to the east side of town, over by the ice rink where this whole mess started. The address was in a neighborhood just off of Spruce Street, near the old Union Carbide site. The map calls it a "spoiled area" now. In the summer it's a big field of weeds and sumac trees that nobody ever touches. In the winter it's covered by a couple feet of snow like everything else so you don't think about it. The houses are small, with windows sealed in plastic to protect them from the wind off the St. Marys River.

I found Leon Prudell's little red car parked in the

driveway of the house. The snowbanks on either side
of the driveway were as tall as the car itself, so I
almost missed it. I had just enough room to park my
truck behind him and then squeeze my way between
the car and the snowbank to get to the front door.
When I rang the bell, it was answered by an elderly
woman with thick glasses and the first real smile I
had seen in days. How she could smile like that in
the middle of winter was a mystery to me, but I instantly loved her for it. She was wearing a thick white
sweater and holding a coffee cup in one hand while
opening the door for me with the other hand. I could
see Leon on the couch, holding a cup from the same
set. "You must be Mr. McKnight," she said.

"Yes, ma'am," I said. "And you must be Mrs. Hudson."

"May I offer you some coffee? Mr. Prudell and I
have been having quite a party here waiting for you."

"I apologize for being late," I said. "As a matter of
fact, some hot coffee would do me a lot of good right
now."

"Mr. Prudell and I just finished some apple pie,"
she said. "Can I cut you a slice while I'm in the
kitchen?"

"You gotta try this pie," Leon said. Now that she
mentioned it, I could see the crumbs all over Leon's
shirt.

"That sounds wonderful," I said. "If it's not too
much trouble."

"You have a seat," she said. "I'll be right back."

When she left, I took a quick look around the place.
There were a lot of old black and white pictures of
children and color pictures of what must have been

grandchildren. The room was small, but it looked comfortable and well-kept. There was a plastic slip-cover on the couch Leon was sitting on. "What took you so long?" he said.

"I had to help out a couple guys who got stuck in the snow," I said. I sat down on the other end of the couch. The plastic made a sound like popcorn popping.

"So I'll brief you, Alex," he said.

"Brief me?"

"Yes, bring you up to date on the information I've developed today."

"Or you could just talk to me and tell me what's going on," I said. "Where was Bruckman staying, anyway? Upstairs?"

"No, there's a big apartment out back, over the garage," he said. "He'd been renting the place for about six weeks."

"How did you find this place?"

Prudell leaned forward and sneaked a look around the corner at Mrs. Hudson in the kitchen. "I had to throw a few Franklins around, Alex, but it was worth it."

"Franklins? You mean, what, fifty-dollar bills?"

"No, hundreds. Grant is on the fifty."

"Leon, what are you talking about? Who did you pay to find out where Bruckman was living?"

"Hockey players, Alex. At the Big Bear Arena. You said you played against him on Thursday night, right? So that's where I started. First I tried the office. I told them I wanted to find Bruckman and I knew he was on one of the teams that played there in the Thursday night league. I got nowhere with that, so I figured I'd just hang around with the players, see if I could get a lead on him that way."

"You hung around with the hockey players?"

"Yeah, I just walked around in the locker rooms. Said hello, how's it going, tried to act like I was playing in the next game or something."

"Leon, no offense, but you don't exactly look like a hockey player."

"I told 'em I was a goalie," he said. "That's where they put the guy who can't skate, right? Just like in baseball when they put the worst player at catcher."

I counted to three in my head. "Okay, right," I finally said. "So eventually you found somebody who knew Bruckman?"

"Eventually," he said. He peeked into the kitchen again. "Alex, I believed you mentioned that this Bruckman fellow may have been involved in drugs?"

"Yes," I said. "Very involved."

"Well, it was certainly no secret to these players I talked to. It didn't take me very long to see what angle to play. I pretended I was looking for him so I could buy some drugs."

I tried to picture Leon Prudell in a locker room, pretending to be a hockey goalie looking to score some coke. The image didn't quite work. "How long did it take you?" I said.

"I had to work several games," he said. "Maybe seven or eight. There was a lot of . . . reluctance to tell me where he lived. I guess they figured that if I had really bought drugs from him before, then I should know where he lived. That's where the Franklins came in. They can be very persuasive."

"Leon," I said, "just how many Franklins did you have to spend?"

"Four or five," he said. "A couple of guys gave me bogus information. I had to go out and check the addresses and then come back again. But one guy finally came through for me. A real dopehead who was playing in the midnight game."

"Here we are," Mrs. Hudson said as she came back into the room. She set a slice of apple pie in front of me, along with a cup of coffee. "The cream and sugar are right there next to Mr. Prudell."

"I can't tell you how much I appreciate this, ma'am," I said. "I understand you had a man named Lonnie Bruckman staying in your apartment out back."

"Oh yes," she said, looking down at her hands which were folded in her lap. "As I was saying to Mr. Prudell, I'm afraid it hasn't been a very pleasant experience, especially the past couple days. He seemed like a nice enough man when he first took the place, but then there were all these people that started showing up. There was always loud music going on, and those snowmobiles that he and his friends would ride. I've always hated those things."

A woman after my own heart. "Mrs. Hudson, I just have to say that this is the best apple pie I've ever tasted." It was a perfect creation of apples and cinnamon and a flaky crust. It made me feel human again, if only for a moment.

"Oh, why thank you," she said. "You have to know how to save the right kind of apples over the winter."

"But go on," I said. "He had all these people over.

Was there one woman in particular who was staying with him?"

"Yes," she said. "There was. I never found out what her name was. I didn't see her much, but when I did . . . I don't know. There was something about her. She always looked very sad and alone to me. Even when all those people were around."

"The police were here on Friday night," Leon said. "And then again on Saturday morning."

"Friday night?" I said. "What time?"

"I called the police around two o'clock in the morning," she said. "I heard all these noises back there. Woke up the whole neighborhood. Things crashing into the walls, glass breaking, like somebody was destroying the place."

"Two o'clock," I said. "The same night he . . . Okay, go on. Did you see who it was? Was it Bruckman?"

"I didn't see anybody," she said. "I was afraid to look out the window."

"What happened when the police came?"

"Whoever was in the apartment was gone by the time the police got here. They just went up and looked around. The place was completely ruined. When I think about all the time Joe spent finishing that apartment—"

"Your husband?"

"Yes," she said. "He's been gone, my heavens, has it been seven years already?"

"You said the police were here again on Saturday morning?"

"Yes, they came back," she said. "They were asking more questions, about the young woman who was with him."

It made sense. He trashed the place Friday night, probably when he saw that she was gone. The next day, the police came back when they found out Dorothy had been kidnapped.

"Can I see the apartment, Mrs. Hudson?"

"I don't see why not," she said. "Let me just put my coat on here. Is it snowing yet?"

"It's snowing," I said.

"All my friends think I'm crazy," she said as she wrapped herself up. "They're all down in Florida now."

"Ah, what's in Florida?" Leon said as he put his coat on. "Besides sunshine and orange trees."

"And old people waiting to die," she said. "I'd rather live somewhere where you have to keep moving."

She led us out through her back door, down a walkway with enough new snow to cover our ankles. The garage was bigger than the house, with enough room for three cars. There was an exterior stairway on the side, leading up to the apartment. "Careful on these stairs," she said. "I didn't get a chance to clean them off." I wanted to hold on to her, help her up the stairs, but she went right up the snowbound treads before I could touch her. When we got to the top, she pushed open the door. The molding was splintered, like mine.

"Did this happen Friday night?" I asked her.

"Yes," she said. "It looks like somebody kicked the door right in."

"But if it was Bruckman—"

"I don't know," she said. "Maybe he didn't have

his key that night. Maybe the young woman had it."

"I suppose so." I took a look inside. "This looks familiar," I said. The place was destroyed. All of the contents of the kitchen drawers and cabinets on the floor, all of the furniture slashed. But there was one difference: I counted three broken hockey sticks here.

"The police asked me not to clean it up yet," she said. "They also asked me not to let anybody inside."

"I understand," I said. "I just wanted to take a look." Leon stood next to me in the doorway, looking the place over like he was memorizing it.

"It's killing me, not being able to clean this mess up," she said. "If Joe had ever seen the place like this . . ."

"Looks like it was a nice place," I said.

"You know the funny thing?" she said. "With all the trouble these people caused, you think this place was ever a mess before this? I came up here a couple times when I knew they were gone, you know, just to make sure everything was okay . . ."

"Yes?"

"I swear to God, Mr. McKnight, this place was spotless. Every single inch of this apartment. The kitchen, the bathroom. It was immaculate. All the noise back here, all the carrying on they did, all those people tromping through here. Say what you want about them, they kept this place *clean*. And now this. Isn't that strange?"

"That is strange," I said. "Although I suppose if something set him off—"

She shook her head. "I don't understand people at all," she said.

"Mrs. Hudson, I can't tell you how much I appreciate you taking the time to help us like this."

"I hope they catch that man," she said. She looked me in the eyes for a long moment. "But you're just looking for the girl, aren't you?"

"Yes," I said. "We are."

"Well, I hope you find her," she said. "Like I said, she didn't look like she belonged with those people . . ."

We both thanked her a few more times, for the help, for the coffee, for the apple pie. When we had seen her back into her house, I walked Leon to his car and took out my wallet. "How much did you say you spent at the hockey rink?"

"Forget it, Alex. We're partners. It's all part of the case."

"Leon, there is no case." The snow was coming down hard now. It had covered Leon's red hair in just the few minutes we had been outside. "And we're not really partners," I said. "I'm sorry. I'm not a private investigator. I told you that."

"You sure are acting like one," he said.

"No, *you* are," I said. "You're the one who found this house."

"But it doesn't tell you much, does it?" he said. "You need more."

"I don't know," I said. "I don't even know what to do next."

"When we were looking at that apartment," he said, "what did you mean when you said it looked familiar?"

"He trashed my place, too," I said. "Sometime yesterday."

"Yesterday? But he took Dorothy on Friday night. Why would he come back?"

"To make a point," I said. "Or to look for his lucky hockey puck. I don't know."

"His lucky hockey puck?"

"Gordie Howe signed it," I said. "Dorothy gave it to me."

"Okay," he said. "His lucky hockey puck. That's good. What else can you tell me? Tell me everything else you know, Alex."

"There's nothing else," I said. "Except . . ." I let out a long breath into the cold air while I decided how much I wanted to tell him.

"Except what, Alex?"

"Except the fact that two men have been following me."

"A-ha! That's something." He was trying to act smooth, but I could hear the excitement in his voice. "Have you gotten a good look at them?"

"Yes," I said. "I don't recognize either one of them. I don't think they were playing on Bruckman's hockey team the other night."

"Interesting," he said. "So what now?"

"I pay you and you go home before the snow gets any worse."

"I'm not taking your money, Alex."

"Yes, you are."

"Give me something else to do," he said. "I want to work on this with you. What else am I going to do? Go back and try to sell snowmobiles? Talk to guys from Detroit all day, pretend I give a fuck what kind of trails they like riding on?"

"Leon . . ."

"This is the only thing I want to do," he said. "Let me help you, Alex."

"If I think of something," I said, "then I'll call you. Okay?"

He thought that over. "Good enough," he said. "We'll stay in touch. You have my number, right?"

"Yes," I said, walking to my truck.

"And my pager number, right?"

"I have it," I said.

"Call me when you need me, Alex. Day or night."

"Okay," I said. I climbed into the truck and closed the door. If he said anything else, I didn't hear it.

I fired up the truck and brushed the snow off my hair while I waited for the heater. Then I picked up the phone and called the sheriff's office again. He still wasn't in, and the woman still wouldn't give me his home number. Instead of trying to leave him a message again, as long as I was in town I figured I'd just go to his office and write it myself.

I pulled out of the driveway and headed west toward the City-County Building. I didn't see anybody following me, but the snow was bad enough now, they probably couldn't even drive in it. I was an idiot myself for being out here, but what else was new?

It took me a good twenty minutes to travel three miles across town. I pulled in behind the building next to the sheriff's office. The little jail courtyard was empty of everything but a waist-high drift of snow. As soon as I got inside the place, a deputy stopped me. "You shouldn't be out, sir," he said. "There's a state of emergency."

"I just have to leave a message for the sheriff," I said. I asked for a piece of paper and pen, and wrote down everything I would have told him if he was there to hear it. My place was trashed yesterday. I know Bruckman's place was trashed, too. Yes, I found out where he was staying. Two men are following me. Don't know who they are. Here's their license plate number. Please run it and call me as soon as you can. Beers are on me. Thank you. Signed Alex.

I put the paper in an envelope and pushed it under his door. "Please tell him there's an urgent message for him," I told the deputy.

"You're not going back out in this snow, are you?"

"This is nothing," I said. "I can still see my truck out there."

The deputy just shook his head as I left. When I was back in my truck and ready to head out, somebody rapped on my window. I turned to see Chief Maven's face a few inches from my own. My bad weekend had just gotten worse.

"McKnight!" he yelled at me. "What the hell is wrong with you?"

I rolled down the window. "Chief Maven," I said. "What a pleasant surprise."

"There's a state of emergency," he said. "That means you keep your ass off the road."

"I appreciate your concern," I said. "But I'm not spending the night here. If you'll excuse me . . ."

"As soon as you hit that street," he said, "you're breaking the law."

"I can see right through you, Chief. You just want me to stay here so I'll be close to you. Isn't that right?"

Maven shook his head and looked up at the sky. When he looked me in the eye again, he was smiling.

It was a horrible sight. "Okay, McKnight. You go right ahead. Don't let me stop you."

I hesitated. This is a trap, I thought. As soon as I go out on that street, he comes and gets me, and then gives me a ticket.

"Go on," he said. "Go home and build a snowman or something."

"Okay, I'm going," I said. He can't give me a ticket. It would be entrapment, right?

"Have a nice day," he said. "Drive carefully."

"I will," I said. I put the truck in gear, looked at him one more time, and then punched it. He stepped backwards, but not quickly enough to avoid the spray from my back wheels. When I was a half a block down the street I looked back and saw him brushing himself off. Then I saw him wave to me. You're hallucinating, I told myself. The snow has finally driven you crazy.

I made my way back to 75. The snowplows were fighting a losing battle, but it was clear enough for me to get through. M-28 was a little worse, but I was fine as long as I kept it under twenty miles an hour. It was a long, hard ride, but I was tired and hungry and thirsty, and I wanted to get to the Glasgow. I pictured a steak sandwich with grilled onions and a cold Canadian in front of the fire and kept going. When I got to the turnoff for Paradise, I had been on the road for a good ninety minutes. I fought my way into town, seeing only the occasional snowmobile. Everyone else was smart enough to be inside.

I finally saw the Glasgow Inn appear on the right side of the road. I was about to pull in when an unwelcome thought hit me. My road was filling up with

snow fast, and if I didn't go plow it a few times during
the evening, by morning there would be too much
snow to plow at all. I'd have to wait for the backhoes
to come dig me out, along with everybody in the cabins. Goddamn it all, I said to myself. I better go give
it a run now before I get comfortable. Or I'll never
do it.

I kept going up the main road and then turned left
onto my access road, lowering the plow into the snow.
It was a hard push, but with all the weight I had in
the back of the truck, I was able to make my way all
the way down the last cabin. I turned the truck around
and came back down. I should plow out Vinnie, I
thought. Was Vinnie's car there? I didn't even notice.
I should probably do my driveway, too.

I slowed down near my own cabin and started
pushing the snow off the driveway. It was the middle
of the day, but with the sun hidden behind the clouds
and the weight of snow in the air, there was an oddly
muted light, dim yet persistent as each snowflake
seemed to glow with its own energy. I stopped for a
moment to watch the snowfall, hypnotized by the
sight of it and by the sound of my own breathing.

And then I noticed that my door was open again.

"Now what?" I said aloud. I left the truck running,
the headlights pointing off into the trees. It must have
blown open again, I thought. I wonder how much
snow will be in there this time.

When I stepped into my cabin, something hit me
in the stomach, knocking the wind right out of me. I
went down on my knees. I couldn't breathe. The next
blow came to the side of my head, sending me sideways on the rough wood floor. I tried to reach into

my coat pocket for my gun, but I never made it. Somebody was grabbing each of my arms and pulling me to my feet. I took a few shots to the ribs, started to sag back down to my knees, and was pulled up again. I couldn't see anything. The room was dark. Finally, my eyes came back into focus and I saw that there were five men in the room. A man holding my left arm, another on my right. Two behind me. And in front of me . . . I knew that face.

I felt his hand on my throat. "Start talking," he said.

I tried to draw a breath. I looked at him and said nothing.

He pulled out a gun. He held it to my forehead. I could feel the cold touch of steel against my skin. "I said start talking," he said. "What did you do to her?"

I found my voice. "What the fuck are you talking about, Bruckman?"

He pressed the gun into my forehead. "She came here," he said. "And now she's gone. What did you do to her?"

I didn't know what to say.

"I'm going to count to three," he said, "and then I'm going to blow the top of your head off." He put his face in front of mine, close enough for me to see the madness in his eyes. "Where is Dorothy?"

CHAPTER ELEVEN

I didn't like the way Bruckman was holding the gun. Beyond the simple fact that he was pointing it at my head. The way it was shaking in his hand, I was afraid he'd shoot me without even meaning to. It had been three days since I saw him on the ice rink. Whatever was racing through his blood that night, there had to be twice as much of it now. He was practically vibrating.

"Put the gun down," I said.

"Talk," he said.

"After you put the gun down."

"You've got three seconds," he said. "Start talking. Where is she?"

"I don't know where she is," I said.

He switched the gun over to his left hand and then hit me across the face with his right. It was more of a slap than an outright punch, but it was enough to make me taste blood.

"Where is she?" he asked again.

"You took her," I said. "Why are you asking me?"

He switched hands, then hit me again. It would have been a lot more efficient to just keep the gun in his right hand and hit me in the face with that, but I wasn't about to make the suggestion.

"I swear to God, Bruckman. I thought you took her. I've been looking for you."

He took a long breath, shivering from the cold or from whatever drugs he was on, or some combination of both. He looked at the men on either side of me. I could feel their grips tightening on each arm. I didn't know what the two men behind me were doing. They were probably just getting ready to kick me again when the time came.

"She was here," he said. "And she brought something with her. Where is it?"

"I don't know what you're talking about."

He didn't hit me this time. He took a two-handed grip on the gun, pointed it between my eyes, and said, "Where?"

"If your friends will let go of me, I'll get it," I said. I thought about the gun in my right-hand pocket.

"Tell me."

"Let me get it."

"Tell me."

"It's in this pocket," I said. I looked down to my left. Please don't go for the other pocket, I thought.

The man on my left dug into my pocket and came out with the hockey puck.

"What is it?" Bruckman asked.

The man threw it to him. Bruckman caught it and looked at it. "What the fuck is this?"

"It's your hockey puck," I said.

"My hockey puck." He kept looking at it like he had never seen one before.

"That's what you wanted, isn't it?"

"This is a joke, right?" he said. "You think I came all the way out here for a fucking hockey puck?"

"It's signed by Gordie Howe," I said. "I knew you'd want it back. That's why I saved it for you. And now that you've got it back, why don't I get us all a beer?"

There was a silence, then a slight flex in his hands. Then the gunshot ripped everything apart. As it roared through my ears I was back in that apartment in Detroit, lying on the floor next to my partner.

The blood. I am dying.

The gunshot ringing in my ears.

I am dying and my partner is dying because I didn't go for my gun.

No. I'm not bleeding. I am in my cabin. Bruckman fired over my head, into the wooden wall. The men have let go of me. My arms are free. The gun. My right pocket.

I went for the pocket. I fumbled around for what seemed like an eternity, finally found the opening and reached in for the gun. I felt the cold weight of it. Pull it out and fire. Shoot the fuckers one by one, starting with Bruckman.

I tried to pull out the gun. I felt a hand on my arm. Then another. My arm bent back, the tendons stretching to the breaking point. The gun falling to the floor; the dull thud of the metal hitting wood.

Then Bruckman's voice against my ear. "I'll fuck you up so bad, McKnight. I swear to God I'm gonna fucking kill you." He gave me a shot to the ribs, the same place he had hit before. My breath was gone again. This time I thought I would never get it back.

"Somebody's gonna hear us," one of the men behind me said. "Did you ever think about that?"

"Joe, we're in the middle of fucking nowhere,"

Bruckman said to him without taking his eyes off me.

Breathe, goddamn it. Why can't I breathe?

"There's other cabins," the man named Joe said. "They're gonna call the police."

The other man behind me spoke up. "The police ain't our biggest problem," he said. "Look at this place."

"Who did this?" Bruckman said. "Who trashed your place?"

Breathe. I still cannot breathe.

"Who did this?"

I held my hand up as I fought for air. Finally, it came to me, as if I had just come up from the bottom of the ocean. "You," I said. "You did this."

Bruckman grabbed my hair and put the gun under my chin. "You're really pissing me off here, you know that? Now listen to me very carefully. I'm gonna go through this nice and slow so even you can understand it."

His face was less than six inches from mine. There was a sickly sweetness to his breath that was worse than any gin drunk.

"She came out here Friday night," he said. "She found you at that bar down the road. Am I right?"

I didn't say anything. He dug the point of the gun into my neck. I swallowed and said, "Yes, she was there."

"She left with you, didn't she? In that piece of shit truck of yours with the window missing."

I nodded.

"Did she give you a little hummer in the parking lot before you left?"

I stared into his eyes.

"Then you came back here to your cabin, right? An old man like you, she probably wore you out in five minutes. Am I right?"

"Lonnie," the man on my left said, "cut the shit."

"Shut up, Stan," he said to the man. And then to me, "How many times did you fuck her, McKnight? I want to know."

"I didn't touch her," I said.

"I know most goalies are faggots, McKnight. But I don't believe you."

"I don't care what you believe," I said.

"Fine," he said. "You were the perfect gentleman. Now tell me where the bag is."

"What bag?"

"She had a white bag with her. Made of cloth or something."

"Canvas," the man on my left said. The man on my right hadn't said a word yet. His only contribution had been nearly twisting my arm off my body and making me drop the gun. Was it on the floor still? I couldn't see it anywhere.

"Canvas," Bruckman said. "Thank you. The bag was made of fucking canvas."

I tried to remember. Yes, she did have a bag with her. It was white, and yes, it looked like it was made of canvas. She wouldn't let me carry it for her.

"I'm telling you the truth," I said. I didn't see any reason not to. Although I knew he wouldn't like it. "The next morning she was gone. The bag was gone, too. I thought you had taken her. That's why I was looking for you."

"You're lying," he said. "That doesn't make any sense."

"Look at this place," one of the men behind me said. "Lonnie, I'm just thinking, you know, about who could've done this."

"Shut up, Stan! Goddamn it, will you just shut up for a minute!"

"Look around, Lonnie! Who else could it be?"

"If it was them and they found the bag here," he said, looking at me, "then this fucker would be dead already."

"Something's wrong here, Lonnie," the man said. "It doesn't make any sense."

Bruckman put both of his hands on the collar of my coat, the cold gun metal against the left side of my face. "I cannot believe this is happening," he said. He was still looking into my eyes but he said it like he was talking to nobody in particular. "I cannot fucking believe that this is *happening!*"

"What are we gonna do?" the man on my left said.

Lonnie let out an animal shriek and hit me in the ribs with the gun again. The other four men took their cue and started beating the hell out of me. Or maybe one of the men held back this time. I wasn't counting.

When they pulled me off the floor, my left eye was starting to swell shut. Everything else was hurting so much, it made me wish I was unconscious.

"Give me that rope," I heard somebody say. I had lost all ability to separate the voices. It was all one monster now, with ten arms and ten legs.

I felt my hands being tied together, so tight that the rough hemp bit into my wrists. And then my legs. I was picked up like a big bag of rock salt and taken out into the cold air. I felt a stinging over my left eyebrow and felt the blood dripping into my eye.

I was dropped into the snow, which opened to receive me, then closed back over me, the cold white powder covering my face. I could see nothing but white.

Footsteps. Walking away from me. I am being left for dead. In the spring they will find what's left of my body, after the coyotes have had their way with me.

It was quiet. Only the distant sound of the wind and the newly fallen snowflakes collecting over my head.

Then the explosion as all five snowmobiles started at once. The metallic whine of engines racing, then the hollow clunk of gears engaging. They will leave me and I will go numb with cold until I am dead.

Then the sudden jerk on my legs. My body moving. I am . . . I am sliding. They're pulling me. Somebody is pulling me behind his snowmobile.

I felt myself rising to the top of the snow as I was pulled feet first into the woods. I could hear the machine laboring through the drifts. Then when we were on the trail he opened it up. The rope strained at the sudden acceleration, almost snapping. And then I became a body in motion. I felt nothing but speed and the smooth blanket of snow beneath me, almost without friction. The snow blew into my face like a thousand tiny needles.

They dragged me for some period of time I could not even register. Then the machines stopped. I heard voices. Words with no meaning. I couldn't feel my face. I couldn't feel my hands. I tried to sit up, to look around me. Through the snow in my eyelashes I saw only trees and more snow. They're taking me into the forest, I thought. They're taking the trail due west, away from town, into the heart of the wilderness. Nobody will see them.

But why have they stopped here? I tried to clear my head and listen to them. Two men were yelling at each other. Fuck you. No, fuck you. You're fucking crazy. Let's just go then.

The machines roared again. This time they were coming right at me. I tried to cover my head, but it was useless. I could barely bend at the middle. The machines passed on either side of me. I could feel the rope pull tight against my body, digging into my neck, and then a sudden violent jerk. My legs were whipped sideways and my whole body flipped over. I hit the ground with my face. I could feel the warm blood flowing from my nose.

They're pulling me back, I thought. Back toward my cabin. I have to stay conscious. I have to think. Somebody has to see me. Somebody else out on the trail. It's my only chance.

I tried to look, tried to keep my eyes open against the onslaught of snow in my face. There was nothing but white.

Until the tree.

I didn't see it until a split second before it hit me. I tried to roll away from it, but it caught me in the ribs, right where Bruckman had already nailed me. It knocked all the air out of my body and sent a shooting pain from my right arm all the way down to my leg.

This is it, I thought. This is how it ends.

We stopped. I was off the trail, back in the deep snow. I sank into it, fighting for my breath.

Breathe, goddamn it. Breathe.

Bruckman's face appeared above mine. He bent down over me. "Are you gonna tell me where it is?" he said.

Breathe. Take a breath.

"I'll kill you," he said. "I'll kill you right here."

One breath. Please.

"Where is it?" he screamed. *"Tell me where it is!"*

"He doesn't know!" a voice behind him said. "Can't you see that? How stupid are you?"

Bruckman's face was gone. I looked up at the branches and the clouds and the snowflakes falling down upon my face. From a thousand miles away I heard the voices blending into one.

"The fuck is wrong with you, anyway? . . . I'll show you what's wrong with me. . . . What're we gonna do, drag his ass all the way back with us? . . . Yeah, that's what we're gonna do. . . . All the way back over the river, that's what we're gonna do. . . . Yeah, that's what we're gonna do. . . . You're so fucking crazy. Stuff has fucked you up so bad you can't even think straight anymore. . . . Just get the fuck out of the way, then. . . . My pleasure, Captain Fuckhead. I'm outta here."

A single machine taking off again. Then another. I waited for the pull. I tried to tense my body but I couldn't even do that anymore. I was dead weight now.

Motion. Slow at first, like before. When we hit the trail he'll open it up again. Can't hold on much longer.

Can't hold on.

No. I must fight it. One more try.

I picked my head up. I opened my eyes.

From the tree. A sudden movement. Something hitting the driver from the side. He is down. The snowmobile has stopped. I am looking at it like it is something in a dream. A snowmobile with no rider on it.

A man. He has a big knife. The biggest knife I have ever seen. He is cutting the rope. He is not wearing a helmet like the riders. I know the man. I have seen him before in my dreams.

Another man. I know him, too. I have seen him in the same dream. He is fighting with the rider. The rider still has his helmet on. They are wrestling in the snow. It is all happening in slow motion.

A gunshot rips through the dream.

"Don't shoot me, you idiot!"

I know that voice.

More gunshots. And then a man's body covering mine, the impact hard enough to wake me, to chase away the warm numbness in my body. I am cold again. And I am in more pain than I have ever felt before.

I heard the whine of the snowmobiles, the sound getting smaller and smaller until finally there was only the sound of his breath against my ear. "Don't worry, Alex," the voice whispered to me. It was Vinnie. "They're gone."

Vinnie rolled off me, sat up next to me. Leon knelt down on the other side of me.

"Help is on the way," Vinnie said.

"You're gonna be okay, partner," Leon said.

I tried to speak. Finally, a short breath. And then another. "I . . ." I couldn't say any more.

"Don't move," Vinnie said. "Don't try to talk."

"Just relax," Leon said. "They'll be here any minute."

"I . . ." I took as much of a breath as I could, swallowed hard and then tried again. "I . . . hate . . ."

They looked down at me. The snow continued to fall all around us.

"I . . . hate . . ." I said. And then with my last ounce of strength, I finished the sentence: ". . . snowmobiles." And then I was out.

CHAPTER TWELVE

When I opened my eyes, I saw white ceiling tiles and a fluorescent light that seemed a thousand times too bright. Then the faces of strangers with white masks on. They were doing something to my side. I felt a vague tugging in my ribs. Then I did not see them anymore and felt nothing but a dull ache all over my body that gave way to a soft rolling sensation like I was lying in a boat in the middle of Lake Superior on a calm day.

I saw Leon's face for a moment. Then Vinnie's.

I slept. When I opened my eyes again the room was empty. I looked over at the door. There was a window in the door, where anyone in the hallway could look into the room and see me lying there. There was a man standing there. He was watching me. He had a blue hunting cap on. The flaps were hanging over his ears. I tried to speak but I couldn't.

I slept again. For an hour or a day or a year. This time when I awoke I felt like I was really awake for the first time since I had come to this place. The pain was stronger now. A lot stronger.

My head hurt, especially over my left eye. My mouth hurt. My legs hurt. More than anything else, my right side hurt. Besides the pain, there was something else. What was it? I lifted my left hand and reached across my body. There was a plastic tube there. It came right out of my body and ran to a machine that was sitting next to the bed. The machine was humming away, doing whatever the hell it was supposed to do to me. God, what was it doing? I felt the tube. It was hollow. It was . . .

Air.

The machine was pumping air into me.

I can't breathe anymore. I'm hooked up to this machine because I can't breathe on my own. Am I paralyzed? No, I can't be. I'm moving my arm. How about the rest of me?

I moved my legs. I tried to sit up. Pain shot through my ribs.

"Bad idea," a voice said.

"Who is it?" I said.

"I'm Dr. Glenn." He appeared next to me, lifting the sheet to look at my right side. He was a tall man, with a beard and eyes that looked right through me. "And you, sir, should not be moving yet." He measured out every word like it was another form of medicine.

"What happened to me?" I said. "Where am I?"

"You are in the War Memorial Hospital in Sault Ste. Marie. You have been here since yesterday afternoon."

"Why am I hooked up to this machine?"

"Do not be alarmed," he said. "It is just to help keep your lung inflated."

"My lung . . ."

"You have two cracked ribs, sir, and a slightly punctured lung. You suffered a fifteen percent collapse. Anything more than ten is serious enough to use this machine. Right now, there is a balloon inside the upper chamber of your right lung. We need to keep the lung inflated for a couple of days to let the ribs heal."

"Wonderful," I said.

"You also suffered a slight concussion," he said. "As well as a cut above your left eye that required fifteen stitches."

I felt the bandage on my eyebrow.

"In addition to all of these injuries," he said, holding up an X ray toward the ceiling light, "were you aware that you have a bullet in your chest?"

"You found the bullet," I said. "I looked *everywhere* for that thing."

He looked down at me and smiled for the first time. The serious doctor routine was gone. "Seriously," he said. "What the hell happened to you?"

"You mean with the bullet or with everything else?"

"Start with the bullet."

"It was fourteen years ago," I said. "I took three in the chest. The doctors left that one in."

He nodded and looked at the X ray again. "Inferior media stinum," he said. "It wouldn't have been worth the risk to go get it."

"That's what they told me."

"I'm sure they also told you that there will always be a danger of the bullet migrating closer to the spinal cord, right? Which is why you have a chest X ray every year to make sure it hasn't moved?"

"Uh . . . I don't seem to recall them saying anything like that."

"The hell you don't," he said. He looked at me and waited for me to confess. When I didn't, he held the X ray up again. "I've never seen this in person before," he said. "Around here, the gunshots are always hunters. They're not little bullets like this one. What is that, a twenty-two?"

"Yes," I said. "From an Uzi."

"You must lead a very interesting life," he said. "Now about this business—"

"Which business?"

"This business that brings you to my hospital with a collapsed lung and more bruises than I can count."

"I was sledding," I said. "I hit a tree."

He smiled again. "There are rope burns on your wrists and ankles," he said. "Do you always have somebody tie you up when you go sledding?"

I looked at my wrists. The ropes had left a three-inch band of red, raw skin. "I need to talk to the sheriff, Doctor."

"He was here. I'll call him, have him come back, now that you're awake. There were two men here, too. The two men who came here with the ambulance."

"Vinnie and Leon," I said. And then I remembered the face I had seen, or *thought* I had seen, in the doorway. "Doctor, were there any men with hunting caps out in the hallway?"

"Hunting caps? You mean with the flaps? I don't know. I mean, I probably wouldn't have even noticed. A lot of men wear hunting caps around here."

"How long do I have to stay here?"

"It's going to be at least two days before we take you off that machine," he said. "Then at least another day after that. We'll do X rays every day to see how the ribs look."

"That's great news," I said. "I've always loved hospitals."

When the doctor left, I sat there listening to the machine for a long while. Now that I knew what was happening, I could *feel* the balloon inside me. For a moment the thought of it was too much and I had to fight the urge to rip the tube out. But then the balloon would still be inside me. In fact, if I pulled out the tube, what would stop me from flying around the room as the air escaped from the balloon, just like in the cartoons?

A nurse came and gave me some pills. When I took them, the pain in my side started to soften again. I took another little ride in the clouds. When I woke up this time, Leon was sitting in a chair next to the bed.

"Hey, partner," he said.

"What time is it?" I said. "How long did I sleep?"

"It's about five P.M.," he said. "You've been here about twenty-four hours now."

"What happened?" I said. "Where did you . . . How did you . . . The last time I saw you, we were both at Mrs. Hudson's house. You were on your way home."

"You told me you were being followed," he said. "So I decided to investigate."

"You followed me home?"

"I followed the men who were following you," I said. He pulled out a notebook. "Jeep Grand Cherokee, dark green . . ."

"Wait a minute," I said. "The guys who were following me were driving a green Taurus."

"Two Caucasian men," he said. "Late forties, wearing hunting caps . . ."

"One red, one blue," I said. "That's them. I helped them get their car out of the snow. They must have wised up and switched to a four-wheel drive."

Leon looked at me. "You helped them."

"Yes."

"Get their car out of the snow."

"They were stuck," I said. "It was the neighborly thing to do."

"And you got a good look at them," he said. "I like it, partner."

"Leon . . . ," I said, but then I didn't have the strength to finish the sentence. "Just tell me what else happened. What did the two men in the car do?"

"I followed them all the way into Paradise. They pulled into one of those little tourist motels on the south end of town, the Brass Anchor. You know it?"

"Yeah, I think I've seen the owner around town," I said. "Those two guys are staying there?"

"It makes sense," he said. "North of you, it's a dead end. All they have to do is sit and wait for you to come down that road, then pick up the tail again."

"So then what?"

"So then after I watched them go into the motel, I came up to your place. I figured you'd want to know. Your truck was there, and the door was open, but you weren't home. I saw a lot of footprints in the snow, and the snowmobile tracks. I wasn't sure what had happened, but it didn't look good. I tried calling the sheriff on my cellular, but it wasn't going through. When the regular phone lines go down, all the cellular channels get jammed. Anyway, I went back down your road, saw Mr. LeBlanc pulling into his place. I tried calling the sheriff again, finally got through, and then we both came back. That's when we heard the snowmobiles. They were pulling you back down the trail. Vinnie grabbed a big stick. I pulled out my revolver. I still have the carry permit. From before, I mean, when I thought I was a real private investigator." He looked down at his hands.

"You are," I said. "You probably saved my life."

"I panicked, Alex. Vinnie knocked that guy off the snowmobile, and I just stood there watching him. The other snowmobiles came back. I didn't know what to do. I just fired the gun into the air. Vinnie yelled at me not to shoot him. I fired the gun in the air again. The men turned around and drove away. I was aiming my gun at them. I could have shot them. One of them, anyway. The guy who was dragging you behind his snowmobile. I could have shot him. But I didn't."

"You did the right thing," I said. "What else were you going to do? Shoot him in the back as he drove away?"

"They were trying to kill you," he said. "They were trying to kill my partner and I let them get away."

"Leon, I don't tell many people this, but when I was a police officer in Detroit, my partner and I got into a . . . well, a bad situation. Both of us got shot. I survived, but my partner didn't. I've replayed that day in my mind a million times, and I always end up feeling responsible for his death. I probably could have drawn my gun in time to stop it. But I didn't."

"That's where the bullet in your chest came from?"

"Yes. The doctor and I were just having some fun with that. Anyway, the difference is, I failed, and my partner died. You didn't fail. I'm alive. So let's knock off all this shit about you letting them get away, all right?"

"Okay," he said. "Thank you for telling me that."

"It's probably just the drugs I'm on," I said.

We both stopped talking for a while. There was only the sound of the machine pumping air into me.

"They were here," I finally said. "At least one of them was."

"Who, the guys who are following you?"

"I think so," I said. "I can't say for sure. I was pretty delirious."

"When?" he said. "Where?"

"He was out in the hallway," I said "I think it was last night."

Leon sprang out of his chair as if he could still catch up to him. "Those bastards. We've got to find out who they are."

"You know where they're staying now," I said. "Go check 'em out."

He looked at me and smiled. "You know, Alex, I've been thinking. Remember how I was saying that we could call ourselves McKnight-Prudell? You know, with your name first?"

"What about it?"

"Well, the more I think about it, I think Prudell-McKnight sounds better. What do you think?"

"I think you're pushing your luck, Leon."

He raised his hands. "Just think about it." He picked up a brown paper bag and put it on the table. "Here, I brought you some stuff."

"What kind of stuff?"

"Some books and magazines. Private investigator

stuff. You might as well make good use of your down time."

"Get out of here," I said. "Go do your thing."

"You got it, partner," he said. "Leon Prudell is on the case."

I watched him leave, a two-hundred-forty-pound whirlwind of flannel and snowboots.

Look out, world.

I spent the rest of the day lying in bed, drifting in and out of a codeine haze. I couldn't get up because of the machine. I couldn't even roll over. The nurses came in to check on me or to give me more drugs or to empty my bedpan. It was not a fun day.

I could see just enough of the window to know that it was snowing again outside, then it was dark and I tried to sleep. I kept waking up every hour as a new pain announced itself. The stitches over my eye started to hurt, then my right hip, then my right shoulder. All the while the ache in my ribs was a constant background.

In the morning I saw the doctor again. He unhooked me from the machine just long enough to do another set of X rays, then had me wheeled back to my room. Bill Brandow was there waiting for me.

"How ya feeling?" he said when I was back in bed.

"Never better," I said. "You got my note?"

"Yes," he said. "I'm working on it."

"What have you got?" I said. "I gave you the description of the two guys who've been following me. I gave you the license plate number. Although now they're driving a different vehicle, sounds like. A Jeep Grand Cherokee. I can even tell you where they're staying now. They're at the Brass Anchor in Paradise. Leon tailed them."

He sat down next to me. "Leon Prudell? That clown who used to be Uttley's investigator?"

"If that clown hadn't showed up yesterday," I said, "Bruckman would still be dragging my ass behind his snowmobile."

"About that," he said. "What can you tell me? Start at the beginning."

"You know the beginning," I said. "I thought he had taken Dorothy. But now, I'm not so sure. He wanted *me* to tell him where she was. And he wanted to know where the bag was."

"What bag?"

"A white bag she had with her."

"You don't know where it is?"

"Of course not," I said. "Bill, are you going to tell me what's going on or not? Are you still looking for Bruckman? And what about those two other guys? Did you run the plate?"

"Alex, I told you I'm working on it. On both of those things. I'm not going to sit here and talk about what I know and what I don't know."

I looked him in the eye. "You're starting to sound like Maven," I said.

"Thanks a lot."

"I mean it. What are you doing to me here?"

"I want you to promise me something, Alex. I want you to promise me that you'll let me take care of this, okay? Just relax and get better. Let me do my job, all right?"

"Will you call me when you find out who they are?"

"Promise me, Alex."

"All right, all right. I promise."

When he was gone, I had nothing to do but lie there and think about it. I took more drugs. I used the bedpan. I can't take much more of this, I thought. I am going to lose my fucking mind.

Vinnie came by around dinnertime. They had just rolled in a tray with some sort of meat in some sort of sauce with some sort of vegetable and a separate compartment of green jello. "That looks almost good enough to eat," he said.

"You're welcome to it," I said.

"No thanks," he said. "I had a steak at the Glasgow. You know, with that brandy sauce that Jackie makes?"

"You're a cruel man," I said.

"I'm keeping the road clear," he said. "I've been using your truck. And I've been taking care of the cabins, although a few guys left already. I don't know if they paid you in advance or not."

"They never do," I said. "But don't worry about it. Thanks for helping me out."

"No problem," he said. He stood there looking at the floor for a long moment. "I'm sorry, Alex."

"For what?"

"For the way I was talking to you the other night. After we went to see Dorothy's parents."

"Forget it," I said. "I should have been a little more understanding."

He looked at the machine. "Is this thing really pumping air into you? What happens if I turn this dial up all the way?" He made a fake for it. I flinched.

"Ow! Goddamn it. Vinnie, I'm so glad you came by."

"I had him, Alex," he said. "I had him right here." He held his hands up and looked at the space between them.

"Who, Bruckman?"

"I wasn't going to let go," he said. "But then Prudell started shooting. I was afraid he was going to hit me."

"He wouldn't hit you," I said. "Don't forget, he's holding a ten-thousand-dollar bond on you. I don't know the rules exactly, but I'm pretty sure he loses the bond if he kills you."

"The bond," he said, like he was sorry I brought it up.

"When's the trial?" I said.

"Next week."

"Now that they know more about Bruckman, they'll have to go easy on you, right?"

"I don't know. They still don't like it when an Indian attacks a cop. No matter what."

"The tribe will represent you, right?"

"Yes," he said, looking at the floor again. "They will."

"Dorothy is still one of you, isn't she?"

"What do you mean?"

"She's still a member of the tribe, even though she's been gone so long?"

"Of course she is."

"So what's the tribe doing about her? Aren't they trying to find her?"

"I think they are, yes. I can tell you one thing. If I ever have my hands on him again, I'll kill him. I'll choke him to death, Alex. He's evil. I could see it in his eyes."

"I know," I said. "I saw it too."

"Well," he said. He seemed to pull himself back from somewhere far away. "I got a shift at the casino. I'm glad you're okay. I mean, all things considered."

"I'm glad you came by," I said. "It means a lot to me." The drugs had me talking mushy again.

When he was gone, I tried to read for a while, but it made my head start to throb. Trying to watch television was even worse. The drugs again, or the concussion, or God knows what. I lay in the bed and thought about baseball, for some reason. I replayed a couple games in my head. How long ago was my last game? It was a triple-A game in Columbus, September 1972. I remembered my very last at-bat, a well-hit ball to left field. It settled into the outfielder's glove, five feet away from a home run. My whole career in a nutshell. It seemed like forever ago, and yet as I looked at my hands I could still see the protrusions from playing four years behind the plate, all the fastballs and foul tips.

And below those old scars, the new wounds on my wrists. The ropes were so tight. In my mind I was there again, sliding through the snow. My heart pounded. I was breathing hard. I could feel the balloon in my chest, this alien *thing* inside me.

Easy, Alex. This is exactly what you don't need right now. Just take it easy.

I put my head back on the pillow, forced myself to relax, to think about nothing. I remembered what an old teammate had told me, that the secret to thinking about nothing is not trying to stop thoughts from coming into your head. Instead, you let them come and then slip right *through* your head. In one ear, across the slippery floor, and then right back out the other ear. But then, this was a left-handed pitcher talking, and everybody knows that lefthanders are crazy.

The nurses made their rounds. Later a man waxed the floor in the hallway. The machine kept pumping air into me. From outside I could hear the sound of the wind.

I slept. Finally, a good night's sleep. In the morning the doctor came around again. We did the X rays again, and then he asked me if I wanted him to take the tube out.

"Is that a trick question?" I said. "Pull the damned thing out already."

He gave me a local before he pulled the tube out. On the end of it there was a deflated balloon, covered with whatever that stuff is that coats the inside of your lung. He stitched up the incision in my side and told me to just lie there for a couple more hours until he got back before I tried standing up. When he left the room, I waited all of one minute before I swung my legs around to the floor. Very slowly, I stood up. It felt good, in a violently sick-to-my-stomach sort of way. I was ready to try it again about an hour later.

Leon stopped in around lunchtime. "Where's your breathing machine?" he said.

"I'm flying solo," I said.

"Great, where are your clothes? Let's get you out of here."

"Leon, it still takes me fifteen minutes to get up and go to the bathroom."

"Well, *I've* been busy, at least. Your two friends

are definitely staying at the Brass Anchor Motel. They have a unit on the end with a window overlooking the main road. With you in the hospital, they haven't had much to do, I guess. I did see them leave one day and drive around the reservation."

"What, you've been watching them the whole time?"

"Off and on," he said. Now that I thought about it, he did look tired. "I couldn't think of any good way to inquire about them at the motel desk. If it got back to them, they'd know somebody's on to them."

"I don't know what else we can do," I said. "Except call Brandow again, see if he's gotten anywhere."

"Cops don't play ball with private eyes," he said. "It's an unwritten rule."

"Leon, you should really listen to yourself sometime. 'Cops don't play ball with private eyes.' For God's sake. This is Bill Brandow we're talking about. He's a good guy."

"Not when he's wearing the badge, Alex."

"Okay, fine," I said. "Whatever you say."

"Now, about the Bruckman situation . . ."

"What Bruckman situation? He didn't take Dorothy."

"Are you sure?"

"The more I think about it," I said. "Nothing else makes sense if he did."

"Then who took her?"

"I don't know," I said. "Maybe the two guys who are following me?"

"But if they have her, why are they following you?"

"I don't know," I said. "Maybe they have Dorothy

but they don't have the white bag." I gave him the quick rundown on the white canvas bag that Bruckman wanted so badly.

"No matter who those guys are, or what they want," he said, "we still have to find Bruckman. He's our only source of information, number one. Number two, don't we sort of owe him something now? After what he did to you?"

"Give me a couple days before I have to think about that, okay? It's all I can do to get up and take a piss."

"Where do you think he is?" he said. "Right now."

"Who knows, Leon? He could be anywhere."

"Think, Alex. What did he say?"

I ran the night through my head, trying to remember what he said. Or what his teammates said.

"One of his guys called him Captain Fuckhead," I said. "That's pretty good."

"Okay, so he has some dissension there," Leon said. "What else can you think of?"

I kept thinking. "Well, let's see. They beat the hell out of me. He wanted to know where Dorothy was. He wanted to know where the bag was. Then they carried me outside, beat the hell out of me again. Then they dragged me behind their snowmobiles for a while. Then they stopped . . ."

"Yes?"

"They argued," I said. "The guy who called him Captain Fuckhead, he asked him if they were going to drag me all way back over the river."

"The river," he said. "The St. Marys. They're in Canada."

"Yes," I said. "They must be."

"They're hiding out over there. Something must have happened."

"And the only reason they came back over," I said, "was to find that bag."

"What do you think is in it?" he said. "Drugs?"

"I don't know what else it could be," I said. "Although if that's true . . ." I didn't want to complete the thought.

But I couldn't escape it. Even when Leon was gone and I spent my last night in the hospital, I couldn't stop asking myself the same question over and over.

I knew Dorothy was in trouble. She was mixed up with some bad people, and she came to me because she didn't know what to do next. She had obviously made some mistakes, but beyond that I thought she was just an innocent victim. That's the part that got to me that night. It's what made me feel so bad when she was taken from my cabin. It's what drove me to go out looking for her. But if that bag she was carrying around was full of speed or coke or God knows what, then what did that say about her?

And after all I had been through in the last few days, what did that say about me?

CHAPTER THIRTEEN

I left the hospital on a Thursday morning, after three nights on the machine and one more night just to make sure my ribs were going to stay put. The doctor took one more X ray, gave me strict orders to do nothing more strenuous than drive home and go to bed for a couple more days, and then I was a free man.

The wind was waiting for me as I stepped out the front door of the hospital. It hit me across the face with a blast of air so cold it made my eyes water. Vinnie was sitting in my truck.

"Welcome back," he said as I eased myself in. "How d'ya feel?"

"Cold," I said. Even with the heater going, the car seat felt like a slab of ice.

"The wind chill is minus forty today," he said as he put it in gear. "I say we point this truck south and keep driving until we run out of gas money."

"I'm not going anywhere until I eat breakfast," I said. "I mean real food."

"Jackie's waiting for you," he said. "Soon as you drop me off at the casino. My car wouldn't start this morning."

"Some day I'll get this window fixed," I said. It

felt strange to be sitting on the wrong side of my own truck, especially with the cold air whistling through the plastic.

"I saw your man Leon this morning," he said. "He looked like he hadn't slept in three days. He came into Jackie's for a cup of coffee. When he saw me he took me outside and told me he was checking on a couple guys at one of the motels. I'm supposed to tell you that he's already working on the other, what did he say, the other individuals at large in Canada."

"He's something else," I said.

"Alex, don't you think he's a little weird?"

"Just drive," I said. "I'm too hungry to talk."

As the snow blew across the road, it swirled in an ever-changing pattern, hypnotizing me as I watched it. I wrapped my coat tight around my body and leaned back in the seat. Somehow I dozed off, even with the cold wind in my ear. When I opened my eyes again, we were just coming to the Bay Mills Reservation. Even on a freezing cold Thursday morning in the middle of January, the casino parking lot was mostly full.

"Thanks for picking me up," I said as he opened the door.

"Watch out for snowmobiles," he said.

I slid over and took the wheel. My head started to hurt again as I concentrated on the road, but I thought about Jackie's omelets and that kept me going. On the main road into Paradise, I looked for the Brass Anchor Motel on the left. There it was, just after the welcome sign. It was a simple string of doors, maybe eight units in all. A dark green Jeep was parked at the end closest to the road.

Alex is back in town, boys.

The Glasgow Inn was mostly empty. It was late in the morning, so the snowmobilers were already out on the trails. Although how the hell they could ride around out there all day in this weather was beyond me. It hurt just to think about it.

"Good God Almighty," Jackie said when he saw me. "If you aren't the ugliest thing that ever walked in here."

"Nice to see you too," I said. "I need an omelet with the works."

"Too late for breakfast," he said. "Kitchen's closed."

"Jackie, even with two broken ribs, I will kill you with my bare hands if you don't get your ass in that kitchen."

"Go sit by the fire," he said. "I suppose you want the paper and a Bloody Mary, too."

"You're a good man, Jackie. God will reward you some day."

He shot me a funny look on his way through the kitchen door. I pulled a chair close to the fireplace and threw another log on. When I was settled in, I promised myself that I wouldn't move from that spot for the next week.

When Jackie came back with the food, he stood over me for a long time, looking down at me.

"What is it?" I said.

"Seriously, are you gonna be all right? You look like shit."

"That's how I feel," I said. "But yes, I'm gonna be all right."

"I got a case of Molson waiting for you," he said. "Just let me know."

"Bless you," I said.

He gave me another funny look and left me to myself. I sat there in the chair and watched the fire. The wind kept blowing outside. An hour later, I finally got off my lazy ass long enough to use the bathroom. While I was up I went over to the window and pulled the curtains open, looked out at some snowmobiles buzzing by and then down the road toward the Brass Anchor Motel. I could just see the corner of the sign through the trees.

This is insane, Alex. There are two men holed up in that motel, waiting for you to do something. And you're holed up here in the bar doing absolutely nothing, waiting for somebody else to find out who they are and why they're watching you.

I went to the bar and grabbed the phone. When I reached the sheriff's office, I asked for Bill. He wasn't in. I left a message for him to call me at the Glasgow Inn. I went back to my chair by the fire for all of two minutes and then I got back up and picked up the phone again.

What was that number? I couldn't remember it. It might have changed by now, anyway. It's been over fourteen years. I called Information in Detroit, asked for the number for my old precinct. When I had the receptionist on the line, I went through every name I could think of—my old sergeant, a couple detectives, every officer I could think of. None of them were in the precinct anymore. I asked to talk to the desk sergeant on duty. When she switched me over, I tried to explain to him that I was a former officer, and that I needed to run a license plate. He wasn't buying it. I couldn't blame him.

I walked around the room a couple times, went back to the window and looked down the road again. Then I remembered a couple more names of old police officers I had worked with. I went back to the phone and tried them out on the receptionist. Nothing. Everybody I had worked with, they were all gone. I wondered if most of them were even cops anymore.

My old partner, I didn't have to wonder about.

Leon came in a little while later, letting in a cold blast of air as he opened the door. You wouldn't confuse the man with a GQ model to begin with, but now he looked horrible. His unruly red hair was even more of a mess than usual, and the rings under his eyes made me wonder if he had slept at all in the last three days. He looked even worse than I did.

"What the hell happened to you?" I said.

"I've been working, Alex. I've been looking for Bruckman. I just wanted to swing by, check on our friends at the motel, see how you're doing." He came over to the bar and sat on a stool.

"Have you slept, for God's sake?"

"Here and there," he said. "In the car. I've been trying to hit the stores and restaurants during the day, and then again during the evening, along with the bars."

"What, are you crazy? Where have you been—"

"In Canada," he said. "Remember? We know he's probably in Canada somewhere."

"You've been going to every store and restaurant and bar in Canada?"

"No, think about it, Alex. They rode their snowmobiles here, right? How far across the river can they be?"

"Anywhere in Soo Canada," I said. "Which is only four times bigger than Soo Michigan."

"It's not that hard," he said. "You just hit one place and then the next. You get into a rhythm. He's gotta be somewhere over there, Alex. He has to eat. And you said he was high, right?"

"Yeah, so?"

"How many cokeheads you know just sit inside all day?"

"I don't know, Leon."

"Potheads are another story. But when you're on coke, you need *action*. You need to be out all night, making the scene. You know, lights, music."

Jackie put a Canadian in front of me, looked at Leon and then rolled his eyes. "I need coffee," Leon said. "As strong as you can make it."

"Don't say that," I said. "His coffee is bad enough already."

"So I've been hitting all the nightspots extra hard, Alex. Because I *know* he's out there somewhere. And there aren't that many places to go at night. I mean, compared to all the places you can go during the day."

"I guess that makes sense," I said. "Have you tried the hockey rinks?"

"Hockey rinks," he said.

"Yeah, you said it yourself. He needs *action*. He's a hockey player."

"Of course," he said. "Goddamn it. Of course."

"If he's anything like the baseball players I've known," I said. "Or the basketball players. Or whatever."

"Even if he's hiding out over there, he's gonna have to get out on that ice eventually. Hurry up with that coffee, Jackie. I gotta get back out there."

"Leon, will you just relax for a minute? You're gonna kill yourself. Eat some lunch at least."

"Okay," he said. "You're right. You're absolutely right. I have to pace myself."

"I've been sitting here thinking about what to do with our guys in the motel," I said. "I tried calling Brandow, but he's not in. I even tried to call some of my old cop friends in Detroit, see if I could get somebody to run the plate."

"I already ran their plate, Alex."

"How did you do that?"

"I called the Secretary of State and gave them the number on my P.I. license. Didn't you know you could do that?"

"Uhh, no," I said. "But then . . . Well, never mind. What did you find out?"

"There is no such license number in the state of Michigan."

"That's impossible."

"That's what the lady told me."

I picked up the phone off the bar and called the sheriff's office again. Bill still wasn't in. "Damn it," I said as I put the phone down. "This is driving me crazy."

"So what are we waiting for?" he said. "Let's go pay them a visit."

"I promised Bill I'd let him handle it," I said. I turned around on the stool and looked at the window. "Hell, I'll give him until tomorrow morning. If he hasn't done anything by then, I'll go over there."

"I'm with you, partner."

I looked at Leon. Maybe for the first time, I really looked at him. "Go home," I finally said. "Get some sleep."

"Couple hours," he said. "Then I'm going back. I wonder how many ice rinks there are in Soo Canada?"

It was dark by five o'clock that evening, the daylight slipping away so fast you wondered if it had really happened. By nine o'clock I had called Bill back three more times. The last message I left for him was simple. My promise expires tomorrow morning. Either call me or come to the Brass Anchor Motel to watch me knock on their door.

With the sun down it had gotten even colder. Just stepping outside was an act of bravery. The snow made a sound like breaking glass when I walked on it. I could see a few lights on down the street. Another bar. A restaurant that catered to the snowmobile crowd. Woodsmoke rising from chimneys. Beyond that the motel. I couldn't see it in the dark, but I knew it was there. I pictured the two men in their room. In their undershirts, maybe. One man sitting by the window. The other man, what? Cleaning his gun? Sleeping? I wished them a good night. Their last night before I came calling on them.

The truck hesitated in the cold. I shouldn't have left it sitting outside all day without going out to start it. Not when it was this cold. Finally, it started. I pumped the heater on all the way and felt nothing but cold air coming out. Goddamn it all to hell, it is too fucking cold, I thought. It's bad enough without being tired and sore, and already feeling like I'm a hundred years old.

I drove home. When I got to my road I put the plow down and cleaned up some of the drifts. Vinnie's car was there. But then he said it hadn't started that day, right? I dropped him off at the casino. Either he's still there or he got a ride home. Whatever. I was too tired to think about it.

You did nothing but sit on your ass all day, Alex, and now you're so tired you can barely keep your eyes open. You are some physical specimen. Okay, so you have broken ribs and stitches over your eye, and it goddamn hurts when it's so cold, and now you're just talking to yourself, so go home and go to bed.

The front door to my cabin was actually closed for a change. But I stood outside the cabin anyway and told myself that nobody was inside waiting for me. Nobody has been here at all today. Nobody is watching you. Those guys are way the hell down the road at the motel. And Bruckman and his boys are way the hell over in Canada, with Leon hot on their trail, God help them. You're feeling spooked because of everything that happened to you, so just forget it and go inside the damned cabin before you freeze to death.

When I finally went in I saw that Vinnie had spent a lot of time there trying to make things right again. There was food in the refrigerator, some new plates stacked on the kitchen counter. He had even put a new mattress on my bed to replace the one that had been slashed. He probably took it from one of the other cabins.

I got a fire going in the woodstove. The air didn't

draw well because it was so cold. I had to fight to get an updraft going but when I finally won that battle the fire burst through the paper and wood and started to give some warmth to the room.

I went into the bathroom and looked in the mirror at the ugliest, most beat-up and broken man I had ever seen. There was a swelling over my left eye where the stitches were, green and purple against the white of the bandage. I didn't even want to look at the bruises on my body. I took the pain pills out of my pocket and read the label. Every four to six hours, as needed.

As needed.

You've been down this road before, Alex. If you take them tonight you'll take them again tomorrow morning and then at noon and then with dinner and then tomorrow night you'll stand here and count how many are left. And then the pills will own you again.

I put the bottle down on the sink and turned off the light. With my clothes still on I climbed into my bed and lay there listening to the wind whistling through the cracks in the walls. I rolled around for a while, trying to find a position that didn't make my side ache. I thought about the pills again. It was going to be a long night.

The phone woke me out of a half sleep. I looked at the clock as I got up. It was just after midnight.

"Alex, it's me," the voice said.

"Leon? What is it?"

"I found him. I found Bruckman." In the background I could hear the low growl of a jukebox.

"Where are you?" I said.

"I'm in a little bar on the east side of town. I caught

up to them over here at the Straithclair Ice Rink. They were just leaving. I guess they got tossed from a game or something. I followed him to this place. They just started playing pool, so I think they'll be here for a while. How soon can you get here?"

"Leon, we should call the police."

"They're in Canada," he said. "What are we gonna do, call the Mounties? You think they're gonna arrest these guys and send them back for us?"

"They're wanted for assault," I said. "We should call the sheriff and let him handle this."

"Like he's handling the two guys at the motel? Listen to me, Alex. We'll call the police if you want to, but don't you want to talk to these guys? Maybe they didn't take Dorothy, but they've got to know *something*. Don't you want to get Bruckman against a wall and make him tell you what the hell is going on?"

I stood there shivering for a long moment. On the phone I heard nothing but the distant sound of music and laughter. And then the sharp crack of a cue ball.

"What's it gonna be, Alex?"

"Give me the address," I said.

I wrote it down, put my coat and boots back on, and headed out into the night.

CHAPTER FOURTEEN

I got the truck up to forty as I passed the Brass Anchor Motel. It was as much speed as I could coax out of an old truck on a snow-packed road, with 1,200 pounds of snowplow on the front and another 800 pounds of cinderblocks in the back. I pictured one of the two men sitting by the window, half asleep, maybe a cup of coffee in his hand. I could only hope he spilled it all over himself when he saw me rumbling by.

I made it all the way down the main road to M-28, then east a good ten miles before I saw the headlights behind me in the distance. Nice to see ya, boys. Glad to have you along for the ride.

They kept a steady quarter-mile behind me the whole way into the Soo, up I-75 toward the bridge. I didn't see them behind me as I paid the toll and crossed the bridge into Canada. Far below me, the St. Marys River lay frozen solid.

As I pulled into Canadian customs, I remembered the gun in the pocket of my coat. "Oh goddamn it all," I said aloud. I've got a carry permit, of course, and somewhere in the glove compartment I think I have my private investigator license. There's probably some official way for a P.I. to bring a handgun into the country. I'm sure Leon knows how to do it. I could pull over and call him on his cellular phone. If he's in his car. If I can afford the extra few minutes. There's probably a form to fill out. Forget it, I'm going through.

The customs agent looked vaguely familiar. I had probably seen him before on a beer run. Why am I coming into Canada this evening? That was an easy one. Canada has strip clubs, Michigan doesn't. Give him a knowing smile. Do I have any drugs or firearms in the vehicle? I looked him right in the eye and said, "No, sir, I don't." He let me go right through.

When I was into Soo Canada, I kept looking in the rearview mirror, waiting to see my two friends. They weren't there. Now why the hell didn't they cross the border?

Because they didn't want to go through customs, Alex. They're criminals, with five or six guns in the car. And they can't lie to the customs agent like I can.

I worked my way through town, heading east. Forget about those guys for now, I told myself. You've got something else to deal with. I wasn't quite sure what I was going to do when I saw Bruckman again. I felt a combination of fear and anger, and something else I couldn't even identify. I started to shiver. I turned the heat up a notch, but it didn't seem to help.

Easy, Alex. Just breathe in and out. You've got to go through with this. You won't be able to live with yourself if you don't face him now.

I need a plan. Some way to get into that bar and get Bruckman out. Think, Alex, think.

I picked up Trunk Road on the east side of town and followed it all the way out past an industrial area toward the Rankin Indian Reserve. The Canadian Pacific Railroad ran next to the road. At this hour the tracks were empty. As I passed the eastern edge of town, the pine trees took over completely. Like most Canadian cities, the wilderness is never far way. I hadn't been down this road before, but I knew from the map that it was bending back toward the northern shore of the St. Marys River. I kept going until I was starting to wonder if I had gone too far. Then I saw the side street I was looking for.

The bar was a little place about a block away from the main road, close to the river. There was no sign on the building, no way you'd even know it was a bar except for two beer signs, Budweiser in one window, Molson in the other. The signs seemed to glow in a way that told me I was far from home and probably not welcome there.

I saw Leon's little red car at the far end of the lot. As soon as I pulled in next to it, Leon opened my passenger's side door and climbed into the truck. "They're still here," he said. He rubbed his hands together and blew on them.

"Don't you have any gloves?" I said.

"I took them off," he said. "We need to be ready for anything." He patted the breast pocket of his coat.

"Remind me to ask you about bringing guns across the border," I said.

"Don't tell me you didn't bring your gun, Alex."

"I did, but I lied about it. I didn't know if I'd get held up in customs."

"Good move," he said. "They would put you through the wringer."

"How many of his friends does Bruckman have with him?" I said.

"Three."

"Hmm, there were four guys with him at the cabin. He must have lost one. Probably the guy he was arguing with."

"I already have our plan mapped out, Alex."

"Wait a minute," I said. "What plan?"

"There's four of them and two of us," he said. "We need to do this just right."

"I know," I said. "I figure I need to get Bruckman away from his friends, take him outside."

"What do you think his friends are gonna do if you try that? And once he's outside, how are you going to contain him? You've got no psychological advantage over him, Alex. He won't feel threatened."

"He will if I stick a gun in his face," I said.

"That's not going to work," he said. "You really think you can walk into that bar and pull a gun on him? They're gonna start breaking cue sticks over your head. Look at this place. I'm sure it wouldn't be the first time. I told you, I've already got it all set up."

"Got *what* set up? Leon, what are you talking about?"

"Alex, we cannot create an overwhelming force here, so we need to need to create the *illusion* of overwhelming force. It's the only thing these guys will respond to."

"The illusion of what? For God's sake, Leon, where do you get this stuff?"

"It's all set," he said. "I just have to go in and give the signal."

"Leon," I said, grabbing the steering wheel. "Please. Let me just go in and bring him out here."

"You want a confined area," he said. "Like the bathroom. You separate him from the others, take him to the area."

"Take him to the bathroom."

"To the confined area. Could be a bathroom. Could be another room. It should be small enough that you're in close contact with him, but not so small that he's within three feet of you."

"Leon . . ."

"I'll be at the bar, creating the illusion of overwhelming force. Just stay here for three minutes before you come in."

"Wait," I said. "Just wait."

"If the plan breaks down and we have to fight our way out of there, go for the knees."

"Hold on, back up to that illusion thing."

"Don't start swinging, Alex. I know you. You're gonna try to start a boxing match with these guys. All you'll end up doing is busting up your hands. Just keep your head down and go for the inside of the knee. Kick outwards and they'll fold up like a cheap suit."

"Leon . . ."

"A cheap umbrella, I mean."

"Leon . . ."

"And don't pull your gun unless they draw first. The last thing we want is a shoot-out. Okay, you ready?"

"No, I'm not. Just wait a minute."

"C'mon, Alex. They're not gonna be in there all night. Let's go do this. Remember, give me three minutes to get things started." He opened the door. "Three minutes!"

"Leon, wait!"

"I gotta go now," he said. "While I'm psyched up."

I tried to grab him, but he closed the door on me and ran through the snow to the bar.

This is a bad dream, I told myself. All of this. I'm gonna wake up and go out and plow the road, and then I'll go wake up Dorothy in her cabin and help her find a good, safe place to go to. Nobody will have taken her or trashed my place or be following me around or dragging my ass behind a snowmobile. And I won't be sitting here in front of a dive bar in Soo Canada, waiting three minutes so Leon can go in and create an illusion of overwhelming force. Whatever the hell that is.

I looked at the clock on the dashboard: 1:13. I can't believe I'm doing this. Two more minutes. I closed my eyes and took a few deep breaths.

When I opened my eyes, the clock read 1:14. One more minute. A gust of wind rocked the truck.

I counted down the last minute, then I gave him one more. Then I got out of the truck. The cold air assaulted me, but it was a short walk to the door, so I was only half numb when I stepped into the place. Like all small buildings, it looked bigger once you were inside. The bar was on the right, a television set high in the corner with a hockey game on. There were Christmas lights still strung around the ceiling. They blinked on and off in the smoky haze. To the left was a pool table and a jukebox. Bruckman was standing there with a cue stick in his hand, watching one of his teammates attempt a shot. His other two teammates stood in front of the jukebox, looking down at the playlist. They had cue sticks, too. Four hockey players with heavy sticks in their hands, at least one of them half out of his mind.

I hesitated. This may not be such a great idea.

Then I saw Leon at the bar. He gave me a little nod. Then he put his glass down and turned around to face the pool table. I counted seven other men at the bar, including the bartender. As soon as Leon turned around, they all fell silent and turned around, as well. Somebody found the remote for the television and turned it off. Then the bartender flipped his magic switch behind the bar to turn off the jukebox. The only sounds left in the room were the impact of the balls on the pool table and Bruckman's rough laughter at a missed shot. As the balls all rolled to a stop, Bruckman stopped laughing.

"What the fuck," he said. He looked up to see eight men staring at him. He scanned the faces left to right. The last face he saw was mine.

"I got next game," I said. I walked to the pool table. It was quiet enough to hear the floor squeak under my feet.

"The fuck you doing here?" he said.

"You know, Bruckman," I said. "Just once I want to hear you say one sentence without the word 'fuck' in it."

Bruckman looked at me and then at his teammates.

"There are eight men in this room," I said. I wish Leon had explained his plan a little better, I said to myself. I hope this is what he had in mind . . . "Every single one of them has a gun. I'd love to see you try something stupid right now."

He looked at his teammates again, and then at the men at the bar. I could practically hear the wheels spinning in his head. "So like . . . what?" he finally said.

"So like I want to ask you a few questions," I said. "That's all. If you play along, I won't shoot you."

"Like you really would," he said.

"In the bathroom," I said. "Unless you want me to kill you right here."

"What?" His eyes were shining with fear, or chemicals, or maybe both.

"You heard me," I said. "Go into the bathroom. While we're in there, all three of your friends are going to just stand here and look stupid. Is that clear?"

He swallowed hard.

"Move," I said.

He looked around the room again, like he was waiting for somebody else to do something. It didn't happen, so he finally leaned the cue stick against the table and moved toward the bathroom. I followed. As we passed the biggest of his teammates, I looked up just long enough to give him a little smile. "Good to see you again," I said.

When we were in the bathroom, I shut the door behind us. There was one stall, one urinal, and one sink. Whoever's job it was to keep the room clean was clearly not an overachiever. I opened the stall door. "Have a seat," I said. I pulled the service revolver out of my coat.

"I'm keeping my pants on," he said.

"Good for you," I said. "Just sit down."

He flipped down the lid and sat on it. In the cheap light he looked tired and thin and used up.

"You don't look so hot," I said.

He didn't say anything. He just sat there staring into some sort of middle distance only he could see.

"Let's see," I said. "If the bullet goes in this way, it should come out like so." I looked past his head at the wall. "Unless it stays in the skull."

"What are you talking about?"

"It's gonna make a hell of a racket in here," I said. I reached down and gave the toilet paper roll a quick spin. I tore off a couple feet, wadded it into a ball, and stuck it in my left ear. Then I made another ball and stuck it in my right ear.

"What the fuck are you doing?"

"I'm getting ready to shoot you," I said. "It's gonna surprise the hell out of everybody, I know. Nobody out there really thinks I'm gonna do it. But I am." I looked over at the sink and the window above it. "I should probably go out that window. What do you think?"

"What . . ."

I made a show of checking the gun and then I held it in both hands. "You ever see a bullet go through somebody's head?" I said. I closed my left eye and looked down the barrel with my right. "It's quite a sight. God, this place is going to be a mess."

"You can't shoot me," he said.

"Sure I can," I said.

"What do you want from me?" he said. He started to rock on the seat.

"I want you to stay still," I said. "So I can get a clean shot."

"You're crazy," he said. "You're fucking crazy."

"Yeah, no kidding," I said. "I guess you should

have killed me when you had the chance."

"No," he said. "I wasn't going to . . ."

"Stop talking," I said. "You're ruining my concentration."

"What do I have to do?" he said. "Just tell me."

I opened up both my eyes and looked at him over the gun. "I suppose you could entertain me," I said. "That might buy you a couple minutes, at least."

"What?" he said. "How?"

"Start talking to me," I said. "What's in that bag?"

"What bag?"

I raised the gun again. "You're not very good at this," I said. "The bag you were looking for when you jumped me in my cabin."

"Drugs," he said.

"What kind?"

"I'm not exactly sure. Some kind of speed. Real intense shit, like it had to be mixed with something. Probably some crack. Maybe something else."

"Where did you get it?"

He hesitated until I closed my left eye again. "A guy in New Jersey," he said. "We stole it off him a couple weeks ago."

"How does Dorothy figure into this?"

"She was with me," he said. "Not when we stole it, I mean. Just that . . . she was with me. We came here together."

"Why did you come here?"

"To sell the stuff," he said. "What else?"

"Why here?"

"We had to get away. Someplace out in the middle of nowhere. Dorothy knows this place because she grew up here."

"It doesn't hurt that Canada is right next door, right? You don't even have to go through customs, just drive your snowmobiles across the river."

"Yeah, something like that."

"And what else, Bruckman?"

"What else what?"

"What else makes this such a great place to sell those drugs?"

He didn't say anything.

"The Indians," I said. "Right?"

"They got the money now," he said. "With those casinos."

"You know about the Northern Cheyenne Reservation, don't you? All the problems they're having with drugs. You figured you could make a big score up here."

"It's not my problem they got no will power."

"Yeah, not like you," I said. "You never touch the stuff."

He looked away from me.

"You were dipping into that bag, weren't you?"

"Little bit," he said.

"What did Dorothy think of your plan to sell that stuff up here?"

"She didn't know about it," he said.

"Ah, now this is starting to make sense," I said. "Let me guess. When she did find out, she took that bag and ran."

"Yeah, maybe," he said.

"How did you know she came to me?" I said.

"Gobi, one of the guys on the team, he was back at that bar with all the deer heads and shit on the walls. There was this waitress there he was working on. He saw her come in and ask about you. She had the bag with her, he thought. He wasn't sure. Nobody else had ever seen it. I had it hidden. I didn't trust anybody. So instead of stopping her and asking her what she's doing, this fucking moron just calls me and leaves me a message on my machine, tells me she was asking about you and I should check it out. You know, on account of he didn't want to leave the bar because he thought he was finally getting somewhere with this waitress. That's the kind of guy Gobi is. Can't play hockey for shit, either."

"You didn't take her from my cabin?" I said.

"No, I didn't even know she was there until a couple of days later. When I went home that night, there was a police car there, so I got the hell out of there, came over here to Canada. I figured I was fucked. Like maybe she turned me in or something. So I'm waiting here and then finally I call Gobi, and I go, Hey, what the fuck is going on over there? Are they looking for me or what? And he goes, No man, didn't you get my message? And I go, What message? And he tells me what happened. Turns out somebody trashed the place that night and Mrs. Hudson called the cops. That's why the police car was there."

"You didn't trash the place?"

"Nah, fuck no," he said. "Why would I do that?"

"And you didn't trash my place?"

"No," he said. "I didn't fucking trash anything."

"So who did?" I said.

He gave me a little smirk. It was almost enough to make me go ahead and shoot him. "You don't know, do you?" he said.

"No, but I'm hoping you're gonna tell me," I said.

"I don't know for sure," he said. "But I'm guessing it was a couple guys named Pearl and Roman."

"Who are they?"

"Just a couple guys who work for Molinov."

"Who's Molinov?"

"He's the guy we stole the drugs off of," he said. "Believe me, you don't want to know about Molinov."

"Is he Russian?" I said.

"I didn't stop to ask him."

"And what about these two guys, Pearl and Roman? What do they look like? Do they wear hunting caps?"

"I've never seen them," he said. "I've only heard of them."

"There's been a couple guys following me around," I said. "You think that's them?"

"From what I hear, they'd probably just kill you instead of following you around, but who the fuck knows?"

"How would they know about me in the first place?" I said.

He rubbed his eyes. His head was probably hurting from all the thinking I was making him do. "The message," he said. "When they trashed my place, they might have played the machine. If they did, you got a big problem."

"Your concern is touching," I said. I put the gun back in my coat pocket.

Bruckman sat there looking at me.

"Here's your chance," I said. "No gun."

He didn't say anything. He didn't move.

"You're pretty tough when you've got four other

guys helping you beat up somebody," I said. "Let's see what you can do all by yourself."

He looked down at the floor.

"You're just a cheap little punk," I said. "You couldn't make it as a hockey player, so for the rest of your life you're gonna take it out on everybody else. Unless they stand up to you."

"Whatever you say, old man."

I stood there in front of him for a long moment, waiting for him to do something.

And then from the other side of the bathroom door came the distinctive sound of all hell breaking loose. Bruckman lunged at me, but he lost a good half a second pulling himself up off the toilet seat. I got my right knee up just in time. I felt a stab of pain in my ribs, but I was sure Bruckman got the worst of it. He went down hard, holding his nose with both hands.

When I opened the door, I saw a good old-fashioned bar brawl going on. "Alex, over here!" It was Leon, over by the door. Two of Bruckman's goons were having it out with two of the men from the bar. I didn't see the third goon. The rest of the men were all standing in the corners, trying to look like they were ready to fight without actually having to do anything. I made my way across the room, ducking a cue stick and a barstool. When I reached Leon, he opened the door just in time for the third goon to come rushing in at me along with a blast of cold air. He took a big swing at me and missed, so I kicked his leg out at the knee, just like Leon had coached me. The guy gave out a high-pitched scream on the way down to the floor.

"Let's get out of here!" Leon said.

"I'm right behind you," I said. We ran out through the snow and jumped into our vehicles. He spun his way out of the lot and I followed, fighting to see my way through the snow his tires were kicking up.

We made our way back west on Trunk Road, back toward the Soo Canada city limits. I kept looking behind me, waiting to see headlights. Leon slowed down when we were in the city again. I settled in behind him and tried to make my own body do the same. My heart was still racing, the adrenaline still pumping through my blood. I could feel the pain in my side now, and in my knee where I had hit Bruckman. I'm gonna pay for all this tomorrow, I thought. I'll be lucky if I can get out of bed.

Leon pulled into a restaurant parking lot on Wellington Street. I parked next to him, got out of the truck, went to his passenger side and opened the door. "You all right?" I said.

"Yeah, I just had to catch my breath a minute."

I got in his car and closed the door.

"I guess we need to compose ourselves before we go back across the border," he said.

"Good idea." I closed my eyes and took a few long breaths. "God, we must be insane."

"I thought that was kinda fun," he said.

I looked at him. He was actually smiling. "How the hell did you get those guys to do that?" I said.

"The guys at the bar? That was easy."

"Oh, don't tell me."

"It's those Franklins, Alex. They can do miracles."

"You paid those guys a hundred bucks apiece to pretend to be carrying guns?"

"Benjamin J. Franklin," he said. "A private eye's best friend."

"Oh for God's sake. So that's like what, seven hundred dollars? And how much did you spend the other night at the hockey rink? Like four hundred? Five hundred?"

"Don't send Ulysses Grant to do a job that only Benjamin Franklin can do."

"All right, already. I get the point. I owe you twelve hundred dollars."

"We'll split the cost, Alex. We're partners."

"I'll give you the money tomorrow," I said. "And you'll take all of it."

He shook his head. "Alex . . ."

"So what happened, anyway? Your, what did you call it? The illusion of overwhelming force? It all fell apart."

"Some local clown walked in the door, wanted to know what the hell was going on. It sort of broke the spell."

"We should both be dead right now."

"What happened in the bathroom? Did you get the information you wanted?"

I told him everything Bruckman had told me. About Dorothy, the drugs in the bag, the men named Pearl and Roman and Molinov.

"So those two guys who've been following you," he said. "That's gotta be them."

"I suppose it is," I said. They didn't cross the border. Maybe they didn't want to risk going through customs.

"Yeah, if they're professional shooters . . ."

"Shooters," I said. "This is getting better every minute."

"So what are we gonna do about them?"

I thought about it for a minute. "I promised Bill I'd give him until tomorrow," I said. "Then I was going to go pay them a visit."

"Maybe we should go over there right now," he said. "Pay them a visit while we still have the kick-ass juices flowing."

"The kick-ass juices. You are too much, Leon."

"Admit it, Alex. You're glad I'm on your side."

I laughed. How I could laugh after what I had just been through, I don't know. "What kind of car is this, anyway?" I said.

"A Plymouth Horizon," he said. "It's a piece of crap, I know."

"How do you drive in the snow in this thing?"

"I've got good tires and I know how to drive in the snow," he said. "Now are we gonna go see those guys or not?"

"Yeah, we'd better," I said. "Tomorrow I'm not going to be able to move."

"You sure you're up for this?"

"Quarterbacks play with broken ribs all the time," I said. "They just put some pads on and hope they don't get hit too hard."

"Yeah, quarterbacks," he said. "*Young* quarterbacks. No offense, Alex . . ."

"Let's go," I said. "I'll meet you at the motel."

I got back in my truck and followed him over the bridge. The clock on my dashboard read 2:40. There was only one customs lane open at this time of night. I watched Leon stop at the window to answer all of the usual questions. Then it was my turn.

When I pulled up, the man looked at me, then down at the truck, then back at me again. I didn't recognize him. "Good evening, sir," he finally said.

"Good evening," I said. I waited for the questions. They never came.

"I'm gonna ask you to pull over into the holding area, sir," he said.

"Excuse me?"

"Right over there, sir. Just pull in right there."

The rest of it was like something from a bad dream. It played itself out in slow motion, under a bank of naked fluorescent bulbs that gave the whole scene a surreal glow.

The customs agents looking through my truck. A small bag pulled from under the front seat. White powder in the bag, held up for all to see. My hands against the wall, my legs spread. The gun taken from my coat pocket.

The bite of steel around my left wrist, then my right.

Then a voice from behind me. "You have the right to remain silent . . ."

CHAPTER FIFTEEN

It was the same cell. Saturday afternoon I visited Vinnie in this cell. This was, what, Friday morning? Six days. But now it was me on the wrong side of the bars.

There weren't as many men in the cells this time. Two in the first, one in the second, two in the third. I had the fourth all to myself. The same fluorescent bulbs hummed and flickered above us.

It was after three in the morning. Whatever strength I had had that day was long gone. I had used it all up dragging myself out of bed, making myself go out into the night, bitterly cold and dark beyond hope. I had ridden a wave of adrenaline and anger all the way across the river to where Leon had found Bruckman. Now I was sitting on a hard wooden bench in the fourth downstairs holding cell in the Chippewa County Jail. I leaned back against the cement wall, feeling the ache in my ribs and in my head. There was no way to get comfortable. I just sat there listening to the lights humming and trying not to throw up.

Just when I thought it couldn't get any worse, the door opened and Chief Maven walked in.

He came down the line of holding cells, casting a quick eye in every cell until he came to mine. He stood there looking at me through the bars. "Evening, McKnight," he finally said.

"Chief," I said.

"You've been read your rights?"

"Yes."

"That's good," he said. "That's good." He pulled a chair over from the far wall. It might have been the same chair I sat in myself when I came here to see Vinnie. He pulled out a pack of cigarettes and a silver lighter. "Cigarette?"

"No, thanks," I said.

He lit the cigarette in his mouth, snapped the lighter shut and blew a thin stream of smoke through the bars. "It's starting to snow again," he said.

I looked down at the floor.

"Just thought you might want to know," he said.

I didn't look at him. "Thanks for the weather report," I said.

"If I ask you a question," he said, "you know you don't have to answer it."

I didn't say anything. Maven's smoke hung in the air.

"I was in bed, you know that? When they called me and told you got stopped on the bridge, I got up and got dressed and came all the way down here in the cold to ask you one question. Are you ready for it?"

I kept looking at the floor.

"Here's my question, McKnight. Do you believe in reincarnation?"

I finally looked up at him.

"Like if you do something bad in a past life," he said. "You might pay for it in this life? Or on the

other hand, if you do something good in a past life
. . . You know what I mean?"

I kept looking at him. I didn't say a word.

"You may not have thought about it too much," he
said. "I admit, I never thought about it either." He
took a long drag on his cigarette. "Until tonight."

He blew the smoke out. The lights kept humming.

"You see," he said, "I think I've led a pretty good
life. Helped out some people along the way. I've been
a good father and a good husband. I'm sure I have
some points stored up. But damn it, McKnight, to be
sitting here looking at you in this cell. It's just too
much, I swear."

He took another drag from his cigarette and
squinted at me through the smoke.

"What do you think, McKnight? I'm thinking
maybe in my last life, I saved a schoolbus full of
children from going over a cliff. Something like that."

I kept looking at him.

"Maybe in the war," he said. "Maybe I saved a
whole town from the Germans. It's gotta be something big like that, I think. This is just too good."

I didn't even blink.

"My cup runneth over, McKnight. I can barely contain myself."

"Are you done?" I said.

"Seriously," he said. "I gotta ask you a real question. Because I thought I had you pegged. You were
a failure as a baseball player. You were a failure as a
cop. You're a broken-down, lonely, miserable man.
So you compensate for that by acting like a bigshot
and shooting your mouth off at everybody. That much
I got. But this business with the drugs. I don't get

that. I mean, I knew you weren't even half as smart as you think you are. But I never dreamed that you were *this fucking stupid.*"

"The drugs are not mine," I said.

"Of course not," he said. "Neither is the gun."

"The gun is mine," I said.

"The gun you admit to," he said. "Of course you don't have a hell of a lot of choice there. It's got a registration number on it. The drugs, on the other hand . . ."

"Are not mine."

"Right. We covered that."

"What will the charge be?" I said. "And when do I get out of here?"

The chair scraped against the floor as he leaned back in it. "What do you think the charge will be?" he said. "The only question is whether it's a felony. They're measuring it right now, I'm sure. Although to tell the truth, it didn't look like there was a full gram in that bag. Maybe I didn't save a whole town after all, eh? Maybe it was just three people and a dog."

"I want a lawyer," I said. "And I want out of here."

"You can have a lawyer if you want," he said. "And we'll get you out of here just as soon as the judge shows up to arraign you."

"What will the bail be?"

"The judge sets the bail. You know that. Your boyfriend Prudell is in the lobby waiting to pay it, whatever it is."

"Tell him to go home," I said. "Tell him I'll call him."

"That's very thoughtful of you," he said. "I'll go

tell him. In the meantime, as long as we're waiting for the judge, I think there are a couple of gentlemen who'd like to speak with you."

"Who?"

"You'll see," he said. "I'll be back in a little while."

"What's going on?" I said.

"Patience," he said. "Just relax." He got up from the chair and replaced it against the wall. "Make your-self at home." He walked back to the door, opened it, and stepped out. The door shut behind him with a metallic clang that went right through me.

I tried to lie down on the wooden bench, but the blood pounded in my head. When I sat back up, my ribs started to ache again. I got up and paced around the cell for a while, then I felt like I needed to throw up again. I went to the corner and leaned over the toilet, one hand against the cement wall. Nothing came up.

I tried to sit down. I hugged myself as I leaned over and hung my head over my knees. This might work, I thought. I'm almost comfortable this way. I started to doze off. Then the door opened again.

Maven came down the hallway. Two men followed him.

It was the men who had been following me. One had his red hunting cap still on his head. The other held his blue hunting cap in his hands.

"Alex McKnight," Maven said, "I'd like you to meet Agents Champagne and Urbanic. They're from the DEA."

The men looked at me. I looked back at them.

"You're not Molinov's men," I said. "You're not Pearl and Roman."

"What the hell are you talking about?" Maven said. "They're not Laurel and Hardy, either. Agent Champagne—" He gestured to the man holding the blue cap, as if introducing me at a party. "And Urbanic." The man wearing the red cap.

"We need to have a little chat, Mr. McKnight," Champagne said. "Perhaps we can use one of your interview rooms, Chief?"

"We have one interview room," Maven said. "I'll show you the way."

Maven pulled out a set of keys and opened the cell door. "What do you think, McKnight?" he said. "Can we do this without the handcuffs?"

"What do you think I'm going to do?" I said. "Try to run away?"

"Ordinarily I'd say no," he said. "But drugs make a man do strange things."

"For God's sake," I said. But before I could say anything else I was led out of the cell and down the hallway. As we passed through the doorway, I looked out the windows. The sun was just starting to come up. A light snow was falling.

Maven led us to the interview room. I had been in the room before. Since my last visit somebody had taken down the fishing map and repainted the walls a light green. I sat in a chair on one side of a long table. Champagne and Urbanic sat directly across from me, with Maven on the end. Urbanic had finally taken his hunting cap off.

"We'd like to ask you some questions, Mr. McKnight," Champagne said. I remembered his dark eyes from our little meeting on the road.

"Go ahead," I said.

"First of all, we'd like you to tell us the whereabouts of Dorothy Parrish."

"I don't know where she is," I said.

"She spent Friday night in your cabin."

"In the cabin next to mine," I said. "The next morning, she was gone."

"She just disappeared?"

"Yes."

"And you have no idea what happened to her."

"No," I said. "I thought Bruckman might have taken her. Bruckman is her . . . boyfriend, I guess."

"Yes, Lonnie Bruckman," Champagne said. "We're familiar with the man."

"I went to see him last night," I said. "To ask him questions."

"To ask him questions."

"Yes."

"You were in the hospital recently," he said.

"Yes," I said. "I saw you there. Your partner, anyway."

Champagne slipped a quick look sideways at his partner. Urbanic shrugged. "Why were you in the hospital?" Champagne said.

"I got beat up and then dragged behind a snowmobile."

"Sounds like somebody doesn't like you very much."

"Your instincts are uncanny, Agent Champagne."

His eyes narrowed just slightly. "What did you do to deserve this kind of treatment?" he said.

"They wanted to know where Dorothy was," I said. "They thought I had her."

"But you didn't."

"I didn't."

"And the fact that they thought *you* had her made you realize that *they* obviously didn't have her."

"Right again," I said. "Keep going while you're hot."

He didn't even bother to react this time. "So if you knew that they didn't have her," he said, "then why did you go over to Canada last night to 'ask him questions'?"

I hesitated. "Because I didn't know what else to do," I said. "I thought he might have some information, even if he didn't know where she was."

"You were trying very hard to find her," he said.

"I was concerned about her," I said. "She was scared that night."

"It must have been very upsetting to you," he said. "Tell me, Mr. McKnight, how did you know where to find Mr. Bruckman last night?"

"We found him," I said. "My . . ." I thought about it for a moment. "My partner and I."

"Your partner."

"Leon Prudell," I said. "He's my partner. When I was in the hospital, he spent some time over in Canada, looking for him."

"How did he know to look in Canada?"

"Bruckman said something about going back over the river. We assumed that meant he was hiding in Canada."

"Chief Maven," Champagne said, "do you know this Prudell fellow?"

Maven cleared his throat. "I believe he's currently a snowmobile salesman."

"A snowmobile salesman," Champagne said, nodding his head. "No doubt a valuable asset to *any* team."

"He's also a bondsman," I said. "And a licensed private investigator."

"I understand," Champagne said. "He doesn't need the other job. He just does it because women can't resist snowmobile salesmen."

"Any chance of me getting some coffee?" I said.

"When you start giving us some answers," Champagne said, "then you'll get your coffee. Hell, we'll wheel the whole breakfast cart in here. So far, you haven't given us anything."

"If there was something to give you, believe me, I'd give it to you."

"We've borrowed some of the county deputies. They're going through all of your cabins right now. You have six of them, right?"

"What do you mean, they're going through the cabins?"

"Turning them upside down would be a better way to put it. You getting stopped with drugs in your truck was more than enough probable cause for a search warrant. What do you think we're going to find in your cabins?"

"At this hour of the morning? Probably a lot of unhappy snowmobilers."

"Sorry about that. I don't suppose this is going to help your rental business."

"All right," I said. "Listen, Agents Champagne and Urbanic, was it?"

Urbanic nodded.

"Champagne and Urbanic," I said. "It's got a nice ring to it. Didn't you guys win a gold medal in ice dancing?"

"That's funny," Champagne said. "Personally, I wouldn't be making jokes if I were sitting on drugs and weapons charges, but that's just me."

"Let me just get this straight," I said. "You guys have been following me around for the past, what, six days? First you're driving around in a Taurus, which gets stuck in the snow so I have to pull you out." I looked down at Maven. "You ever hear of such a thing, Chief? I helped them out of the snow so they could keep following me."

Maven looked at them without saying a word.

"And then when I tell the sheriff I'm being followed . . ." I stopped. A couple thoughts hit me at once. I didn't like either of them. "He stalls me," I went on. "Because you must have told him to. Which means that you kept following me even though you *knew* I was on to you."

Champagne rubbed his hands together. Urbanic just sat there. Maven kept looking at them with a face of stone.

"You didn't come to me and tell me who you were," I said. "You just kept following me. In a new car. A four-wheel drive this time. But with the same brilliant disguises. Those Elmer Fudd hats really look good on you, too."

"Mr. McKnight . . ."

"All because you thought I had something to do with Dorothy's disappearance. And let me guess, that white bag she had with her."

That perked them right up. "What do you know about the white bag?" the man named Urbanic said. It was the first time he had spoken.

"Bruckman was looking for it," I said. "That's all I know."

"When did you see the white bag?" Champagne said.

"I told you. Dorothy had it with her Friday night. The next morning she was gone, and so was her bag."

"Just like that," Champagne said. "Just . . . *poof!* She was gone."

"Yes, she was gone," I said. "Somebody took her. I thought it was Bruckman, but it wasn't."

"So now you don't know *who* took her."

"No."

"Or the bag."

"No."

"We're not getting much here, are we?" He looked at his partner and then down the table at Maven.

Maven sat totally still, watching us.

"If you had come to me before last night," I said, "then I wouldn't have gone over to see Bruckman by myself. You would have him right now, and you could be asking him these questions."

"I thought you said you met him in Canada."

"I didn't meet him," I said. "I found him. I mean, Leon found him. But you could have had the Canadian Mounties there. I'm sure you've worked with them before."

"What makes you think we're not working with them now?" he said.

I thought about that one for a moment. "Wait a minute," I said. "When you followed me to the bridge last night, did you have the Mounties pick up the tail on the other side?"

"What do you think?"

"I think you probably did," I said. "Which means they followed us to the bar. Which means . . ." I replayed what had happened. Bruckman and me in the bathroom. His guys by the pool table. The fight starts. I go out, see what's going on, make my way across the room, we go out the front door and meet one of his guys coming in. From outside! "He planted the drugs in my car," I said. "When the fighting started, he went outside and put the bag in my car. Just to fuck me over. And then, let me guess, they called the bridge?"

Nobody said anything.

"That's what happened, right? They got an anonymous tip? They must have. They were waiting for me."

Champagne kept staring at me. Urbanic frowned and looked away. And Maven . . .

I knew that face. Maven was looking at the agents with that same face he used whenever he talked to me. He was squinting his eyes, the left a little more than the right. His mouth was set hard like he was biting the head off a nail. It was the worst tough cop face I had ever seen, but right now it was a welcome sight. It gave me a glimmer of hope.

"If you had Mounties watching the bar," I said, "then they must have seen the plant. Am I right?"

Champagne let out a long breath. "There were Mounties on the scene, yes. And yes, they did see an individual come out of the bar and open up the door to your truck. But that doesn't have to mean that he was planting drugs."

Maven slapped his hand on the table. "What the hell do you *think* he was doing? Leaving a mint on his car seat?"

"Chief Maven," Champagne said. He raised his hands as if to calm a child. "Please."

"Please my ass," Maven said. "When were you going to tell me you had the Mounties involved in this?"

"Can we discuss this outside?" Champagne said.

"We'll discuss it right here," Maven said. "You come all the way up here looking for this guy Bruckman and a bag of drugs he's got with him. You're walking around here like you own the place, ordering my men around, talking on the phone about the 'football.'" He held an imaginary phone up to his face. "Yes, sir, we're closing in on the football, sir. We'll have Bruckman and the football any minute now."

"The football?" I said. "You guys really call it that?"

"Shut up, McKnight," Maven said, "or I'll throw you back in that cell."

"Sorry," I said. "Go on."

"God knows how many times you could have taken him," Maven said. "But no, you gotta wait until you're absolutely sure you got the right guy and you're absolutely sure he has the drugs with him. "'Can't tackle the man without the football in his hands.' Right? How many times did you say that? So then of course this Parrish girl takes the bag out of the place and goes to see McKnight with it. And you two are running around like idiots, splitting up, one of you trying to follow Bruckman, the other guy trying to follow the girl. And then you *still* won't move in, because now your man doesn't have the football anymore. Now the next morning she's long gone, God knows where, run off or kidnapped by God knows who. McKnight's running around like an idiot now, trying to find out where she is. And what do you guys do? You start following *him!*" He pointed at me. "Like this jackass is going to take you right back to your football!"

I nodded my thanks but didn't dare say anything.

"How many days did you follow him around?" Maven said. "Six days? The dumbest man on the planet and it takes him what, not even a day to figure out he's being tailed?" Maven paused for effect and then drew out his next line like a torturer who enjoys his work a little too much. *"McKnight even pulls you out of the snow when you get stuck trying to follow him?"*

"You're out of line, Chief Maven," Champagne said.

"But now I'm still supposed to play along with you guys even though you didn't tell me anything about the Mounties, or them seeing the plant, or any of this horseshit?"

He stopped for a breath. Champagne looked like he wanted to kill me or Maven or both. Urbanic just looked sick.

"Did they get Bruckman, at least?" Maven said. "As long as McKnight is doing all your legwork for you, did they at least pick up Bruckman in Canada?"

"No," Champagne said.

"No?" Maven said.

"No," Champagne said. "There were two undercover officers on the scene. The local police arrived to break up the fight. The undercover officers attempted to apprehend Bruckman, but he had, um . . . he had escaped through the bathroom window."

I raised my hand. "I think I sort of put that idea in his head," I said. "Sorry about that."

"There was a lot of blood on the floor," Champagne said.

"His nose was broken," I said. "Me again."

"We did apprehend two of his friends," Champagne said.

"So go talk to them," Maven said. "Why are you wasting everybody's time over here?"

"Chief Maven," Champagne said, "I think I've been showing a great deal of patience and restraint here. This man was stopped on an international boundary with drugs and a loaded handgun in his vehicle. If you're not going to cooperate in our investigation, then we'll proceed without you."

Maven looked at Champagne for a long, terrible moment. If I wasn't so tired and sore and scared, I would have pitied the poor agent. The DEA has a district office in Detroit, so I had met a couple of them when I was a police officer there. They were good. But they *knew* they were good. They knew it maybe a little too well. So they may have come off as a little arrogant when they dealt with the local police. And that was in a major city. God knows how much they would look down on the police in a little town in the middle of nowhere, with a force so small it shared the same building as the county deputies.

Maven hated me. I knew that. But how much more would he hate a couple hotshot DEA agents who treated him like a backwoods hick?

"McKnight," he said, "the judge will be here at nine o'clock. When you're arraigned, I'm going to ask the DA to dismiss the charges."

That's how much.

"What are you doing?" Champagne said.

"What does it look like I'm doing?" Maven said. "I'm kicking him."

"You can't do that."

"Sure I can. There was less than a gram in that bag, so it's a misdemeanor. The gun was licensed. It just wasn't reported on the way over. So that's a misdemeanor, too. Any misdemeanor charges on that bridge belong to the city. You know that."

Champagne pointed a finger right in his face. Another great idea. "You are making a big mistake," he said.

"The next finger you point at me gets separated from your body," Maven said.

"This is how it works up here, huh? This is how you run a police department?"

"Excuse me, boys," I said. "You said I could leave, right Chief?"

"Get out of here," he said. "Just be in the court building at nine."

Champagne stood up, knocking his chair over. "This isn't over, McKnight," he said. He stood right in front of me, his face just a few inches from mine. "I'll be watching you."

"You go right ahead," I said. "I hope you like watching a man shovel snow, split wood and drink beer. Because that's all you're gonna see."

He stood there, probably trying to think up another tough guy line.

"If you'll excuse me," I said. "I need some fresh air." I stepped around him and went out the door, stopping just long enough to give my new buddy Chief Maven a little salute.

CHAPTER SIXTEEN

I had two hours to kill before my appointment in the courthouse, so I took a walk down Water Street in a winter light that made everything look gray and soft around the edges. The snow was wet and heavy. Ten minutes of walking and I was already wearing the snow around my shoulders like an old woman's shawl.

I stopped at a little restaurant over by the Locks Park. The locks were closed, of course, but there was just enough business from the snowmobilers and the locals to keep the place open. I sat down in a booth with the newspaper and a cup of coffee, and asked for eggs and bacon and sausage and anything else they could fit on a breakfast plate.

While I was waiting for the food, I called Leon's home number and left a message. Two minutes later he came banging through the door.

"My wife paged me," he said. He was breathing hard as he pulled his coat off. "God, you look awful."

"Were you at work?" I said.

"Yeah, I can't stay long," he said. "I just wanted to come down and see what the hell happened."

I ran it all down for him, starting at the bridge.

"They left you a nice little present," he said.

"A souvenir from our visit to the bar," I said. "It was very thoughtful of them."

"They could have really jammed you up," he said.

"They should have put a full gram in the truck," I said. "*Then* I would have been fucked. I guess they didn't want to part with that much of it, though."

"Ha, you're probably right."

"If you see two guys with hunting caps walk in here," I said, "you better duck."

"Maven really let you go?"

"The charges get withdrawn at nine o'clock," I said. "I hope he doesn't come to his senses by then."

"Those guys were feds," he said. "I should have known."

"I was sure they were Molinov's guys. Those two men Bruckman was talking about."

"Molinov," he said. He worked the name around a few times while the waitress brought over my breakfast.

"Gotta be Russian," I said.

"Gotta be," he said. "I could look him up."

"Where?"

"I've got a computer now," he said. "There's all sorts of places on the Internet."

I smiled and shook my head.

"You can't be a private eye in the nineties without a computer," he said. "Or at least a partner who has one."

I stopped eating and looked at him. "I told those agents that you were my partner, Leon. And I meant it."

"That's good to hear, Alex."

"But this is the only case we're going to work on," I said. "And I think it's about over."

"We make a great team, Alex. You know that."

"This is a small town," I said. "If there's any business here at all, you're more than enough to handle it. I told you that before. Look at everything you did, the way you found Bruckman. You're a real private investigator, Leon. I'm not. And I don't want to be."

"I think we should find him again," he said. "He's gotten you twice now. Don't you want to even the score? He might know more about this Molinov guy, too."

"I don't think we're gonna get anything else out of him," I said. "We'll probably just get ourselves killed this time."

"Alex, if I have to go back and sell snowmobiles every winter and outboard motors every summer for the rest of my life, I swear to God I'm gonna lose my mind. Just don't close the door on this thing yet, okay? Wait a few days and see what happens."

"All right, we'll see what happens," I said. I didn't feel like fighting over it.

"Good man," he said. "I'm going back to work. I'll let you know if I find anything on Molinov." He stood up, zipped his coat and left the place. He gave me a thumbs-up as he passed the window.

I sat there and watched the snow for a while. Then I paid my bill and went back out into the snow. I walked back directly this time, shielding my face from the wind. I saw Bill Brandow walk in the door just ahead of me, but by the time I got into the lobby he had already disappeared into his office.

I went over to the receptionist's desk and asked her

if the sheriff was free. She picked up the phone and talked to him for a few seconds, then looked up at me. "And you would be . . . ?" she said.

"I'm the drug kingpin everybody's looking for," I said.

"Okay," she said, not missing a beat. She gave Brandow my title and watched me as she listened to whatever Brandow was saying on the other end. "The sheriff will see you," she finally said.

"Thank you," I said. I went through his door and found him sitting at his desk with the newspaper.

"Every time you come in here," he said, "you track in enough snow to make a snowman. You look terrible, by the way."

"Why didn't you tell me those guys were DEA agents?" I said.

He put the paper down. "They asked me to stall you," he said. "I wasn't happy about it, believe me."

"They have no leverage over you," I said. "You're an elected sheriff."

"They asked me for one week, Alex. I *told* them they were wasting their time following you. But come on, they're agents from the federal government. I was just trying to do the right thing. You were a cop once. You know how it works. I really didn't have a choice."

"Of course not," I said. "That's why you sent your deputies out to search my cabins this morning, too."

"I could have let them call in their people, Alex. They would tear your cabins apart. I figured at least this way we could be a little more careful about it."

"I appreciate the gesture," I said. "Remind me to pick up the tab the next time we drink together."

"We did that once," he said. "And only once. It's not like we're best friends."

"No," I said. "We're not. And we never will be. Because I'm not from around here, am I? I wasn't born here. I didn't grow up here. No matter how long I live up here, I'll always be a downstater to you. I'll always be from 'below the bridge.' " It was a term I had heard used many times in bars all over the county. The bridge, in this case, being the Mackinac Bridge that separated the two peninsulas. Back in the sixties and seventies, when I was down being a cop in Detroit as it burned all around me, a lot of guys up here were actually talking about blowing up that bridge. They were scared to death that we'd all come up there and ruin the Upper Peninsula.

"One more day," he said. "I would have made them come to you directly. If you don't like that, then I don't know what else to say."

"This has been some morning," I said. "I always thought you were the good guy and Maven was the bad guy. But you're the one who rolls over for these clowns, and he's the one who tells them to go fuck themselves."

He folded his hands together and looked at me. "Are you about done?" he said.

"I'm done," I said. "I'll see you around."

I left his office, went out to the lobby and walked around for a few minutes, trying to make some sense out of everything that had happened that morning. It didn't happen. At nine o'clock I went over to the courthouse and watched my charges get dropped. It would have been better if Champagne and Urbanic had been there to see it, but maybe that's asking too

much out of life. When I was free to go, I went looking for my truck and finally found it in the parking
lot behind the City-County Building. I went inside and
asked for the keys. After a few minutes of poking
around, an officer finally found them and gave them
to me. When I opened the door to the truck, the interior door panel fell out into the snow. Everything
that could be taken apart had been taken apart, just in
case I had any more drugs stashed away. They hadn't
bothered putting anything back together.

I threw the door panel onto the other side of the
seat and started her up. I'll put this all back together
later, I thought. Just get the hell out of here.

The sun was actually trying to shine a little bit as
I left Sault Ste. Marie, but it was a losing battle. By
the time I made it to Paradise, the snowclouds had
returned. The agents' car wasn't in the motel lot as I
drove by. Too bad. I wondered what they were going
to do to amuse themselves now that they couldn't follow me anymore?

Or could they? It wouldn't have surprised me, although I knew they weren't behind me on my way
back home that morning. Maybe they'll take the day
off and start again tomorrow, I thought.

I put the plow down when I hit my access road,
pushing off the few inches of snow from the night
before. Vinnie's car was parked in front of his cabin.
There was maybe one inch of snow on his windshield,
meaning that he had worked a late shift at the casino
and driven home around dawn. Brilliant detective
work on my part. I pushed the snow from his driveway all the way up to where his car was parked, and
then I laid on the horn for a few seconds to make sure

he was awake. If I was tired and sore and miserable, I didn't want to be alone.

When I got to my cabin and opened the door, I stood there in the doorway for a full minute before I could bring myself to go inside. This is too much, I thought. A man shouldn't have to have his cabin trashed twice in one week. Every drawer was open, every single item taken out and left out. At least they didn't intentionally break everything and slash the furniture, I thought, like when Bruckman was here. Or no, I, I guess it wasn't Bruckman, was it? It was whoever the hell those other guys were, the guys who work for Molinov. Whoever the hell he is. God, listen to me. I have no idea who I'm talking about.

I got a fire going in the woodstove, and then I cleaned up the place just enough to make it livable again. I didn't feel like seeing what the other cabins looked like, but I knew I wouldn't be able to relax until I did. So I put my coat back on, went back out to the truck, and drove the quarter mile to the second cabin.

It had gotten the same treatment. Everything opened up, turned over, taken out and left out. It took about thirty minutes to clean the place up. There wasn't as much to put away, at least. Nobody actually lived there. This is where you keep your guests, I said to myself, when you want them to be kidnapped. You leave them alone in this cabin and then you go to bed. In the morning, they'll be gone.

I stood there and looked at the bed where she had slept. The pipes are probably still frozen, I thought. And the leg on that table needs to be glued back on.

Hell with it, I'll deal with it later. I can't stand being here.

The third cabin was another quarter mile down the road. My father had built this one in 1970, on enough of a hill to make it higher than the others. It was bigger than the first two, and it had a porch on it so you could see Lake Superior through the trees. He had learned a little more about plumbing, so the pipes didn't freeze as long as the temperature stayed above minus twenty. I put that place back together and then kept working my way down the line. My father had gotten tired of drilling new wells for each cabin, so the fourth and fifth cabins were close to each other and shared the same well. The two cabins together would sleep twenty people, maybe twenty-four if they liked it cozy.

When I got to the sixth and last cabin, I saw the same kind of mess, and the same kind of emptiness. Every single renter had left. I didn't imagine any of them would be sending me money, either. Not that I blamed them. If federal agents woke me up to search the place I was renting, I'd stiff the landlord, too.

The only consolation, I thought, was that I wouldn't have to hear as many snowmobiles for a while.

But wait. There was an envelope on the table. I opened it up and found three hundred-dollar bills. Benjamin Franklin, Leon's best friend. I couldn't help smiling.

When I had cleaned up the place, I stood in the center of the room and looked at it. It was the last cabin he had built. The biggest and the best. There was a real kitchen, separated from the rest of the cabin, with its own woodstove. There was even a second floor in this cabin, with a balcony overlooking the living room. My father had built the fireplace with all the stones he had moved or dug up while making the other cabins. Standing there in that cabin, I actually started to feel human again, so I figured I'd stay a while. I brought some wood in and made a fire. I even found a can of good coffee in the kitchen. After I had made a cup and sat there looking out at the snow, I couldn't stop myself from leaning back on the couch. The warmth from the fire felt too good. In less than a minute, I started to fall asleep. In a half-dream, I was behind Bruckman's snowmobile again, sliding over the snow.

The tree coming up fast. I can't avoid it. I'm going to slam into it.

Impact. A loud bang like a gunshot.

I sat up straight, instantly awake. The front door opened and Vinnie walked into the cabin.

"Oh, it's you," I said. "You woke me up."

"Who was laying on the horn in my driveway a couple hours ago?" he said.

"I thought you said Indians only need three hours of sleep every night."

"I never said that," he said.

"Must have been somebody else."

"You been cleaning up after the deputies?" he said. He looked around the room.

"Yeah, did you see them this morning?"

"They were just finishing up when I got home," he said. "They stopped at my place and asked me some questions."

"You're kidding."

"I told them you had a major drug ring going for years. About time they busted you."

"That's it," I said. "No more freebies for you."

"I brought you some beer," he said. The bottles clanked in his hands. "Sorry, they're American." He gave me a bottle, opened one up for himself and pulled a chair over from the kitchen table.

"Thanks," I said.

"I figured you'd be having a tough day," he said. "God, you look terrible."

"Thanks again. Wait a minute, are you drinking beer?"

"It's non-alcoholic," he said, holding up the bottle. "I tried one a couple years ago, figured it was time to try again. See if they got any better at making it."

"So how is it?"

"I think they need a couple more years." He tried to screw the cap back on the bottle but couldn't quite get it to work. "So, now what?" he said. "You're not still looking for her, are you?"

"Not really," I said. "There's no place to look anymore. Why do you ask?"

"I'm just wondering why you've gone to this much trouble. You only just met her that one night."

"Vinnie, she got kidnapped and it was my fault." My head started hurting again, just having to say the words. "She came to me for help and I fucked up. What do you want me to do, just forget it?"

"She was in trouble long before she got to you."

"Yeah, I know," I said. "She chose her own path. Step by step. All that shit again."

"All right," he said. "All right. Let's not go through this again."

"You brought it up," I said.

"I'm sorry," he said. "It's just . . ."

"What?"

"You're killing yourself over this. And it's not your fault. No matter what you think. That's all."

"Okay," I said.

"Okay," he said.

A long silence reigned. We watched the last of the fire go out in the fireplace.

"Alex, this has got to be the best fucking cabin I have ever seen in my life," he said. "Your father was a genius."

"He got pretty good at it," I said.

"You'll sell it to me one day, won't you?"

"When you've got a million dollars, come talk to me."

"After all I've done for you," he said.

"Make it two million."

I finished my beer and then he helped me clean up the place a little more. I could never leave that cabin without making it look perfect. One more reason to never live there myself. When we went back outside, the sun was making another rally, fighting its way through the snowclouds. A single brilliant beam swept slowly over the snow-covered trees like a searchlight.

"What are you gonna do now?" he said.

I thought about it. There weren't many options. "See what Jackie made for dinner," I said. "Read the paper."

"Don't you get sick of that place? I'm starting to hate going there."

"It's either that or sit in my cabin," I said. "At least this way I have somebody to annoy."

"Save me a seat by the fire," he said. "I'll be in later."

I drove down to the Glasgow. You've got some life, I said to myself. A cabin and a bar and snow up to your ass. When I walked into the place, Jackie took one look at me and winced. "You look terrible," he said.

"That seems to be the consensus," I said.

I sat in that bar for the rest of the day. There was nothing more I could do about Dorothy. I didn't even have any renters to take care of anymore, thanks to the agents. I just sat there by the fire, feeling almost normal again, except for the fact that everything hurt and it took me five minutes to get up to go to the bathroom.

When the sun had gone down, the place started to fill up. Snowmobilers came in fresh from the trail, their faces red from the cold.

The men were all talking about their snowmobiles and where they would ride the next day. There was laughter. Somebody lit a cigarette next to me.

The smell of it. The smoke.

Dark outside. The sound of the men in the room.

It all came back to me. The night she was here in this room. Sitting right here talking to her. The way she looked into the fire when she was talking.

She was so afraid.

I know this. It is not a new thing to me. But now it hits me in the stomach. Now I feel it myself.

She was so afraid.

I thought it was Bruckman she was afraid of. The boyfriend she ran out on. The usual story.

But no.

It was something bigger. Bruckman was nothing.

It was Molinov. I didn't even know his name that night, didn't know that he existed. But now I see it. It all comes to me at once. It runs down my spine and into my gut.

What did she say about the wolves? You shoot the wolf closest to your door. But there are other wolves behind him. Bigger wolves. With bigger teeth.

Molinov was the bigger wolf. That's who she was afraid of all along, from the very beginning.

And now he has her.

CHAPTER SEVENTEEN

A voice, from far away: "Alex."

I came back. I was in the Glasgow Inn again, sitting in front of the fire.

"Welcome back to planet Earth," Jackie said. "Do you want dinner or not?"

"I need the phone," I said. "Can you bring it over here?"

"That's why I have a cordless phone," I heard him say as he left me. "So you don't have to get out of your chair."

When he brought the phone back to me, he set it down on the little table next to my chair and bowed. "Your highness," he said.

"Thank you. Now go away."

He shook his head and went back to the bar. "I can't believe I'm doing this," I said aloud as I punched in the numbers. An officer answered.

"Is Chief Maven still there?" I said.

"He's just about to leave," the man said. "May I tell him who's calling?"

"This is Alex McKnight," I said.

I heard some muffled voices on the other end and then Maven's said, "McKnight, what do you want?" he said.

"Chief Maven," I said. "I just called to thank you again."

"The hell you did," he said. "State your business. I'm on my way home to dinner."

"I want to talk to Agent Urbanic," I said. "Can you have him call me?"

"What am I, your secretary now?"

"I figured you'd know how to reach him," I said. "They don't seem to be staying here in town any-more."

"All right, all right," he said. "I'll have them call you. Let me guess, you're at the Glasgow Inn."

"Not Champagne," I said. "I want to talk to Ur-banic."

I heard him muttering something to himself. "Is there anything else you want me to do, McKnight? Come out and shovel your driveway for you?"

"No, thanks," I said. "I have a plow. Oh, but while you're having the DA drop charges, how about throw-ing out Vinnie's assault charge?"

"That officer came back to work today," he said. "He looks almost as bad as you do. Good night."

"Good night, Chief," I said, but he had already hung up.

The phone wasn't lying on the table more than two minutes before it rang. "McKnight," I said.

"This is Champagne."

"I wanted to talk to your partner," I said.

"You'll talk to me."

"That's what you think," I said, and hung up.

The phone rang again a minute later.

"This is Urbanic. What the hell's going on?"

"I wanted to talk to you," I said. "You seem like you might be half human."

"So talk."

"Tell me about Molinov."

"Why do you want to know about Molinov?" he said.

"Because he took her. We have to find him."

"Who's 'we,' Mr. McKnight?"

"You, me. I don't care. Damn it, Urbanic. If you could have seen how scared she was that night . . ."

"We're working on it," he said.

"No, you're not," I said. "You're looking for that stupid bag. I know how you guys operate."

"The bag came from Molinov," he said. "Find the bag and you find the man. Find the man and you find Dorothy. At least according to you. Am I right?"

"I don't know," I said. "Just." I hesitated. "What's your first name? I don't want to keep calling you Agent Urbanic."

"My name is John."

"Okay, John. John Urbanic. Is that German?"

"Polish," he said.

"John, you gotta tell me what's going on. Who is this Molinov guy?"

There was a long pause on the other end of the line. I sat there listening to the silence, watching the fire. "We don't know that much about him," he finally said. "The name is Russian, that much is obvious. Whether it's his real name or not, we don't know. Nobody has ever seen him, not in America anyway."

"Bruckman said he saw him," I said. "He said he stole the bag from him in New Jersey."

"We heard that much," he said. "We've been trying

to catch up with Bruckman for about two months. We were about to put a move on him last week, but we weren't sure where the bag was."

"The football," I said.

"That's my partner talking," he said. "He likes code words."

"What's in the bag?"

"It's methcathinone," he said. "It's a synthetic stimulant, similar to methamphetamine."

"Speed," I said.

"It's *like* speed," he said. "Maybe a little worse. They call it 'cat,' or 'wild cat' if it's got a little crack mixed in. It's got the same energy boost on the way up, but sometimes it's a hard ride down. Paranoia, hallucinations. Seizures, even."

"So that powder they put in my truck," I said. "That wasn't from the bag?"

"No," he said. "That was good old-fashioned cocaine. Not even good cocaine. I guess they didn't want to waste any of the good stuff just to set you up."

"If she took the bag, they must be running pretty low on this, wait a minute, did you say they call this stuff 'wild cat'? Like the cat's in the bag?"

"It sounds cute, I know, but believe me, this stuff is a killer. It's been tearing up Russia for years."

"It comes from Russia," I said. "So Molinov . . ."

"Yes," he said. "Whoever he is, it looks like he's testing out the market, see if he can start a little import business."

"And these two guys who work for him," I said. "Pearl and Roman? What kind of names are those?"

"You got me," he said. "They don't sound like nice guys."

"What was she doing?" I said. "Why did she take the bag? She should have just run away."

"We'd like to talk to her about that," he said. "We know she came to you on Friday night. On Saturday, we had no Bruckman, no Dorothy. Only Alex McKnight. You can see why we were interested in you."

"I suppose so," I said. "I was your only lead."

"I'm sorry it . . . well, it didn't turn out to be a very pleasant experience for you."

"John, you're moving up from half human to almost human here. Why are you telling me all this?"

"Because you had nothing to do with it," he said. "I could see that as soon as we questioned you."

"You should do something about your partner," I said. "Make him shut up while you do all the talking."

"He's better with the guilty ones," he said. "And believe me, they're almost always guilty."

"John, you've got no idea where this Molinov guy is now? Or these guys who work for him?"

"No idea," he said. "But if they got the bag back, you gotta figure they're not sticking around."

"And if he has Dorothy?"

Another pause. An awful silence before he said what I already knew. "If they got to her, then I don't like her chances."

I squeezed the phone. There was not a word I could think of saying.

"Alex, are you there?"

"I'm here."

"We've got the Mounties looking for Bruckman. If we find him, we'll try to trace Molinov back to New

Jersey or wherever the hell he is right now. You've had no involvement in this from the beginning, right?"

I said nothing.

"Alex?"

"Right," I said.

"Okay, so now it's time to let us do whatever we can do. Just let it go, Alex."

"Let it go," I said.

"Stay home and stay warm," he said. "If we find out anything, I'll let you know. In the meantime, if my partner sees you again, I think he's going to kill us both. I can't imagine what he's going to say when he finds out I told you all this."

"You mean he's not right there, listening in?"

"No, I made him wait in the next room. I think I hear him tearing the drapes down."

"Send me the bill," I said.

"Take care of yourself, Alex."

I thanked him and hung up.

Let it go, he said.

I picked the phone back up and dialed Leon's number.

"He's Russian," I said.

"We figured that," he said. "From the name."

"Now we know for sure. He's from Russia." I told him everything Urbanic had told me, and then I gave him the punch line. "Any ideas on how we can find him?"

"Not that I know of, Alex. Not any way that the DEA couldn't do a hundred times better."

"No, I didn't think so," I said. "I'm sorry, I shouldn't have bothered you. You've got me thinking you can do miracles now. The way you found Bruckman's place, and then the way you found Bruckman himself."

"That was just common sense and hard work," he said. "With Molinov we don't even know where to begin. I thought you said this was over, anyway?"

"It is," I said. "I shouldn't have called. I'm sorry."

"Don't worry about it," he said. "If I think of something, I'll call you."

"Thanks, Leon."

"Good night, partner."

"Good night, Leon."

I hung up the phone, put it back down again. Now there was nobody else to call, nothing else to do.

I stood up. From across the room Jackie expressed his amazement at the feat. Then he asked if he could have his phone back sometime that evening.

When I stepped outside, I regretted it instantly. I pulled my coat tighter around my body and went to my truck. I just couldn't stand the idea of sitting in that place all night again. I didn't feel like going back to the cabin. The renters were all gone, anyway. I didn't know *what* to do with myself.

You're going to drive yourself crazy, I thought. You're going to keep thinking about this until you're ready to kill yourself.

I got in the truck and drove. I didn't even know where I was going. I just wanted to keep moving.

Let it go, he said. He actually said that.

Out of sheer habit, I drove east toward the Soo. Maybe I'll go to the casino, I thought. See how much money I can lose playing blackjack. I'm already sitting on five empty rentals at the height of the season. Let's see just how low I can go.

"There's nothing you can do," I said out loud. My voice sounded thin against the roar of the heater and the cold air whipping against the plastic window. "They're gone. You can't find them."

When I thought it was Bruckman, at least I had a shot at him. I had reason to believe he was still around. I had a way to find him. Or Leon did, anyway. But Molinov. Pearl and Roman. The names were absurd even, like something out of a James Bond movie. What could I do with names like that? These men were ghosts to me. They were invisible monsters in the night.

"You can't find them," I told myself again. I was in the Soo now, driving north on I-75 toward the International Bridge.

I seem to be driving to Canada, I thought. Why am I doing this? What am I going to do in Canada? Try to find Bruckman again? What will that get me?

I want to get back at him.

No, it's not worth it.

Yes, I want to hit him again, with my hands this time. I want to feel the point of his chin against my right fist. None of this would have happened if he hadn't brought her here.

It doesn't matter. I won't be able to find him, anyway. He won't be at that bar. And besides, I don't think I should go over that bridge again for a while. Not after what happened the last time.

I pulled off the freeway, just before the bridge. I took Easterday Avenue into the center of town, past the college. There was a hockey game going on at the arena. Alaska-Fairbanks was in town to face the hometown Lakers. What a long way to come to play hockey, in a place that's just as cold as the one you left.

Hockey. Bruckman's teammate. What was his name?

I kept driving. A right on Spruce, another right on Shunk Road. I was going south now, toward the other arena. The Big Bear, where we played our game. The first time I saw Bruckman.

What was his teammate's name?

When we were in that bar, in the bathroom. Bruckman talking finally, with a gun pointed at his head. A teammate who lived in town, the one who was at the bar when Dorothy asked about me. He called Bruckman, left a message. Bruckman came home, saw the police cars, took off to Canada. Never got the message. He called the teammate back a couple days later, asked what the hell had happened. What did that guy say? He told Bruckman about Dorothy then, two days after she was kidnapped. So Bruckman couldn't have taken her. But what else? "He was freaking out." I heard Bruckman say the words again in my head. "Said he was getting fucking paranoid, like they were coming to get him."

They. He said they were coming to get him. When Bruckman had told me that, I thought it was just something this guy would say because he was coming down off a high, with no more speed to take him back up. But maybe there was more to it. Maybe this guy knew where this stuff came from, and who was looking for it.

Gobi. His name is Gobi. Like the desert.

What the hell, I thought. I pulled into the parking lot. It looked like the Big Bear was having a busy league night. I went into the arena, stood against the glass and watched the game for a while. It was another "slow puck" league game, but this one seemed to have a real referee. Then I went back into the locker room. A dozen players were getting dressed for the next game. They were making a racket, so I had to shout. "Hey! Anybody here know a guy named Gobi?" The shouting made my ribs hurt.

The players stopped what they were doing and looked at me. There was one man who was sitting on the bench, lacing up his skates. "Don't tell me Gobi did that to you," he said.

"Did what?" I said.

"Destroyed your face. Gobi's that little shit who plays with Bruckman, ain't he?"

"He didn't do this to me," I said. If there's one good thing about having bruises on your face and a bandage above your eye, it's that you have no trouble passing for a hockey player. "I'm just looking for him."

"I haven't seen him since last week," he said. "I think Bruckman's team is out of the league."

"Ain't that a shame," somebody else said.

"Do you know where he lives?" I said.

"Nah, no idea," he said.

"Anybody else?" I said. Nobody did.

I went back out to the rink and sat in the stands, waiting for the game to end. When it did, the Zamboni came out and cleared the ice, then the teams I had just talked to came skating out. About ten minutes later, I figured more players would be in the locker room, suiting up for the next game. I was right. There were a dozen new faces in the room when I walked in.

"Anybody here know a player named Gobi?" I shouted again. I was already getting tired of this game. I couldn't imagine how Leon had done this for hours on end.

"Who wants to know?" said one player.

"I do," I said. "Why do you think I'm asking?"

"I might know him," he said.

"Either you do or you don't," I said. "When you make up your mind, let me know. Anybody else know him?"

He stepped up to me. He was young, not more than twenty years old. There was a shine in his eyes like maybe he wasn't always on the same planet as the rest of us. "I might know him," he said, "if the price is right."

"I just need to find Gobi," I said. "It's important. Can you help me or not?"

"For a hundred bucks I can."

"What? Are you crazy?"

"There was a guy in here a few nights ago looking for somebody. He paid me a hundred bucks for the information."

"I'll give you twenty," I said.

"No way, man. The way I see it, this guy sort of set the market value at a hundred, you know what I mean?"

"Fifty bucks," I said.

"He had hundred-dollar bills, man. He was flashing them around like they were nothing. It was my pleasure to help the man."

"Thanks, Leon," I said as I reached into my coat pocket. I took a hundred-dollar bill out of the envelope the renters had left me and handed it to him. "Where does he live?" I said.

"I don't know," he said. "But Eddie does. Hey Eddie!"

A teammate came hopping over, one foot in a skate.

"Eddie's gonna need a hundred, too, man. He's the one actually knows where Gobi lives."

"Then why am I paying you?" I said.

"Finder's fee," he said.

"Finder's fee," I said. "This is great. How about the two of you just share that hundred?"

"I guess you don't want to find Gobi too bad," he said.

I pulled out another hundred and gave it to Eddie. "All right, that's it. Now where does he live?"

"Whoa, who's this dude?" Eddie said, peering at the bill.

"That's Benjamin Franklin," the first player said. "Don't you know your presidents?"

"Where does he live?" I said.

"He lives in a little cabin," Eddie said. "Just south of town. He had a party one time, invited like fifty people. You couldn't get more than twenty people in that place. We were all outside standing around in the cold."

"Where was I?" the first player said. "I didn't get invited."

"You were there, man," Eddie said. "You were just too stoned to remember. That was the night Mike pissed on you."

"Give me the address," I said.

"*Mike* pissed on me? I'm gonna kill him. I'm gonna fucking kill him."

"The address," I said.

"Shit, I wasn't supposed to tell you that," Eddie said.

"Eddie," I said, trying very hard to control myself. "Will you please give me the address now?"

He gave me an address on Mackinac County Road.

"Thank you," I said. "Have a nice game, boys."

"Do you know what it's like to wake up and have human urine all over you?"

I didn't stick around to find out. I went back out to the truck, fired it up and took the business loop through the south end of town. The bank sign flashed the time, 9:28, and the temperature, an even zero. When I looked again in the rearview mirror it had gone down to one below.

I got off the loop near the state police barracks and went south down Mackinac Trail. I passed a small subdivision of houses and then it was just pine trees and the occasional driveway leading off into darkness. I watched the numbers on the mailboxes, counting them down until I found the one I was looking for. When I pulled into the driveway, I hit snow. There had to be at least two feet of it. I could see the driveway snaking through the trees, beyond the reach of my headlights. There were no tracks, no footprints. No sign of life.

I sat there and thought about it. The wind came and rocked the trees, sending down a fine white mist from the branches. He might use a snowmobile in the wintertime, I thought, instead of trying to keep this driveway clear. I knew of a few people who did the same thing in Paradise.

I backed up onto the road for a running start and then put the plow down. What the hell, I thought. I'll do him a favor. I gunned it down the driveway and started pushing the snow off. It was heavy work on a narrow track. I had to be careful to keep the truck away from the trees. More than once I had to back my way up all the way to the road and take another run at it. A good fifteen minutes later, I broke through into the clearing and saw his house. It was dark.

I pushed the snow all the way up to the back of his car. I got out, leaving the truck running with the headlights on. As I walked past his car I saw that it was buried in snow so deep you could barely tell what color it was. I made my way through the snow to his cabin and knocked on the front door. As I stood there waiting for an answer, I gave the cabin a close look. Even in this light I could see that it was a cheap job. It would have made my old man sick to his stomach to see all the chinking somebody had packed in between the logs to keep the wind out.

I knocked again. No answer.

I stepped back and looked around the place. There were two windows on either side of the door, but they were small and set high off the ground. I walked all the way around the cabin, working hard to get through the snow. It was a simple rectangle, with two more high windows in the back and a big skylight.

"Now what?" I said to myself. "How bad do you want to know what's inside this place?" I knew the answer right away. Bad enough to break in, but not bad enough to try to crawl through one of those windows.

I went back to the front door and leaned against it. It seemed solid. It's hard to build a good cabin, I thought, but it's easy to buy a good door. I had a set of lock picks, but they were back in my cabin. Plus I had no idea how to use them.

Leon. He could do it.

I went back to the truck, took off my gloves, picked up the cellular phone, and called him. "Leon," I said, "I'm outside somebody's cabin. He was a teammate of Bruckman. I think he might have had some connection to Molinov and his men. From what Bruckman told me, he might have at least known about them."

"Sounds promising," Leon said. "What's your plan?"

"My plan is for you to come out here and pick the lock," I said. "We might be able to find something useful. Phone numbers, addresses, who knows what."

"That would be breaking and entering," he said. "Unlawful trespassing."

"Are you coming out here or not?" I said.

"I'm on my way," he said. "Give me the address."

I gave him the address. "Just look for the freshly plowed driveway," I said.

I put my gloves back on and held my hands down by the heater until they stopped hurting. Then I sat back and waited. I figured it would be a twenty-minute drive from Leon's house in Rosedale. He was there in eighteen.

He pulled up in his little red car and jumped out. "You rang, partner?"

"Right this way," I said. I led him to the front door.

"Nobody can see us," he said, looking around the place. There was nothing but trees. "This is good."

"Can you get in?"

"Let's see," he said. He went down on one knee and gave the doorknob a rattle. "Hold this flashlight."

I took the flashlight from him and aimed the beam at the doorknob.

"The trick to picking any lock is applying the right degree of tension," he said. "You do this by first choosing the correct size tension bar."

"Leon, save the lesson for a warm day, okay? Just get the door open."

"Such gratitude," he said. He put a tension bar into the lock with one hand, and then with a pick in the other hand he started to work at the tumblers. "It's kinda tricky. It's hard to get a good feel for it in this cold." He blew on his hands and tried again. "Damn, I'm losing the feeling in my hands."

"Are you gonna be able to do this?" I said.

"Have no fear," he said. "I just have to warm my hands up. Let's go sit in your truck for a minute."

We went back to the truck. He held his hands down by the heater, rubbing them together. "That's good," he said. "That's very good. Let's go give it another shot."

We went back out into the cold, back to the door. He went down on one knee again and set the tension bar, working more quickly this time. "I'm losing the back tumbler," he said. "It won't stay put by the time I get up to the front." He worked at it for a few more minutes. In the faint light I could see him gritting his teeth. "Goddamn it all," he said. "I'm losing my hands again. I almost had it! Let's go back to the truck."

We went back to the truck again. He warmed up his hands again. Then we got out of the truck and went back to the door.

"All right, this time I'm going to get it," he said. He worked at the lock. I could hear the faint ticking of metal against metal until the sound was swallowed by a gust of wind. "Almost there," he said. "I'm almost there."

"Leon, this isn't going to work," I said. "Come back to the truck."

"Wait," he said. "Wait . . ." He worked at it. "Wait . . ." The pick fell from his hand. "Damn it! All right. Let me warm up my hands one more time."

We went back to the truck. "Let's go through the window," I said.

"I can do this, Alex. Give me one more shot."

I put the truck in gear. "I've got a better idea," I said.

"What are you doing?" he said.

"I'm gonna pull the truck up to the front of the house," I said. "We can climb up on the plow and go right in." I pulled off the driveway and started plowing a path to one of the front windows. When I had pushed my way to within five feet of the cabin, my wheels started slipping. I slammed it in reverse and backed up to the driveway again.

"Alex," he said, "be careful."

"Don't worry," I said. I put the truck back in drive and started down the path to the window. I gave it a little extra this time, just enough to punch my way through the last few feet of snow.

I gave it too much. When I tried to hit the brake,

my boot with all the snow on it slipped right off the pedal. I tried again and hit the gas pedal instead.

"Alex, look out!"

I slammed all twelve hundred pounds of snowplow into the side of the cabin. The wall caved in. The window frame hung from a corner for a second and then fell on top of the plow. Then the roof buckled, sending a full load of snow onto my windshield. We couldn't see a thing.

Neither of us said anything for a long moment.

"Well, this is one other way of getting in," I said.

"Alex," Leon finally said. "Have you lost your mind?"

"I knew this was a cheap cabin," I said.

He choked out a few words, unable to put a sentence together.

"Come on," I said. "As long as we're in." I opened my door.

"As long as we're . . . I cannot believe this."

I stepped around the snowplow and into the cabin. I stopped.

Leon came up behind me. "Do you have any idea what's going to happen to us if . . ."

He stopped.

There was a body in the center of the room. On the floor.

Another body in a chair.

Blood.

Blood everywhere.

Old blood. Dried hard and black. The body on the floor spread out, face up. A man. What was left of the face. A man.

The body in the chair slumped over. Long hair. A woman.

Blood everywhere.

I couldn't see the woman's face. The hair hanging down to the floor like a final curtain.

Blood everywhere.

Leon swallowed hard next to me. "Sweet Jesus," he said. "Let's get out of here, Alex."

I couldn't move.

"Come on, Alex. Let's go." I felt his hands on my arm. "I said let's go."

I turned around and went back to the truck. I opened the door and got in. Leon was still outside the truck, wiping the snow off the windshield. When he finished and got in the truck, I turned the key in the ignition. There was a sudden grinding sound that went right through me.

"The truck is already running, Alex. Put it in reverse."

I put it in reverse. As I pulled backwards, part of the wall came with it. In the beam of the headlights, we could both see into the cabin. The light hit the blood and somehow made it come alive again, a brilliant shimmering red.

"Nice and easy," he said. He sounded calm. "Look where you're going. Right back to the driveway."

"I got it."

"Keep going," he said. "Straight back."

"Okay, I got it."

I moved back slowly, all the way back to his car. "Oh God," he said when I had stopped. His calm was gone. He started to rock back and forth in the seat. "Holy God in heaven."

"Take it easy," I said. "Are you going to be all right?"

"God, did you see all that blood?"

"Yes," I said. I was fighting it. I couldn't let the blood overwhelm me.

"It looks like they've been dead for a couple of days," he said. "At least a couple of days."

"I wonder why nobody came looking for them?"

"We have to call the police," he said.

"Hold on," I said. "Think about it for a minute."

"Think about what?" he said. "What's there to think about?"

"Leon, think. What good is it going to do to have them come out here and see what we've done to this place? It's not going to do *them* any good. Gobi, and . . . it was a woman, right?"

"Yes," he said. "His wife maybe?"

"We'll both go home," I said. "And then I'll call it in, anonymously."

"I don't know, Alex."

"Think about it," I said. "Play it in your head, both ways. Think about what happens in the end."

He took a long breath and sniffled. "Let me call," he said. "They might know your voice."

I looked at him. "Are you sure?"

"Yes," he said. "I'll call. I'll wait about an hour after I get home."

"Okay," I said. "Okay."

"I'll talk to you tomorrow," he said.

"I'm sorry, Leon. I'm sorry I dragged you out here."

"Don't worry about it, partner." He took one more breath and let it out. "Okay," he said. "I'm good now." He got out and went to his car. I followed him down the driveway, both of us backing our way down through the trees. He hit the road and went south. I went north.

When I was back on M-28, heading toward Paradise, I tried not to think about what I had seen. I couldn't keep the image out of my head.

The waitress. Bruckman said something about Gobi working on the waitress from the Horns Inn. That's who the woman was.

I pulled over, kicked the door open. I threw up all over the road, everything I had until I was heaving up nothing but air. I tried to breathe. So cold it hurt. I closed the door and kept going.

By the time I got to Strongs, I was having second thoughts about our plan. I've got to call the police myself, I thought. I can't just go home and let Leon do this, pretend we weren't there.

I picked up the phone, put it down, then picked it up again. I dialed 911.

Then to my left, something flashing by. A vehicle. It pulled over into my lane, cutting me off. I hit the brakes, started to skid on the icy road. I saw the car in front of me sliding sideways, then straightening out again. It was a Jeep. Champagne and Urbanic.

The Jeep was coming to a stop. I pumped the brakes. I wouldn't be able to stop in time. Closer, closer. Goddamn it, stop! I swerved to the right, hitting the snowbank. The impact sent me bouncing off the steering wheel and then back against my seat.

When everything finally stopped moving, I looked up at the Jeep in front of me. They must know about what happened, I thought. This is going to take some explaining, why I'm driving back home, why I didn't call it in.

Maybe if I can cut Champagne out of this, don't even talk to him. I'll have a better chance with Urbanic.

I winced as I got out of the truck. The sudden stop hadn't done my ribs any good.

Go right to Urbanic and throw yourself at his mercy, I thought. Pretend Champagne isn't even here.

The Jeep's doors opened. Two men stepped out.

It wasn't them.

I reached for my gun. It wasn't there. My right pocket was empty. I never got it back from the police.

The road was deserted. Nothing to see in any direction but trees and snow. No sound but the wind.

"Good evening, Mr. McKnight," the driver said. "At last we meet. You're a hard man to find."

CHAPTER EIGHTEEN

I sat in the back seat, directly behind the driver. I could see the back of his head, the fur on his collar, and nothing else. The other man sat next to me, wearing the same kind of coat. Fur on the collar, maybe sable. He had a strong chin and a nose that might have been broken once or twice. He kept looking straight ahead. He did not turn to look at me. He did not speak.

You're a hard man to find, they said. The words rang in my head. You're a hard man to find.

The driver had opened the door for me. He had stood there waiting for me. It would have been a perfect imitation of a chauffeur, except for the gun in his hand. The other man stood on the other side of the car, waiting patiently for me to accept the invitation. He had a gun, too.

I had gotten into the car. What else was I going to do?

You're a hard man to find. It didn't make any sense.

The driver kept going west on M-28. He turned north on the road to Paradise. I cleared my throat. "You're Pearl and Roman," I said.

They said nothing. The man sitting next to me didn't even turn his head.

"You trashed my cabin," I said. "Saturday."

"We will not talk now," the man said. He looked straight ahead.

We kept going in silence. When we came into Paradise, I saw the lights on all along the road, all the places that made up my town. The gas station. The post office. I tried to keep the fear down, someplace deep inside me, in a little box where fear can have its place without controlling you. I knew if I let it out of that box, I would have no hope of thinking clearly.

You're a hard man to find. Meaning that they had been looking for me, but could not find me until tonight? They broke into my place on Saturday. How many days have passed since then? What day is it today? *Think, Alex.*

We came into the center of town. I could see the Glasgow Inn up ahead. Jackie is in there right now. He has a cold Canadian waiting for me. But no, we're turning.

The driver took a left at the blinking light, taking 123 west out of town. "Where are we going?" I said.

"We will not talk now," the man said.

We kept going west. The driver held the steering wheel with hands in black gloves. He was a good driver. He was confident in the snow, but he never drove too fast.

You're a hard man to find. It's starting to make sense now. They trashed the place on Saturday. I didn't sleep in the cabin that night. I was in the other cabin. The next day Bruckman put me in the hospital. I spent four nights there, then most of yesterday at the Glasgow, then I went over to Canada last night, spent the rest of the night in jail. I haven't been in my cabin more than ten minutes at a time since Dorothy disappeared. That's why I'm a hard man to find.

But now they've found me.

These men took Dorothy, I thought. They probably killed her. They killed Gobi and that woman. The nightmare I saw in that cabin, they did that. Now they're going to kill me. They're going to drive me deep into the woods and then kill me.

I closed my eyes. Breathe in, breathe out. Think.

I could open the door, try to make it into the woods.

They'd shoot me down like an animal. I'd have no chance.

If they wanted to kill me, they could have done it when they stopped me on the road. Nobody would have seen them. Maybe they want something else.

Yeah, maybe they want something else *first*. And *then* they'll kill me.

Okay, then. If they're going to kill me, they're going to kill me. As long as I'm still alive, I have a chance. Hold on to that.

We kept going deeper into the woods, past the turnoff for the Tahquamenon Falls. The road was getting narrower, the snow deeper. The driver kept a steady hand on the wheel, working the Jeep through the snow.

I kept talking to myself, trying to make myself believe that I was going to live to see another day.

A small sign told us that we were leaving Chippewa County, entering Luce County. I knew this road. It went through nothing but forest until it finally hit Newberry, a good thirty miles southwest. Just as I started to wonder how much farther we would go, the

driver slowed down. There was an access road running north. It had been plowed recently, by whom I
could not imagine. As far as I knew, there were no
cabins in this part of the woods, just small lakes and
snowmobile trails. We went up the road for three
miles, maybe four. The driver had to work a little
harder to keep going. The wheels started to slip in the
snow.

Then we stopped.

The man next to me spoke. "We get out now."

The driver opened his door, got out and then
opened mine. The other man stayed where he was
until I stepped out of the car. It was dark. With the
headlights off it took a while for my eyes to adjust.
The driver took out a flashlight and turned it on.

"This way," he said. I saw his face for an instant.
His features were more delicate than his partner's.

"Where are you taking me?" I said.

"This way," he said again. He turned and walked
down the road. The other man was behind me. Neither
of them had their guns out. They didn't jab the barrels
into my back and tell me start walking and to not try
anything funny. They didn't have to. It was an unspoken understanding between us that as long as I
came with them, they would not pull the guns out of
their coats and shoot me.

We walked down the road, following the thin beam
from the driver's flashlight. The road ended. The
snow got deeper. It was almost up to my waist. I
fought my way through it, pulling one leg out and
then the other. It wasn't long before I was breathing
hard. The other two men moved through the same

snow, but it didn't look like they were working nearly as hard as I was.

"I'm too old for this," I said. But my words were lost in the cold night.

We came to a clearing and walked toward its center. Finally, I started to see a building ahead of us. It was small, no bigger than a shed. It's an ice shanty, I thought. We're walking on a lake now. I tried to picture a map in my head. It could be Little Two Hearted Lake, or it could be one of a hundred other lakes whose names I could not remember. Wherever we were, I knew that we were alone. If there was another building within five miles of us, besides other empty ice shanties, I wouldn't know how to find it.

We walked the last hundred yards to the ice shanty. There was a faint glow coming through the cracks. The driver opened the door and held it open for me. Another polite gesture. Right this way, sir.

I stepped inside. The building was made like most ice shanties I had seen. Unfinished walls and ceiling, bare two-by-fours everywhere, one small window. A rough wooden floor with a square hole in the middle, where someone had opened up the ice to expose the dark water. I saw the fishing line first, traced it up out of the water to the pole and then to the man who was holding it. I saw a long fur coat. The same fur as on the two men's collars. Black leather boots and gloves. The man's face was like something carved from stone. He looked up at me with eyes as dark as the square of water at his feet. A propane lantern sat on the bench next to him, casting its pale light. "Mr. McKnight," he said. "Welcome."

"Is your name Molinov?" I said.

"Yes," he said. "Please come in and join me. I believe you've already met Mr. Bruckman."

I stood there in front of him, wondering what the
hell he was talking about.

And then I saw Bruckman.

He was behind Molinov, huddled against the back
wall near a kerosene heater. He was completely naked, his skin like blue steel. I didn't know if he was
dead or alive until I saw him move. He was shaking.

"Sit down," Molinov said. He gestured to a rough
wooden bench to his left. I sat down on it, moving
slowly as if I were in a dream. I looked down at
Bruckman again. His face was turned away from us.

The other two men sat on the bench across from
me. Molinov picked up a cigar, took a long puff, and
then put the cigar back on the bench. The smell of
cigar smoke mixed with the smell of burning kerosene. "Perhaps you will answer a few questions for
me," he said. "As long as you are here." I didn't hear
much of an accent in his voice, but he said each word
as carefully as a man drawing notes from a violin.

He took out a handheld tape recorder from his coat
pocket and pressed a button. The tape began playing,
filling the room with Bruckman's voice. "This is Lonnie. Leave a message." That was all he said. There
was a long silence, and then the messages came one
by one.

"Yo, Lonnie, this is Miles. You coming over here
or what? Give me a call, man."

"Yeah, Bruckman, this is Charles. Patty gave me
your number, said I should hook up with you. I'll be
at the ice rink tomorrow around ten o'clock. Maybe
I'll see you there."

"Hey, Lonnie, this is Gobi . . ." Molinov looked at me. He held the machine up a little higher. "You ain't gonna like this, man, but I think you got a problem. I'm over at the Horns Inn here and I saw your girlfriend come in here. She was up at the bar asking about that McKnight guy who was playing goal against us last night. Turns out he's some sort of private investigator or something. I don't think she saw me there, but I didn't know what I should do, you know? She had a white bag with her. If that's what I think it is, you better get over there and find her, man. I got something going with that waitress who works here, and it's like a lot colder out there than it is in here, you know what I mean? So if you want to find him, he lives up in Paradise. That's all I heard. I'll talk to ya later, man."

He hit the stop button and took the tape out. "Do you know where this tape came from?"

"I think so," I said.

He put the tape back into the machine and then put it back in his coat pocket. "This girl, Dorothy Parrish," he said. "She came to you that night, did she not?"

"Yes."

"I understand that she was gone the next morning."

I looked over at the two men. I still didn't know which was Pearl and which was Roman. They looked back at me without an ounce of emotion between them.

"Yes," I said. "She was gone."

"Perhaps you could tell me where she went."

The words hit me like a slap in the face. "I don't understand."

"The girl," he said. "Where is she?"

"You're asking *me?* You kidnapped her." I pointed at the men. "*They* kidnapped her."

"That is not true," he said. "By the time these men inspected your cabin, she was already gone."

"Inspected my cabin? Is that what they did?"

"It was necessary," he said.

"I don't know where she is," I said. "I swear."

Bruckman made a noise behind him. It was a low, gurgling moan that made me bite my lip to stop from shaking. Pearl and Roman looked over at him as casually as you'd look at the family dog whimpering in the corner.

"Mr. Bruckman seems to be feeling a chill," Molinov said. "Perhaps you'd be so kind as to give him your coat."

I looked at him. Was he serious?

"Please," he said. "Your coat."

I stood up and took my coat off. Nobody moved, so I figured the rest was up to me. I went behind Molinov, to where Bruckman was huddled against the wall. He had his face next to the kerosene heater, so close I could smell the singed hair. "Bruckman," I said. He didn't respond. I touched his back. His skin was so cold, I couldn't see how he could still be alive. I put the coat over his body.

"Thank you, Mr. McKnight," Molinov said. "I'm sure Mr. Bruckman appreciates that."

"Why did you do this to him?"

"Come back to the party, Mr. McKnight. I'll explain."

I sat back down on the bench. I could barely feel the warmth from the kerosene heater. The cold air came rattling through the cracks in the shanty, making me shiver.

"Mr. Bruckman took something that belongs to me," Molinov said. "This is the result."

"He'll die," I said.

"I've been fishing for quite a while now," he said, pulling his line out of the water. A metal lure, the kind you'd use for trolling in the middle of summer, gleamed in the lantern's light. "Perhaps I'm not doing it correctly. Would you like to try?"

"No, thank you," I said.

"Perhaps Mr. Bruckman would like to try," he said. "Why don't we find out?"

Pearl and Roman stood up in unison. They picked up Bruckman from the back wall, one arm apiece, and lifted him over to the bench they were just sitting on. I saw his face for the first time. His eyes were swollen shut. I could barely recognize him. My coat slid off of his naked, blue body.

"Please, his coat," Molinov said. "We wouldn't want Mr. Bruckman to catch cold."

The men pulled his arms away from his body and somehow managed to get my coat on him.

"Much better," Molinov said. "Now, Mr. Bruckman, perhaps you'd like to try your luck at some ice fishing?"

Bruckman started to fall sideways. One of the men caught him.

"I think Mr. Bruckman needs some more assistance," Molinov said.

With one smooth motion, the two men picked him up and dropped him head first into the water. The splash hit me across the front of my shirt and across my face, as cold and shocking and painful as a thousand icy needles. Bruckman's body hung against the edge of the opening. It was barely big enough for him to fit through. But then as my coat soaked up the water it pulled him down until only one foot was left above the surface. And then that too was gone.

I kept staring at the water. I could not move.

Pearl and Roman sat down. Molinov looked at his wet cigar for a moment and then threw it behind him. "Mr. McKnight, I can understand your reluctance to reveal her whereabouts."

The surface of the water was still trembling. I kept expecting Bruckman's head to come bursting back up through the hole.

"But I should think at this point you see how important it is to me that I find her, as well as a white bag that was in her possession."

"I don't know where she is," I said. "I don't know where the bag is."

He nodded slowly. "When I found out that Miss Parrish had come to you, naturally I was curious about who you were. The man on the tape states quite clearly that you are a private investigator. I made some inquiries and discovered that yes, you do in fact have a license. I was surprised to find, however, that you have no office, you have no listing in the phone directory, you apparently make no attempt whatsoever to advertise your services. I thought that rather odd, until I learned more about your recent past. Is it true that your last clients were the Fulton family?"

I looked up at him.

"It's a very wealthy family, is it not? I understand they have a vacation home on the lake, just north of your cabin. I actually paid the house a visit today, did you know that? It's an impressive building. Of course, it's empty now. I couldn't imagine living here in the winter if one had a choice. We have places just like this where I come from, you realize. I can assure you, though, that nobody ever builds a vacation home there."

The water on my clothes was soaking through to my skin. I tried not to shake.

"I made some more inquiries, Mr. McKnight. It seems that the Fulton family suffered a great misfortune recently. The Fulton heir, Edwin the third, was tragically killed. Of course, this is not news to you. I understand that you were employed at the time by a lawyer named Lane Uttley, and that Mr. Uttley was in fact representing the Fulton family. Am I correct?"

"Yes," I said.

"Mr. Edwin Fulton," he said, "the man who died so suddenly. He led a rather interesting life, did he not? I have heard many rumors. Voices in the wind, if you will. It made me think, here is a man, Alex McKnight, who has a license to be a private investigator, but doesn't seem to do any investigating. Yet when a wealthy man with many problems disappears, Mr. McKnight is close by. Then comes a young woman with many problems, different problems to be sure, but just as serious. When this woman disappears, once again Mr. McKnight is at her side. It makes me begin to wonder if perhaps this is ... Am I using the correct word here? His specialty?"

The room was getting colder. The kerosene heater was hissing like it was running out of fuel.

"This place," he said. "It does seem to be perfectly suited for disappearances, does it not?"

"I don't know what you're talking about," I said.

"The next question, of course," he said, "is does Mr. McKnight *help* these people disappear, or *make* them disappear?"

"I don't know what happened to Dorothy," I said. "But I *do* know what happened to Edwin Fulton. He's dead." I was starting to feel dizzy. My own voice sounded far away from my body.

"I wonder what Edwin Fulton's widow might say if I took up this matter with her? What is her name again? Sylvia?"

"No," I said. "Not her."

He drew the gun out from his breast pocket. He didn't point it at me. He didn't hold it away from his body or wave it around in the air like most men would. He held the gun close to his body, as naturally as holding a telephone or a fountain pen. "I am offended," he said. "Do you believe that I would harm this woman?"

I looked at his gun. I didn't say anything.

"To harm a woman," he said. "An innocent woman. That you would even think such a thing. I'd like to show you how strongly I object to the very idea."

I looked up at this face.

The heater had gone out. There was silence.

"Gentlemen," he said, without taking his eyes off me. "Please remove those coats. They are quite expensive. I would not want them to be ruined when we perform our little demonstration."

The two men stood up and took their coats off.

They put them on the bench behind them. The bigger one, the one with the hard face and the nose that had been broken, he looked at me with the cold eyes of a natural killer. He flexed his hands in their black leather gloves.

I waited for what would happen next. My whole body was tight. I will not shake, I told myself. I will not let them see me shake.

The other man. I saw him blink. He sneaked a look at his partner, and then at Molinov.

Molinov raised his arm sideways and shot both of the men.

They fell backwards, first one, then the other. The bench fell over with them. The shots rang in my ears. Molinov's upraised arm did not move.

"I understand," he finally said, lowering his arm, "that when my associates were questioning Mr. Gobi and his female companion about Mr. Bruckman's whereabouts, they committed an act of extreme brutality. The woman was innocent. There was no reason to kill her."

"You're crazy," I said.

"Not at all," he said. "Now I wonder if you'd be so kind as to collect their coats. I believe you'll find the keys to the vehicle in Mr. Pearl's pocket."

"Which one is he?"

"They didn't introduce themselves? How impolite. Mr. Pearl is on the left."

When I stood up, the room began to spin around me. I grabbed the bench to stop from falling over.

"Careful, Mr. McKnight," he said. "You wouldn't want to fall through that hole and join Mr. Bruckman."

I shook my head clear and went over to the two men on the floor. They were both staring at the ceiling, with holes perfectly centered in their chests. I pulled the coat out from under him, the one named Pearl. I found the keys and pulled them out.

"Bring them to me," he said.

I turned and took two steps toward him. I looked him in the eyes.

And then I dropped the keys into the water. They disappeared instantly.

He looked down at the water, then back up at my face. He smiled.

"You have seen death before," he said.

"Yes," I said.

"You're not afraid of me right now, are you? Not enough to beg me for your life."

"I don't have to," I said. "We're both stuck out here together."

"Are you cold?"

"Yes," I said.

"You don't know what it is to be cold," he said. He slipped his free hand out of its glove, switched the gun, then took the other glove off. His fingers had all been amputated down to the first knuckle, all of them except his right index finger. His trigger finger.

"I believe the heater has run out of kerosene," he said. "This room is not comfortable anymore. The smell of death isn't very pleasant, either." He stood up, his fur coat reaching all the way to the floor. We were exactly the same height, his dark eyes dead-even with mine. He picked up the lantern and walked to the door. On his way, he pulled the other coat out from under the other dead man. He looked at it closely, brushing away some sawdust.

"Where are you going?" I said.

"To the car," he said.

"You don't have the keys."

"I have my own keys," he said. "I asked you to take Mr. Pearl's keys because I wanted to see what you would do with them. If you had given them to me, I would have been very disappointed. But you didn't. I believe you when you say that you don't know where Miss Parrish is. As for the matter of Mr. Fulton, I will need to look into that situation a little further. I believe I see some unique . . . opportunities there. If you really are a private investigator, I assume that your services are available for hire. Sometime in the future, I may wish to retain those services."

"You're going to leave me here," I said. "I'll freeze to death."

"Perhaps you will," he said. "Perhaps you won't. If you survive, then that will tell me something very important about you. It will tell me that you are a man who may be of great use to me."

I stood there watching him. There were no words to say.

"If you survive," he said, "we will have something in common. Something very rare. You see, I was in a similar situation myself once. I didn't freeze to death. But I must warn you. The cold can take away a piece of you. Not just your physical body. I mean inside of you."

He opened the door, then stopped. The brutal air rushed in. I could feel my shirt frozen against my chest. "Once you freeze all the way through to your soul," he said, "you will never feel warm again. You'll see."

He closed the door, leaving me in the cold darkness.

CHAPTER NINETEEN

I was alone in the ice shanty, alone except for two men dead on the floor and Bruckman underneath us somewhere, wearing my coat, either sinking to the bottom or bobbing against the ice itself. The heater was dead. Molinov had taken the lantern. It was completely dark and getting colder by the minute.

Okay, think. You're alive. You want to stay alive. What do you do?

I started to remember something. I'm sitting in the barber shop, waiting for the chair. An old copy of *Michigan Out of Doors* there, pick it up, there's an article about hypothermia and frostbite. What the hell did it say? I wish I had paid more attention . . .

I felt my shirt, frozen solid where I got splashed, like having a block of ice strapped to my chest. That was the first problem.

No, wait, my hands. They are so cold. Where are my gloves? I went down on my knees, felt around on the floor for them. I couldn't even remember taking them off. Maybe when I went digging in the dead man's pockets for the car keys.

I felt around on the rough wooden floor. There! There's one of them. I put it on my left hand. Now, where's the other one? I felt around with my bare right hand. It's here somewhere.

What's that? *Oh fuck!* I shifted my weight before I realized what I was doing, felt the icy sting of the cold water all the way up to my elbow.

That's just what I need right now. Fall through the fucking hole in the ice. Say hello to Bruckman on the way down.

I sat back and shook my hand. When I put it back down, I felt leather.

Great, it was right under me. I put it on. Okay, now what do I do about this wet shirt? What did that article say? Something about how snow soaks up water. When you're wet, you're supposed to roll around in the snow.

No, I don't think so. I'm not going out there and rolling around in the snow. I don't care what the magazine said.

The dead men. What about their clothes? Molinov took their coats. What a wonderful thing to do. But what about the rest of their clothes? Two shirts, two pairs of pants.

Yeah, I'm going to go find the two dead guys in the pitch black, strip their clothes off.

Easy, Alex. Listen to your breathing. You're using up all your energy. Just sit here for a minute. Relax and think about it.

I found the bench, the one I had been sitting on from the beginning. My hands felt cold even with the gloves on, especially my right hand after the ice bath. I tucked them under my armpits. The wind picked up again outside, rattling every inch of the place. I put my head down and felt the shivers take control of my body.

This is not good, Alex. This is not good at all.

I tried to remember what the place looked like. I went down on my hands and knees again and crawled toward the back corner, feeling for the heater. When I came to it, I picked it up. It was too light. I shook it. Nothing. Maybe there was more kerosene somewhere. I felt around the back wall. I came upon the heavy metal ice spud that they used to break through the ice. I kept feeling against the wall.

There! A metal can! I picked it up. It was empty.

Matches. Could there be matches somewhere? I could start a fire, burn some wood or something. I came to a wooden box, took my gloves off and opened it. A fish hook bit into my finger. It was just a tackle box.

What a stupid fucking sport, anyway. Sitting in a little shack in the middle of a frozen lake with a fishing pole.

As my eyes became adjusted to the darkness, I saw that there was some light coming through the back window. It was the faintest light you could ever imagine, just one shade above black, but it was enough for me to start making out the general shape of the room. I stood up and looked out the window. There was enough ambient light from wherever the moon was hiding to see an endless expanse of snow and nothing else.

All right, you're going to have to do this. You have no choice.

The two dead men were just shadows on one side of the floor. I went down on my hands and knees again, crawled over and reached out toward them. I touched a hand, recoiled from the shock of it.

You've got to do this, Alex. Don't think about it. Just do it.

I reached out again, felt the arm, moved up to the chest. I started to unbutton the shirt. I could feel the blood. It was still warm enough not to have frozen.

Blood. This is all I need right now.

I made myself breathe in and out a few times. Then I kept unbuttoning the man's shirt. When it was un-buttoned, I struggled to lift the man's body. I had to get the shirt off him. His arms wouldn't bend. It's just a mannequin, I thought. A big heavy mannequin with some blood on it.

When I finally got the shirt off, I thought about what to do next. Take my wet shirt off, put this one on instead? This one might be just as bad, now that this blood is freezing. I tried putting the shirt on over my own. It smelled like cigarettes.

Core body temperature. That's what the article said. That's the number one priority. Keep the core body temperature up. When it starts falling, you've got big problems. There was even a little table with the different temperatures, what kind of symptoms you get as your core body temperature goes lower and lower. When you're shivering, when your hands are starting to go numb, that's mild hypothermia, right? That's me right now. I'm off to a running start.

I moved over to the second man. It was harder to unbutton the shirt this time. My hands were getting worse. Not a good sign. He was the heavier of the two, so I had to strain to lift him, working the shirt off his body. I put it on over the other shirt.

Okay, Alex, you're all set now. You've got three shirts on now, one wet with water, the other two with blood. Now you're all ready to freeze to death.

Do I take their pants, too? I could stuff them inside my shirt.

Yes, Alex, you have to.

"I hope you gentlemen will excuse me for what I am about to do," I said. I took the boots off of each man, unzipped their flies and then pulled the pants off them. I stuffed one pair of pants inside my shirt, between the frozen fabric and my skin. The other pants I wrapped around my neck.

This is much better. Now I might live for a whole hour.

That smell again. Cigarettes. The shirts, the pants. They all smell like cigarettes. And when you smoke cigarettes, you have matches. Or a lighter.

I felt the pants around my neck, felt for the pockets. I took a wallet out, threw it aside, felt around for anything else. Nothing.

I pulled the other pair of pants out from under my shirt, felt the pockets. Another wallet. And something else. I reached inside with numb fingers.

A lighter. One of those little butane lighters you see everywhere. God bless you.

I can break up the bench, maybe pull some wood off the walls if I have to. Just a few minutes of fire, that's all I need.

Better make sure it works. I put my thumb on the little wheel, tried to give it a turn. Nothing. Damn it, I can barely feel what I'm doing.

I blew warm air on my right hand. Come on, thumb, don't fail me now.

I gave it another try. Nothing.

Another try. Nothing.

I blew on my hand again. Come on, baby. Who wrote that story, Jack London? The guy who had to start a fire to save his own life. I think he had matches, though. Not a fucking piece of shit lighter that wouldn't light.

I gave it a good turn. Nothing.

I shook it. I didn't hear anything. Does that mean it's empty? Why the fuck would he be carrying a fucking empty lighter in his pocket?

I cranked it again. And again. And again.

I can see the spark, Goddamn it. I know I'm doing this right. I'm giving you the fucking spark, why don't you *light already?*

Crank. Spark. Nothing.

Crank. Spark. Nothing.

I gripped it like I was going to throw it, then stopped myself. Hold onto it. Give it another try in a few minutes. Maybe it'll work.

I put my gloves back on, then found the nearest corner and sat down against it, drawing my knees up to my chest. I rocked back and forth slowly, riding a wave of shivers.

I breathed warm.air on the lighter. Hell, maybe that'll help. I took my glove off, gave it a try. And then another. And then one more.

And then I dropped it.

Okay, so I'm not going to build a fire. I'm as warm as I'm going to get here. Which isn't a hell of a lot. Goddamn it, I'm cold. Am I supposed to wait here until morning? I'll never make it. I'll just sit here all night with two dead bodies on the floor. In a little while I'll start hearing Bruckman knocking on the ice, trying to crawl his way back up.

If I move, I'll feel warmer, right? I'll generate body heat? Or will I just use up my energy faster? But if I can make it back to the main road, maybe somebody will see me. Maybe. If I make it that far.

I pulled myself up off the floor. "Okay," I said. "Okay, okay. Here we go." I went to the door. "Don't get up, guys," I said. "See you around."

I opened the door and stepped out into the snow. The cold air attacked me, seeking every inch of my body. "Oh, this was a great idea," I said. "I am such a fucking genius." I started making my way over the lake, back toward where the Jeep had been parked. I looked in all directions as I fought my way through the snow. The surface of the lake disappeared into total darkness no matter where I looked. There were no lights, no sign of life anywhere. Lacking any other idea, I would have to try to make it back down the access road. I had no other choice.

I kept my hands tucked under my arms as I stepped through the snow. Even with good gloves on, I could feel my fingers growing more and more numb. I tried to follow whatever trail we had made coming out to the ice shanty. Molinov must have come back the same way, as well, but the wind was filling in the deep footprints.

Keep going. The road should be here somewhere. You'll get a little more shelter from the wind.

I looked back at the ice shanty. It was just a shadow. I tried to remember how long we had walked on our way out. Ten minutes? Maybe fifteen? It felt like more than that already. The lake should have ended by now. I felt the panic rising through my body, starting in my stomach. I'm going to get lost and wander around in circles on the lake. They won't find me until the spring.

This was a mistake. I should have stayed in the shack and taken my chances. You can't do anything right, McKnight. Now you're gonna die out here because you're such a fucking idiot.

No, wait. Up ahead, I began to make out a dark band. It had to be the edge of the lake. I kept going, fighting through the snow, keeping my head down as the wind picked up again, blasting me with a million tiny bullets. The insane howling of the wind rang in my ears.

When I got closer to the shoreline, I looked for the opening where we had come through. All I saw were trees.

Goddamn it, I can't waste energy like this. I've got to get to the main road. Where did we come through?

I walked along the edge of the trees, looking for the opening. The snow hung on the branches, making a solid curtain. I tried walking close to the trees, hoping they would shield me from some of the wind.

Down here, a few more yards, then you gotta double back. You can't get lost. You cannot get fucking lost here or it's all over. Is that it there? No. Wait, maybe. Yes, there it is!

I found the depression in the snow where the Jeep had been. This must be a boat launch in the summer, I thought. Now, how long did we have to drive down here once we left the main road?

I headed straight down the access road. In the dim light it was no more than a narrow opening in the trees. My feet were numb. My hands were hurting. I didn't know which was worse.

I lost my footing and fell into the snow. When I got up, I wrapped the pants more tightly around my neck and kept going. What did that article say about the next level of hypothermia? You get the "umbles." Fumble, stumble, mumble, grumble. Is that me yet? I kept walking, rhyming the words in my head. Fumble, stumble, mumble, grumble, bumble, rumble, crumble.

At least the snow isn't as deep here. And the wind isn't so bad. It's downright balmy, isn't it? I do believe I'm starting to feel quite warm here. This would make a lovely vacation spot.

I fell down into the snow again. I pushed myself back up to my knees and stopped.

Get up, goddamn it. Get on your feet. If you stop, you're dead.

I got up. I kept going.

Just keep walking. Straight ahead. The road is this way. Get to the road.

Bumble. Tumble. Trumble. What's trumble? It's the name of a street. But it's spelled Trumbull. Michigan and Trumbull. Tiger Stadium is on the corner of Michigan and Trumbull.

Keep walking. Get to the road.

Things to do when I get back home. Take a hot bath. Sit by the fire. Drink some hot coffee.

I fell down again.

Get up. Get up or die.

I got up, snow clinging to my face.

Move to Florida. Lie on a beach. Get a suntan.

I kept walking. One foot and then the other, through the snow, straight ahead through the trees.

How long did we drive down this road? I don't remember. How long have I been walking? I don't remember starting. I've been walking in the snow all my life.

God, my hands hurt. God, my face hurts. My feet aren't numb anymore. My feet hurt now, too. This is how Bruckman felt. Curled up there in that shack. Waiting to die. I wonder if he felt that water when he went in.

Humble. Lumble. Is that a word? Jumble.

Finally, I came to the main road. There was only a few inches of snow. It had been plowed recently.

This is it, Alex. This is the main road. Where's the rescue party? Where's the receiving line? Where's the man with the big trophy and the beauty queen ready to kiss you on the mouth? Sorry, ma'am, my lips are frozen.

Which way? Right or left? Which way did you come? Which way did you turn when you came in? If you turned right then you gotta go left. If you turned left then you gotta go right. Or is it the other way around?

Fuck, like it matters. Like it makes any difference. Just keep walking. Or don't. Just lie down right here and wait for them to come get you. They'll be here any minute.

I'll walk. Might as well. It's such a lovely night. I'll go this way. There seems to be a little more light this way.

What's that, headlights? Here they come. I see headlights.

No, false alarm. Just your eyes playing tricks on you. Eyes are funny that way. Always playing tricks.

You know. Maybe I'm crazy. I don't even feel that cold anymore. My hands aren't cold. Wherever they are. My hands. I'm sure they're here somewhere. I hope I didn't leave them somewhere.

Headlights. Here they come. For real this time.

Nope. No headlights. I keep seeing lights. Down the road. But not headlights. Maybe it's a UFO. That could be it.

The trees. On the side of the road. All that snow on them. They look like monks wearing white robes.

What's that music? It sounds like a saxophone.

I should lie down here. Take a nap. I'm sleepy. What time is it? It must be late.

No. Keep walking. Alex. Alex.

The music is getting louder. It's too slow to dance to. Just as well. I'm too sleepy to dance. I should lie down.

No. Alex.

It doesn't matter. I don't care anymore.

This snow is soft. I'm going to lie down now.

What is that music? I know this song. I hear it every night.

What is that light? It's a UFO. I was right. The aliens are here. I'm going to lie down now.

I'm lying in the snow. It is so soft.

The aliens are here now. The machines are next to me. One on each side. The aliens are looking down at me. One big eye in the center of their heads.

Welcome to the planet Earth. I hope you like it here. We call this white stuff snow. It's very soft. Perfect for lying on. Now if you'll excuse me. I'm going to sleep.

CHAPTER TWENTY

I spent two more days in the hospital, the same hospital I had gone to after Bruckman—make that the late Lonnie Bruckman—and his friends did their number on me. The same doctor shined a light in my eyes, asked me what the hell was wrong with me. I was supposed to go home the last time and rest for a few days.

"I missed the hospital food," I said.

"You're lucky to be alive," he said. "You're also lucky to have your fingers and your toes still attached to your body."

A couple snowmobilers had found me, a man and his son. The man was a scoutmaster and a volunteer fireman, one of those guys who are ready for anything at any time. He had the emergency heat packs. He had the electric hand warmers that connected to the snowmobile battery. He even had the pad on the seat that warmed your ass while you were riding.

"Those snowmobiles are amazing machines," the doctor said. "Do you own one?"

"No," I said. "Not at the moment."

"You need to get one," he said. "They're a lot of fun, too."

When the snowmobilers got back to Paradise, they

called the sheriff's office. An ambulance was sent out
to bring me to the hospital. My core body temperature
was eighty-seven degrees, three below the severe hypothermia line. They applied heat to my neck, armpits
and groin on the way to the hospital. When I got there,
they put me in a full body wrap. My temperature came
back up, about two degrees an hour.

"Ninety-six degrees," the doctor said, looking at
the display on the thermometer. "How do you feel?"

"I still feel cold," I said.

"You'll feel better," he said. "You're still dehy-
drated from the vasoconstriction."

"The vasoconstriction," I said. "Of course."

"We were concerned about all the blood," he said.

"The blood . . ." I said.

"You were a mess," he said. "But you didn't have
any bleeding injuries. That wasn't even your blood,
was it?"

"No, it wasn't," I said. "It's a long story."

"Somebody else's blood," he said, shaking his
head. "Do me a favor. When you're ready to tell the
story to somebody, make sure I'm in the room. This
I gotta hear."

I did tell the story to Sheriff Brandow, and I did
make sure the doctor was there to hear it. Brandow
listened to everything I said and wrote it down without saying a word, then he sent his men out to find
the ice shanty.

"They're going to find two dead men in their underwear," I said. "I don't know what you guys are
going to do about Bruckman."

"As far as I'm concerned," he said, "we can just
wait until spring. If Champagne and Urbanic want

him now, they can go in after him themselves."

I passed those exact words on to the agents when they came by to see me. They weren't happy.

"Let me get this straight," Champagne said. "We've got two of Molinov's men. Dead. We got Bruckman. Dead, and under the ice somewhere. We got no live bodies. We got no bag."

"You've still got each other," I said.

"It's a good thing you're in the hospital," he said. "Because you're going to need some type O in about one minute."

I caught Urbanic's eye. He was trying not to smile. After Champagne stormed out of the room, I asked him how he could stand having a guy like that for a partner.

"You were a cop once," he said. "You ever had a partner you couldn't stand?"

"Yes," I said. "He got killed."

"Do you miss him?"

"Every day," I said.

"I'd feel the same way," he said. "And besides, you should see him hit a golf ball. We've won the DEA Two-Man Best Ball seven years in a row."

I was still thinking about that when Leon stopped by. He had more private investigator magazines for me and a small box.

"I've got a present for you," he said.

I opened the box. Inside were at least a couple hundred business cards. "What's this?"

"Read it," he said.

I took out one of the cards. "Prudell-McKnight Investigations," I read. There were two guns under our names.

"You see, that's your service revolver, and that's my Luger."

"It's looks like they're shooting at each other," I said.

"No, no," he said. "It's like the two musketeers. All for one and one for all. Or both. Or whatever."

"You actually had business cards made up," I said.

"I thought they'd cheer you up," he said. "I'll be back later, after work."

"You don't have to do that," I said. "I'm fine."

"I don't like seeing my partner lying in a hospital bed," he said. "I won't feel right until you're back on the case."

"The case," I said. "How much time have we spent thinking about this? How much trouble did we get into? Well, me, anyway. Not to mention two trips to the hospital. What do we have to show for it?"

"Well," he said. He thought about it. "We've eliminated some suspects."

I couldn't help laughing. "You're right," I said. "We have done that."

"Just get better," he said. "Then we'll get back to work."

"Leon," I said. "Seriously, I don't know what the hell we've been doing, but I will say this. I'm glad you were helping me."

"See ya later, partner," he said.

"See ya later," I said. "Partner."

When he was gone, I looked through the magazines he had left for me, then I took a nap. When I woke up, the two snowmobilers were there to see me, a man and his thirteen-year-old son from Traverse City. They both had crew cuts and firm handshakes. I thanked them and gave them my phone number, invited them up for a week in one of the cabins, whenever they felt like coming up again.

Bill Brandow came back again that evening. This time he had a brown paper bag with a cold Canadian beer in it. "I figured you could use this," he said.

"The doctor will kill you," I said.

"I'm going to be buying you drinks for a long time," he said, "so I thought I might as well get started now."

"And it's just what I need right now," I said, feeling the bottle. "Something cold."

He looked down at the floor. "Guess I wasn't thinking."

"Don't worry about it, Bill."

"I shouldn't have played along with those agents," he said. "You were right. I'm an elected sheriff. They can't do anything to me."

"Yeah, but that Champagne guy is such a smooth talker, you couldn't help yourself."

"I see I'm going to be paying for this for a long time," he said.

When he was gone, Jackie came by, the man who would rather kiss his ex-wife than leave his bar and go out driving in the snow.

"What did you do," I said, "close the place?"

"My son's there," he said. "I just had to come by and make sure you were okay."

"You didn't come here the last time I was in the hospital," I said.

"Yeah, but you were just beat up then. By the time I even found out about it, you were out. If you're going to freeze to death, on the other hand, I wish you'd pay your tab first."

"Good seeing you, too," I said.

The doctor came by again, and then Leon again after work, and then around dinnertime I looked up and thought I must be hallucinating. Chief Maven was standing in the doorway.

"What, no flowers?" I said.

"I just had to come by and see for myself," he said. "They found you lying in the snow in the middle of Luce County, without a coat on, and you didn't even lose a body part to frostbite?"

"My parts are all here," I said. "All the original equipment."

"How's that saying go?" he said. " 'God looks after fools and idiots'?"

"I think it's fools and drunkards," I said.

"Either way," he said, "ain't you the living proof."

When he came close enough to stand over me, he put his gloves in his pockets and folded his arms. He looked tired.

"Why did you come here?" I said. "Really."

"I came here to ask you a few questions," he said.

"Go ahead."

"That cabin on Mackinac Trail," he said. "I've already read the statement you gave to Brandow, but I have to ask you this myself. Did you really hit that thing with your snowplow?"

"Yes," I said. "It wasn't intentional."

"You meant to plow the driveway and missed."

"Next question," I said.

"You saw what was done to those people," he said.

"After you accidentally caved in the whole side of the place with your snowplow."

"Yes," I said.

"And those men in the ice shanty," he said. "The dead men they found lying in their underwear. Pearl and Roman? Is that what they called themselves? They're the ones who killed those people in the cabin?"

"Yes."

"You sure about that?"

"Yes."

"And the other man?" he said. "Molinov? You saw him kill Pearl and Roman?"

"Yes," I said.

He nodded his head. "Okay, last question. Was it fast or was it slow?"

"What are you asking me?" I said.

"You saw what those men did," he said. "When they died, was it fast or was it slow?"

I looked at him for a long moment. "It was fast," I finally said. "They never even saw it coming."

He nodded his head again. "Okay," he said. "Okay." He took his gloves back out of his pocket and put them on.

"That's all," he said. And then he left.

I sat there, staring at the far wall. The doctor came in a few minutes later and broke the spell.

"I'd like to keep you here a couple of more days," he said. "Make sure your stomach is ready to digest food again. Hell, I'd like to keep you here for a month this time, make sure you don't do anything stupid as soon as you get out of here."

"I feel fine," I said.

"You don't feel cold anymore?"

"No," I said. Which was a lie. But I couldn't take the hospital anymore, and the endless parade of visitors. Everybody I knew had come by to see me.

With one exception.

I left the hospital at eight o'clock the next morning. I was wearing the new coat Leon had brought me. My old one was under the ice, after all, presumably still wrapped around Lonnie Bruckman's body. But that was okay with me. I had gotten twelve good years out of that coat.

My truck was waiting in the parking lot, just as Leon had promised. I told him I didn't want him to pick me up. I didn't want to see anybody that morning. I just wanted to have a few hours by myself to do something important. He understood that, without needing any kind of explanation. The mark of a good partner.

I headed west that morning. It was cold, like most days. It looked like it would snow again soon, like most days. But I wasn't thinking about the weather. When I hit the turnoff for Brimley, I took the road north onto the reservation. I parked the truck in the casino lot and went inside.

It didn't take me long to find him. He was working a five-dollar blackjack table. There were three players, two women and one man. I joined them.

"Alex," he said, without looking up. When he was done shuffling, he slid the shoe to one of the woman and handed her the cut card.

"Vinnie," I said.

After the cut, he started dealing. "Are you playing?" he said. He kept looking at the cards as he dealt them. He dealt himself a jack, so he pushed the other card over the sensor to see if he had blackjack. He didn't, so the hand continued.

"I'm playing," I said. I took out the envelope from my pocket, the one the renters had left for me. After my adventures at the ice rink, I had one hundred-dollar bill left.

When the hand was finished and the bettors paid off, he took the bill from me. "Changing a hundred," he said. The pit boss gave him a nod.

I waited until the next hand was underway. "You didn't come see me in the hospital," I said.

"I've been working," he said. "Dealer shows nine."

"You came and saw me the last time," I said. "Suddenly you're too busy? Did they change your hours?"

"Twenty-two," he said, after the first woman drew a ten to her twelve. "Alex, I can't talk right now."

"I've got an idea," I said. "I think I know why you didn't come by."

"Twenty-five," he said, after the man drew a nine to his sixteen. "Alex, please."

"You should have split the eights, sir," I said to the man. From the look on his face, my advice was not appreciated. "I think you didn't come by," I said to Vinnie, "because you were consumed by guilt."

He showed no reaction. He kept dealing. The third player stood on seventeen.

"Your turn," he said to me. "Would you like a card?"

I just looked at him. The other three players looked at me.

"A card for you, sir?"

I slipped my hands under the table and gave it a little experimental nudge. "This thing isn't too heavy," I said. "I wonder what would happen if I flipped it right over."

"You would be removed from the premises, sir," he said.

"It would make a hell of a show, though, wouldn't it?"

"Would you like a card, sir?"

"What I would like," I said, "is for you to come outside with me."

"Alex, I just got on this table," he said. "I can't leave."

I gave the table another nudge. This time all the little piles of chips fell over. The three other players looked around like they were expecting somebody to help them.

Vinnie closed his eyes. "Finish the hand," he said. "Then we'll go."

"Give me a card," I said.

He put a six on my fourteen. Then he threw over his hole card and showed nineteen. "You win," he said. He cleaned up the table, then signaled for the pit boss. "I have an emergency," he said to the man.

The boss looked at me and then gave a little wave. Another dealer was there in three seconds to take Vinnie's place.

I waited until we were in the parking lot. Then I started thinking about where I should hit him first. The problem was, I wasn't sure that I had the strength to lift my arm high enough to swing at him. And I didn't feel mad enough to start kicking him. Not yet, anyway.

"Tell me something," I said. "What happened to that big lecture you were giving me about Indians not interfering in each other's lives? That whole story about how your mother didn't even make you go to the dentist. You make your own way, you choose your own path, all that bullshit."

"What are you talking about?" he said.

"What about kidnapping Dorothy from my cabin?" I said. "Isn't that interfering with her life? Just a little bit?"

He looked out at the road. A cold wind picked up. I barely felt it.

"So when are you going to explain this to me?" I said. "Before or after I beat the living crap out of you?"

"Alex, don't."

"Why do you say that? Because you don't want to hurt me? You don't want to have to use some secret Indian chokehold on me?"

He looked at me. "Stop it," he said.

"How many of you guys did it take?" I said. "She must have put up quite a fight."

"In case you're forgetting," he said, "I was in jail the night she was taken."

"Yes, you were. But you've only got, what, seven hundred cousins? How many came out that night?"

"How did you find out?" he said. "Who told you?"

"Guess what, Vinnie. Nobody had to tell me. Some of us white people can figure things out ourselves. I knew it wasn't Bruckman and it wasn't Molinov. Neither of them even knew she was with me until the next day. Even if they did know, they wouldn't have known to go to that second cabin. It had to be somebody who actually saw me take her there. Somebody who was in the woods, watching us."

He looked away again.

"It also explains why she opened the door that night. They must have tricked her. What did they do, call her by her Indian name?"

"I didn't know about any of this," he said. "I swear. I didn't know. I told you Jimmy and Buck were with me when I went after Bruckman. When I got arrested, I guess they kept following them. Bruckman and Dorothy, both. When Dorothy ran out on him that night, they split up. Buck followed Dorothy to the bar, then to the Glasgow, then to your place."

"Of course he's good at following people," I said. "He's an Ojibwa."

"Will you knock it off?" he said. "He's a college student. He's gonna be a lawyer one day. He and my other cousins, I don't know how to make you understand this, Alex. They've seen too much. This guy Bruckman, he had taken one of our people from us. Then he brought her back, like he was rubbing our noses in it. And he was trying to sell drugs to our people, Alex. To some of us, the ones who don't know better. He was another white man trying to destroy us. They decided it was time to start doing something about it."

"I came to that jail the next day and bailed you out," I said. "You're telling me you had no idea any of this was happening?"

"No," he said. "I swear to you."

"So when *did* you know, Vinnie?"

He hesitated.

"When did you know?"

"The night you were arrested," he said. "I saw her."

"Wait a minute, the night I was arrested? On the bridge? The next morning you came over and helped me clean up that last cabin, and you were asking me why I was still trying to find her."

"I wanted you to stop," he said. "You'd been through enough."

"My God, Vinnie. Why didn't you just *tell* me?"

"I didn't think I had to," he said. "It sounded like you were done with it."

"I can't believe this," I said. "And all this time, up until that night, you didn't have the *slightest* idea that your own cousins took her?"

"I don't live on the reservation," he said.

"That's not a very convincing answer."

He looked at me. He didn't say anything.

"When we went to talk to her parents," I said. "When I thought they were acting strange and you gave me your big speech about the way of the Ojibwa, was that all a sham? Did *they* already know?"

"I think her parents knew she was safe," he said. "That's all. They didn't know anything else."

"And everybody just let me run around trying to find her?" I said. "Do you have any idea what I went through?"

"You were looking for Bruckman," he said. "My cousins probably didn't want to stop you from finding him."

"You mean if I found him . . . ," I said.

"They would have taken care of him," he said.

"Listen to you," I said. "You sound like the Mafia or something."

"No," he said. "Just a new generation, Alex. We've

been through too much. We'll do whatever it takes to save our people."

"Beautiful," I said. "I'm moved."

He didn't say anything.

"So where is she now?" I said. "Where did you see her?"

"In Canada," he said. "She wanted to call you."

"Why didn't she?"

"They didn't want her to," he said. "They didn't want . . . I mean, they wanted to wait."

"Who's 'they'?"

"The people who are taking care of her."

"The people who kidnapped her," I said.

"No."

"They came into the cabin," I said. "And then they dragged her out of there."

"It didn't happen that way," he said. "That's not what they told me."

"There were people in that cabin," I said. "And they did a nice job of busting up the furniture."

"No," he said. "They're helping her. They're getting her cleaned up . . ."

"Is that what she told you?"

"Yes," he said. "And she asked me to tell you something, too. She said to say that she's sorry she got you involved in this, and something else about your pipes."

"My pipes?"

"Something about your pipes freezing."

"Oh, yeah. I've been losing a lot of sleep over that. It's been my biggest problem this week."

"I'm just telling you what she said."

"Okay," I said. "You delivered the message."

"Alex, I don't know what else to say. I swear, I really didn't know anything until . . ."

"Save it," I said. "I don't want to hear any more. You didn't know about this because you didn't *want* to know. If you knew, you would have had to tell me. And you didn't want to do that. And we both know why."

I looked in his eyes. For the first time since I had known him, I felt the distance between us as he looked back at me. I knew that, even if we ever found a way to get over this, the distance would always be there.

"Tell me this," I said. "Whatever happened to that bag? I hear there's quite a load of, what did they call it, wild cat in there?"

"I don't know anything about it," he said. "As far as I know, she didn't have it when they took her."

"Of course she did," I said. "Your cousins are sitting on enough drugs to stay high for the rest of their lives. Or whoever those people are in Canada. And they're not even sharing it with you?"

He just looked at me, his shoulders back like he was ready to jump on me. "I was feeling pretty bad about what happened to you," he said. "You're making it a lot easier on me."

"Why don't you go ask them?" I said. "Ask them where that bag is. If they say they don't even know what you're talking about, then you know you've got a problem. That stuff is poison, Vinnie. For anybody. Indians, white, black, anybody. If the drug doesn't hook you, what about the fact that you could sell that stuff for, God I don't even know, a couple hundred thousand dollars, at least? You think that every single one of your cousins can resist that temptation? Talk about the white people destroying you. It looks like you guys are gonna do a pretty good job of it without anybody's help."

"It's time for you to walk away," he said. "Walk away before I do something I'll regret."

"We wouldn't want that," I said. "God knows you've done enough already."

When I left, he was still standing there in the parking lot, staring off into the distance.

I spent the heart of the day in my cabin, sitting by the woodstove. I didn't feel like going to the Glasgow, even when the sun was starting to go down and I'd normally feel the urge for a little company. I sat by the woodstove, putting in log after log, trying to get even heat going to dispel the chill in my body. I felt cold all the way through.

I tried not to think about Molinov, or about what he said as he left me. The cold takes away a part of you. It didn't make any sense at the time. Now I was beginning to feel the truth of his words.

I was tired, but I dreaded the thought of going to sleep. I knew as soon as I closed my eyes, I would be back in that shack. It took me fourteen years to get over that day in Detroit, I thought. Fourteen years until I didn't see that apartment every night, my partner lying on the floor next to me. Now I've got some new dead bodies to dream about. Maybe this time it'll only take me thirteen years.

I got up and walked around the place, looked out the window as the day gave way to darkness. I could see my own reflection in the glass.

"Do something," I said. "Anything. Don't just sit here going crazy."

I put my coat on and went out to the truck. I fired it up and drove the quarter-mile to the second cabin. It felt strange to open the door and walk in, now that I knew what had really happened there. I picked up the leg that had broken off the table. It was solid oak. My father had made this table down in his basement in Dearborn, turned the legs by hand on his lathe and put the whole thing together without using one nail. Somewhere I still have a couple of his old pipe-clamps, I thought. If I can find them, I'll try to glue this thing back together.

I felt the weight of the table leg in my hands, holding it like a bat without even thinking of it. I tried to swing it. It hurt like hell. You're a real specimen, Alex. You used to be able to drive the ball when you got hold of it. Now it hurts just to swing a fucking table leg.

Wait a minute.

I stared at the table leg in my hands. In my mind I was back in this very same cabin the morning this had all started, the morning I came to find Dorothy and found nothing.

Nothing but chairs scattered around the room. A table overturned. A leg broken off. And the faint marks of snow melting on the floor.

They came to her that night. They knocked on the door. She was afraid. She thought it was Bruckman. Or Molinov's men. Or Molinov himself.

She panicked. She looked for something to defend herself. She opened the drawers. There was nothing but plastic silverware. She knocked a chair over.

And then she turned the table over and tore the leg off. She was strong enough to do it if she used a little leverage. There was nothing holding the table together but glue that had become brittle after years of cold air.

She held the leg and waited for the door to be kicked in. I could see her standing right here, breathing hard, ready to make her stand.

And then they called to her. Voices from her past, calling her by her Ojibwa name.

She dropped the table leg and opened the door. Come with us, they said. We'll take you away from here.

She must have wanted to tell me she was going. I had to believe that.

No, they said. There's no time. We must go.

Maybe they told her they would call me later. Maybe they tried to convince her that they *couldn't* tell me, that I couldn't be trusted.

Or maybe they just grabbed her at that point, and took her away.

No matter how it happened, she didn't have the bag with her when she left.

The melted snow on the floor. That was her. After I left her, she went outside, then came back in.

Which explains her message. The frozen pipes.

I put the table leg down, went back outside to the truck, grabbed the flashlight from the cab and the shovel from the back.

I went to the back of the cabin and started digging through the snow. I had done the same thing the night I brought Dorothy here. I had gone under the cabin to turn the water on, and told her to keep the tap dripping so the pipes wouldn't freeze.

When the deputies searched this place, I thought, they didn't really have their hearts in it. They didn't think about what was *under* the cabin.

I dug all the way down to the little access door. By the time the deputies got here, there had been enough new snow to cover it.

I crawled under the cabin and turned the flashlight on. There it was in the corner. I backed my way out, pulling the bag with me. When I was out, I stayed on my knees and unzipped the bag.

White powder, in small clear bags, the powder glittering as I passed the light over it.

"So this is wild cat," I said. "Brought here all the way from Russia."

I zipped up the bag and took it back to my truck. I needed to get back inside, next to that woodstove. A good stiff drink wouldn't hurt, either.

Then I needed to figure out what the hell to do next.

CHAPTER TWENTY-ONE

Two weeks passed. It snowed. I plowed the road. New renters came to stay in the cabins. They drove their snowmobiles on the trails, filling the cold air with noise.

I didn't spend much time at the Glasgow Inn those two weeks. I chopped some wood. I cleaned up after the snowmobilers. I even got the passenger side window in my truck fixed. Mostly I stayed in my cabin by the woodstove, trying to get warm.

I saw Vinnie's car by his cabin. But I didn't see the man himself. Not once.

Until he came knocking on my door. When I opened the door, he was standing there on the walkway I had just shoveled.

"Get your coat on," he said. "You're coming with me."

"The hell I am," I said.

"There's a ceremony at Garden River," he said. "She wants you to be there."

"Who does?"

"Dorothy," he said. "Who do you think?"

"I thought she was locked away somewhere."

"She was never locked anywhere," he said. "She

was just getting herself together. Now she's ready to move on."

"Where's she moving on to?" I said. "Last I heard, those DEA agents still wanted to talk to her."

"They're not going to," he said. "She's not coming back to the United States."

"She's in Canada?"

"No, Alex, she's in Ecuador. Are you coming or not?"

"Take it easy," I said. I went to get my coat.

"Why's it so hot in here?" he said.

"I've been cold lately," I said. "Ever since I almost died of hypothermia."

"All right, all right," he said. "I hear you."

"Ecuador, did you say? Where did you come up with that one?"

"Come on, let's go," he said. "I'll drive."

I followed him to his car. When we got in, I turned the heat up.

"The car's warm enough," he said. "You're gonna suffocate me."

"That would be a shame."

He let out a long breath and backed out onto the access road. "She asked me to bring you," he said. "So I'm bringing you."

"So drive," I said.

"I am," he said.

He drove through Paradise, between piles of snow that were a good seven feet high. He didn't say anything for a few minutes. I didn't say anything back.

When we were on M-28 heading east, he finally cleared his throat. "I know what you did," he said.

"Do tell."

"With those drugs," he said. "The day I go to trial on the assault charge, there's Maven on the front page of the paper, bunch of bags on a table, those two agents on either side of him. What did you do, give the stuff to Maven directly?"

"I don't know what you're talking about," I said.

"Soon as I get to the courthouse, the public defender tells me the charge has been dropped down to a misdemeanor. I get a fine and a lecture from the judge. That's it."

"Lucky you," I said.

"Just stop it, Alex. I know what you did."

"Look," I said. "I still feel like shit, okay? But when I get my strength back, I'm coming over and knocking you on your ass. How am I gonna do that if you're sitting in jail?"

He laughed. "You've been plowing out my driveway, too," he said.

"When I come over to knock you on your ass," I said, "I don't want to get all tired out having to climb over three feet of snow. When I come through your door, I want to be fresh and ready to go."

"Fair enough," he said.

"Just a little warning," I said. "I think I'm almost back to one hundred percent."

"You know where to find me," he said.

He kept driving, through the Soo to the International Bridge. It was the first time I had been across since I was arrested. The customs agent asked Vinnie the usual questions, took a look at me, then let us through.

"Where are we going, anyway?" I said.

"Garden River Healing Center," he said. "It'll be a quick ceremony. It's kind of a secret."

"How come I get to be here?"

"I told you," he said. "She asked for you."

"But I'm the enemy."

"Don't even start, Alex. You helped her. She wants to thank you."

"What about all your cousins, the ones who told you not to trust me? Are they going to be there?"

"Some of them."

"Great," I said. "This will be a lot of fun."

"They feel bad about what happened," he said. "For what that's worth."

"It's worth nothing," I said. "Exactly nothing."

"Reminds me," he said. "I think you probably ended up spending some money. Didn't you?"

I didn't say anything.

"You were in the hospital twice," he said. "That must have cost a lot of money."

"I'm covered," I said.

"Not all of it," he said. "You had to end up paying for some of it . . ."

"Vinnie," I said. "If you're talking about somebody paying me because of what happened . . ."

"I'm just saying, Alex. You shouldn't have to—"

"So help me God," I said, "if you say one more word about money . . ."

"All right," he said. "All right. I'm just saying."

"Vinnie . . ."

"No more," he said. "I'm done."

He drove all the way through Soo Canada, then east into the forest. A few miles outside the city, we came to the Garden River Reservation. It was another of the

Ojibwa tribes, along with the Bay Mills and Sault tribes in Michigan, a few others in Wisconsin and Minnesota. Garden River didn't have casinos, and they weren't going to get them. The government of Ontario would soon be opening their own casino in Soo Canada, cutting the Canadian tribes right out of the game.

"All these buildings are white pine," he said as we drove in. "That's to honor Chief Shingwaukonce. His name means 'pine.'"

"You don't say."

"The healing center we're going to has thirteen sides, one for each month in the old Ojibwa calendar. The white man stole one of our months, did you know that?"

"I apologize on their behalf," I said.

"I'll shut up now," he said.

"Thank you."

We parked next to the healing center. There were maybe a dozen cars there. I looked at my watch. It was almost midnight.

When we got out of his car, the snow crunched under out feet as though we were stepping on fine crystal. It was impossibly, inhumanly cold, all the clouds gone from the sky. We could see every star above us, and in the east a full moon burned brightly, casting a blue light on everything below.

"Look at that moon," Vinnie said.

"It's a moon, all right."

He shook his head and led me into the place.

In the center of the healing center there was a round meeting room, with a high tin exhaust pipe rising through the ceiling. Below the pipe there was a large circle where the floor opened up all the way to the ground. There was a great mass of sand there, and after my eyes adjusted to the dim light, I could see that the sand had been formed into the shape of a turtle. On the turtle's back was a hearth, also made from sand. The sweet smoke rose and hung in the air before leaving the room through the exhaust pipe. A man stood next to the sand turtle, his shirt decorated with ribbons, red, yellow, black and white.

There were chairs placed in a circle all around the turtle, at least thirty tribal members already sitting. They all looked up at us as we came in. I recognized Dorothy's parents on the far side of the room.

"I take it they don't see many white men in here," I whispered.

"I hope you realize what an honor this is," he said.

"Uh-huh."

"This is a sacred place," he said as he sat down. "You know, like church? Think you could put a lid on it for a little while?"

I shut up and sat down next to him.

When Dorothy came into the room, I could barely recognize her. Her face was scrubbed clean, her hair pulled back straight as if it were still wet. She wasn't wearing any makeup, or any of the earrings she had on the night I met her. As she came through the circle and stood next to the man, she caught my eye and gave me a quick smile.

The man unwrapped a clay bowl from a red blanket that was lying at his feet. From the edge of the fire he took an ember and lit whatever was inside the bowl. Dorothy whispered something into his ear, and then he looked up at me. Slowly he walked over to me, carrying the smoking bowl in front of him.

"What's happening?" I whispered to Vinnie. But it was the medicine man who answered me.

"We call this smudging," he said. As he held the bowl next to my heart, the smoke rose all around my head and then filled my lungs as I breathed it. "This is Shkodawabuk, or sage," he said. "It was one of our four medicines. Tobacco is from the east, cedar from the south, sweetgrass from the north and sage from the west."

I closed my eyes and listened to his words. For the first time in many days, I started to feel warm. Just a little bit.

"We use sage today, because sage is the medicine of purification and rebirth. As the sun sets in the west, the day dies and is reborn again after the night."

When I opened my eyes again, I looked around at all the men and women, young and old. They were all watching me with quiet faces. Then the medicine man took his bowl to Vinnie, and then on to the next person until he had worked his way through the entire room.

Then he came back to Dorothy and performed the same ritual, enveloping her with the smoke from the bowl. When he finally spoke to the room, his message was brief.

We are many tribes, divided by borders and boundaries, but one people.

Dorothy Parrish has come back to our people, but in a way she never left, because we all belong to each other, and to the Earth.

We welcome her back to us and wish her well on her journey.

When the ceremony was over, the tribal members approached her one by one to hold her hands and give her their best wishes. I stood on the outside of it all, watching her.

When she finally looked over at me, I saw the medicine man look at his watch and say something to her. She nodded and said something in return, and then came over to me.

"Alex," she said. "Thank you for coming here."

"You look good," I said.

"I don't know what to say. You helped me so much."

"I'm glad you're safe," I said.

"I'm sorry about everything that happened to you. I didn't mean to pull you into the middle of everything."

"I'm sure you didn't plan it that way," I said.

"You know, as soon as I met you, I knew I could trust you. I had been running so long, and I just wanted to stop. I knew you'd do the right thing, no matter what. You know what I mean?"

"I think so," I said. I looked around the room and lowered my voice a notch. "When you took that bag . . ."

"I was still trying to decide what to do with it that night. Either take it to the police. Or else give it back to Molinov, ask him to go away and leave me alone. Leave *all* of us alone."

"You get points for guts," I said.

She smiled. "Did you see that moon tonight?"

"Yes, I did."

"There was a full moon the night I met you. Do you remember?"

"Yes," I said. "You called it the wolf moon."

"Yes," she said. "The wolf moon, for protecting those close to you."

"What's this one called?"

"This is the ice moon," she said. "For resting until it's warm again."

"Sounds like my kind of moon."

"I should go," she said. "I hope I see you again some day."

"Where are you going?"

"I don't know yet," she said. "A reservation somewhere. Here in Canada. I just want to be somewhere where I can have a little peace for a while."

"I hope you find it," I said.

"I will. I have my family back now."

"Hey, you never did tell me your Ojibwa name."

"It's Waubun-anung," she said. "It means 'Morning Star.' "

"That's a good name," I said.

"Thank you."

"Take care of yourself," I said. "Morning Star."

She gave me a kiss on the cheek, then left with the medicine man.

Vinnie and I walked back out into the night. We got into the car without saying a word. We drove back through Soo Canada, back over the bridge, into Soo Michigan and then west toward Paradise. The only sound in the car was the steady hum of the heater. "I've been thinking about getting a hockey team together again," he finally said. "Do you want to play?"

"Are you kidding me?" I said.

"You were good in goal," he said. "We could use you."

"You are kidding," I said. "Please tell me you're making a joke."

"You should play," he said. "It's not good being by yourself all the time. You think too much."

When we were in Paradise, he asked me if he could buy me a drink at the Glasgow.

"It's late," I said.

"Jackie will still be there," he said. "He'll let us in."

"No, thanks," I said. "Not tonight."

"Suit yourself," he said. He dropped me off at my cabin.

"It was good to see her," I said.

"I'm glad you got the chance," he said. And then he left.

I stood outside my cabin for a while, breathing in the cold air, looking up at the ice moon.

So now what? Before any of this happened, I had made a vow to myself, of all the things I was going to do when the springtime came. The debts I was going to repay.

I pulled my coat tight around my neck.

Where is all my anger now? Where is the fire? I just feel tired and sore and cold.

Everything hurts. It hurts to breathe. It hurts to move.

It hurts to live.

The hell with it. Vinnie's right. I think too much.

Whatever happens will happen. I'll make things right again someday, no matter what I have to do, or where I have to go. And this man Molinov, it sounds like he may be hunting the same game. I have a feeling I'll be running into him again.

But not tonight. Tonight I will close my eyes and feel the smoke touching my face again, the smoke of burning sage with its promise of a new day.

I need to rest. I need to heal myself.

For now, there is nothing to do but sleep under the ice moon.

When the lefthander found me, I was sitting in my usual chair in front of the fire, trying to stay warm. The calendar said April, but April in Paradise is still cold enough to hurt you, and I could feel the sting of it in my hands and on my face. I sat there by the fire, watching the baseball game on the television over the bar, nursing a cold Canadian beer as the lefthander made his way in the darkness. He knew where he was going, because he had a hand-drawn map in his back pocket, with a little star on the right side of the road as you come north into Paradise. The Glasgow inn, that was his destination. He knew I'd be there. On a cold Tuesday night in April, where else would I be?

His trip began early that morning in Los Angeles. He boarded a 747 and flew to Detroit Metropolitan Airport. He had to wait two hours there, and he had already lost three hours in the time change. So the sun was going down when he finally got on the little two-propeller plane with twelve passengers, a pilot, and a co-pilot who doubled as the flight attendant. That plane took him first to Alpena, where he sat on the runway for a half-hour while half the passengers got off. The co-pilot got out and sprayed the ice off the wings, and then they were in the air again. The plane was noisy, and cold, and it bounced around in the wind like a paper kite. It was after eleven o'clock at night when they finally touched down at Chippewa County Airport. There are only two flights per day that land there, two little airplanes like the one the lefthander was on that night. The funny thing is that those little airplanes land on a runway that's over two and a half miles long. It's one of the longest runways in the country, long enough to be on the space shuttle's emergency back-up list. The lefthander asked one of the other passengers why the runway was so long, because that's the kind of thing the lefthander does. He asks strangers questions as if he'd known them his whole life. And they always answer him, because he has this way of making them feel at ease.

"This used to be an Air Force Base, ay," the stranger said. He was a local man from the Upper Peninsula, so he had that yooper rise in his voice. "Kincheloe Air Force Base, back in World War Two. Did ya know the Soo locks were the most heavily defended position in America back then? I guess they figured if the Japs or Germans were gonna bomb us, they'd start at the locks and cut off our ore supply."

"That's interesting," the lefthander said. I'm sure he said it in a way that made the stranger feel that it really *was* interesting, and that therefore the stranger must be an interesting man himself. That's the kind of thing the lefthander can do, with just two words.

The airport terminal itself is a one-room hut sitting next to that long runway. The lefthander went into the terminal and picked up his luggage. It didn't take long because the co-pilot just grabbed the suitcases two at a time and carried them in himself. If the lefthander was worried about getting his rental car at such a tiny airport at eleven o'clock at night, he had no reason to be. A woman named Eileen was there waiting for him, keys in hand. That was her job, after all. When somebody reserves a car, she stays up late that night and waits for the plane to come in. The lefthander signed a form, took the keys from her, and thanked her. He thanked Eileen with a smile that she'd remember for months afterward, I'm sure. Then she went home to bed.

He found his rental car in the parking lot. Across the street from the airport there is a factory where they recondition auto parts, twenty-four hours a day. The factory sends up a constant stream of smoke, and the light from the airport makes the smoke look silver against the night sky. He must have stood there and looked at the smoke for a moment, breathing in the cold air. The coat he had just taken out of his suitcase was not warm enough. He had started his day in California, where it was seventy-one degrees. Here in the Upper Peninsula of Michigan, on an April night a good three weeks after the official start of spring, it was twelve degrees.

He left the airport and drove down a lonely road with no streetlights. It must have seemed then like he'd come to the end of the earth. There were still piles of gray snow on either side of the road, what remained of the mountains made each year by the snowplows. When he found I-75, he took that north toward Sault Ste. Marie. The Soo, as the locals call it. But he didn't get to see the Soo itself that night, because the map he had laid on the seat next to him told him to take M-28 west, right into the heart of the

Hiawatha National Forest. He passed through a couple of small towns named Raco and Strongs, and then he hit M-123. He took that road north. After a few miles he could see Lake Superior in the moonlight. There was ice on the shore.

When he saw the sign, he knew he had finally reached Paradise. "Welcome to Paradise! We're glad you made it!" He paused at the single blinking red light in the middle of town, and then he found the Glasgow Inn a hundred yards up on the right. He pulled his rental car into the lot and parked it right next to my twelve-year-old Ford truck with the wood-stove in the back, covered in plastic.

I didn't know about any of this at the time, of course. About the plane to Detroit and then the plane to Chippewa County, about the words to the stranger or the smile for Eileen the rental car lady. I didn't know he was coming all this way to see me on that night. The Detroit Tigers were playing a late game out on the west coast, the same coast Randy had spent all day flying away from. I was just sitting by the fireplace at the Glasgow Inn, watching the game on the television that hung over the bar. The place is supposed to resemble a Scottish pub, with the big overstuffed chairs and footrests. It's a lot more inviting than most bars I've seen. And Jackie, the owner of the place, cannot be trusted to do anything right on his own, so it is my duty to stop in every night and share my wisdom with him. He never listens to me but I keep going back anyway.

I own some land up the road, with six cabins my father had built back in the sixties and seventies. I live in the first cabin, the one I helped him build myself in 1968. The other five I rent out to tourists in the summer, hunters in the fall, and snowmobilers in the winter. Spring is the off season in Paradise, a time to clean out the cabins and wait for the snow to melt.

There was a time when spring meant something else, the four years I was catching in the minor leagues. A lifetime ago. I didn't think about those days much anymore. A lot of time had passed since then, and a lot of things had happened. Eight years as a police officer in Detroit. A dead partner and a bullet still inside my chest. And then fifteen years up here in Paradise, spending nights like this one watching baseball on television and not even thinking about the days when I played the game myself. I certainly wasn't thinking about Randy Wilkins, a lefthander I had caught back in triple-A ball in 1971. When he opened the door and stepped into the place and shouted my name, I couldn't believe it was really him. If the Pope himself had come through the door wearing his big hat, I wouldn't have been more surprised.

Almost thirty years later, the lefthander had found me.

"Wilkins," I said. "Randy Wilkins. I don't believe it." He looked about twenty pounds heavier, and the curly black hair he once had was mostly gone. What was left was cut close to his scalp. As if to compensate for the loss, he had grown a mustache and goatee.

The eyes, they hadn't changed. He still had that look in his eyes. Some days you'd call it a twinkle, other days you'd call it insanity. Which was totally appropriate considering the side of the mound he threw from. There are some simple truths in baseball, after all. One of them, whether it would be considered politically correct these days or not, is that lefthanded pitchers are not normal. They can't throw the ball in a straight line, for one thing. Everything a lefthander throws has a little movement on it, no matter how hard they try to throw the straight fastball. A lefthander, being a total freak of nature, is fragile and more likely to hurt himself. One bad throw and the arm is done forever. I've seen it happen.

And lefthanders think differently, too. They might be a little absent-minded maybe. Or eccentric. Or downright crazy.

"Alex McKnight," he said. He grabbed my shoulders and didn't let go. "How long has it been?"

"It's what, almost thirty years?" I said. "How in the world . . . What are you doing here?"

"I was in the neighborhood," he said. "I thought I'd drop by."

"In the neighborhood, huh? You wanna try that again?"

"Do I get a drink first?" he said. "It's been a hell of a long day."

"A drink," I said. "Of course."

I introduced him to Jackie. "This man right here," I said, "played ball with me in Toledo, believe it or not. He was a pitcher."

"Pleased to meet ya," Jackie said, shaking his hand. "What are you drinking?"

"Whatever Alex is having," Randy said.

"Alex is having a beer," Jackie said. "A beer from Canada. Alex doesn't drink beer if it's bottled in America. He makes me go all the way over the bridge just to pick him up a case of beer every week."

"He doesn't need the sob story," I said. "Just get him the beer."

"You look good," Randy said to me. "You've been working out?"

"Working out, ha!" Jackie said from behind the bar. "Alex McKnight working out. That's a good one."

"I'll tell you something," Randy said. "This man right here was one hell of a catcher. I don't think I ever saw him give up a passed ball."

"Too bad he couldn't hit his weight," Jackie said as he brought the beer around.

"Just give the man his beer," I said. I sat him down in front of the fire and watched him take a pull right out of the bottle.

"So this is Canadian beer," he said.

"Can you taste the difference?"

"Um, sure," he said.

"You're lying," I said. "No matter how long it's been, I can still tell when you're lying."

He laughed. "I can't lie to my catcher."

"Damned right," I said. "But seriously. It's great to see you. Except for that mustache and that goatee thing."

"Makes me look pretty smooth, doesn't it?"

"Yeah, in a Satanic serial killer sort of way. What's that on your arm, a tattoo?"

He looked at the back of his left wrist. There were three parallel lines. The line farthest from his hand had a gap in the middle. "That's a trigram," he said. "You know, from the *I Ching*. It's called 'the joyous lake.' A Tibetan monk used a needle dipped in spider blood."

"You're lying again," I said. "I told you, don't even

try it. I can see right through you. Even thirty years later."

"How about I got drunk one night in San Francisco?" he said. "When I woke up, I had no wallet, no shoes, and a brand new tattoo?"

"That's sounds more like it," I said.

He laughed again. It was the same laugh. For one year of my life I heard that laugh at least twenty times a day.

"So tell me already," I said.

"What?"

"What's going on? How far did you have come to get here, anyway?"

"Well, I've been living in L.A. for the last few years," he said. "I was watching a Cactus League game a couple weeks ago, and the guy on TV was talking about how a good catcher is a pitcher's best friend. I said to myself, 'Ain't that the truth,' and I started thinking about the old days in Toledo. I was wondering whatever happened to you, so I started poking around on the Internet to see if I could find you. I saw your Website, man, and I figured, hey, I'm gonna go see him!"

"Whoa," I said. "Back up. My Website?"

"Yeah, I did a search on Alex McKnight and it came up."

"Randy, I don't have a Website. I don't even have a computer."

"I'm talking about your business Website, Alex. Prudell-McKnight Investigations."

I just looked at him for a long moment. And then it came to me. "Oh my God," I said. "What did he do now?"

"Your partner, Leon?"

I closed my eyes. "Yeah, my partner, Leon."

"Well, it looks like he's put a nice little Website out there advertising your services. There's this drawing with two pistols on it, pointing at each other. It kinda looks like they're shooting at each other."

"Yeah, I know what you mean," I said. "He used the same thing on our business cards."

"I gave Leon a call," he said. "Real nice guy. He told me you'd be here. I made him promise not to tell you I was coming. I wanted it to be a surprise."

"Well, you certainly did surprise me. But why—"

"There's something on there about you having a bullet in your chest, too. Is that true?"

"I'm going to kill him," I said. "He is absolutely dead."

"So you do have a bullet in there?" He snuck a look down at my torso, the same way everybody does when they first hear about it.

"Yes," I said. "It's a long story."

"All right, save that one, then. Are you married? You got any kids?"

"No and no," I said. "Married once, divorced. No kids. How about you?"

He looked at the ceiling for a moment. "I'm divorced, too. Three kids. Jonathon just passed the bar. He's a lawyer in San Francisco. His wife's expecting a baby soon. Can you believe that, I'm gonna be a grandfather! Annie's a chef, just got a new job at a really nice restaurant down in San Diego. And Terry just went off to school at UC–Santa Barbara. Hey, guess what." He reached over and punched me in the leg.

"Ouch. What?"

"Terry's a ballplayer. He's on the freshman team. Guess what position he plays."

"Oh great," I said. "Another pitcher. I bet he's a crazy lefthander."

"He's a catcher," he said. "Can you beat that?"

"That's even worse," I said. "He has to *catch* crazy lefthanders."

"He's a switch-hitter," he said. "God, he can drive the ball, Alex. Just like you used to."

"I see your memory went along with your hair."

"Oh man, you haven't changed, Alex." He took another pull of the bottle. "Canadian beer. I can't believe I'm in Michigan drinking Canadian beer. And why is it so cold here, anyway? Haven't you guys heard of spring?"

"Sure," I said. "Just wait until June."

"Hey, Jackie!" he yelled. "Get your butt over here so I can tell you some stories about your boy Alex here. Stuff I bet you never heard before. And bring some more beer while you're at it."

Anybody else who came into the place for the first time and talked to Jackie that way, he'd be back out in the parking lot in ten seconds, wiping the gravel off his ass. But Randy had always had this knack for making you feel like you've known him your whole life, even if you just met him. I saw it all the time when we were playing together, and even more when we became roommates. Randy had already gone through a couple roommates by the time he got to me. Something about the way he'd keep talking all night, even if you had to get up early the next morning and ride on a bus all day to the next game.

But you couldn't hate the guy for it. As much as you wanted to kill him sometimes, he'd always say something funny and disarming, or even worse, he'd put his arm around you and sing in your ear. "You know you love me, Alex," he used to say. "You've got the hots for me. You dream about me all night long. That's why I drive you crazy."

A whole busload of guys in their twenties, most of them from farms or little towns around the midwest, all of them dirt tough or at least trying to act like it. And I get Randy Wilkins for a roommate.

So now almost thirty years has passed, and out of nowhere he's sitting in the Glasgow Inn on a late Tuesday night in April. It's taken him exactly twenty minutes to feel comfortable. Hell, in twenty minutes he owns the place. Even a crusty old goat like Jackie is treating him like royalty. I kept waiting for him to tell me why he had come so far to see me, after all these years, but he kept talking about baseball, the games we had played in, old teammates I had all but forgotten.

"So tell me, Randy," Jackie said at one point. "Did you ever make it up to the big leagues?"

There it was. I knew it would come up eventually. I certainly wasn't going to mention it myself.

"Why, yes," Randy said. "As a matter of fact, I did make it up to the big leagues. I pitched in one game." By this time, Jackie had pulled a couple of the tables over by the fireplace, and at least twelve men were sitting there listening to him. "You want to tell this story, Alex?"

"I wasn't there," I said. And that's all I said, because I didn't want to touch it. I had never even heard him tell it before, because after that September call-up, I never saw him again. Until tonight.